Forever and a Day

Jae Henderson

Forever and a Day
RiverHouse Publishing, LLC
5100 Poplar Avenue
Suite 2700
Memphis, TN 38117

All **RiverHouse, LLC** Titles, Imprints and Distributed
Lines are available at special quantity discounts for bulk
purchases for sales promotions, premiums, fund-raising
and educational or institutional use.

First RiverHouse, LLC Trade Paperback Printing:
2/11/2013

1

ISBN: **978-0-9839819-9-2**
ISBN: **0-9839819-9-2**

Printed in the United States of America

This book is printed on acid-free paper.

www.riverhousepublishingllc.com

This book is dedicated to all my readers. Thank you for following me through this literary journey. This is the end of the Someday series but it is the beginning of my quest to make you fall in love with a new set of characters that can't wait to share their amazing lives with you.

Acknowledgments

Thank you to my Heavenly Father who has allowed his message to flow from my fingertips onto these pages. I pray that my words bless each and every reader in some way.

Thank you to my publisher and friend, Latrivia A. Nelson. Your wisdom and assistance have been immeasurable. I will be forever grateful that you believed in me enough to help me bring my books to life.

Thank you to my editor and proofreaders, Alanna Boutin, Kiara Rainey, Rachelle Butler and Esther Crain-Holden. I'm getting better at this part and you are definitely part of the process.

Thank you to my wonderful church family at Olivet Fellowship Baptist Church. You truly exemplify our slogan "The Place of the Outpouring." You have blessed me collectively and individually. Dr. Eugene Gibson, Jr. and Lady Nicole, I love you!

To Pastors Kevin and Linda Willis of New Life in Christ Fellowship Church. Thank you for your support and words of encouragement.

To my amazing family, I don't know what I'd do without you and I thank God that I don't have to find out.

To my girls Tracy, Shana, Gwen and Dorsha, thanks for keeping me sane when this world tries to make me crazy. Thank you to my amazing sorority sisters of Zeta Phi Beta Sorority, Inc. for your love and support.

To my readers, you are invaluable. Your emails, words of encouragement, suggestions, and criticism have helped me to make each book better.

And to every bookstore, book club, and business that saw fit to make me and my books a part of your lives, thank you for the doors you opened. Let's keep the momentum going! May everyone that I mentioned an those I didn't experience God's blessings, grace, favor, and peace in abundance!

Chapter 1

MiTee Management at Your Service

"Thank you for calling MiTee Management, how may I help you?" asked Sheba in her sweetest voice.

"Yeah. Can I speak to my momma?" said a young male.

Sheba hated prank phone calls. She had better things to do with her time than play with somebody she couldn't see.

"Sir, I think you have the wrong number. Everyone in this office is childless," she said rudely.

"No. Tina Stokes is my momma. Tell her that her son is on the phone. She'll know exactly who you're talking about," the young man insisted.

Sheba was sure he was crazy. Tee didn't have any children yet, and if she did, whoever was on the other end was way too old to be her child, but she decided to humor him. "One moment please," she said and pressed the button to put him on hold. She then pressed the extension for Tee's office. "Boss Lady, there's a young man on the phone who says you're his momma. Do I need to get rid of him?"

Tee giggled. "No, Sheba, that's my baby. I'll explain later. Put him through."

Her phone rang two seconds later. "MiTee Management, where we are lifting our clients to new heights. Tee Stokes here. How may I help you?"

Tee loved to say the name of her and Michael's new management company. They selected MiTee because it was a combination of their names and it sounded like the word *mighty*. That's exactly what they planned to be—stronger, bigger, and badder than any other management company in the nation. Together, they were a force to be reckoned with. They had only been in business two months, and MiTee Management was currently responsible for maintaining the I'm A Good Woman brand and executing the I'm A Good Woman Empowerment Conference. They also managed Michael's career as a motivational speaker and book author, Tiffany's Magic Touch Mobile Massage, and now gospel hip-hop artist Icy Blak. It was an eclectic bunch, but nothing she and Michael couldn't handle. So far, their assistant Sheba was the only employee, but they were looking to add an additional manager to the team so Tee could attend solely to the baby after he or she was born.

Things took off much faster than either of them could have imagined. After the word circulated that MiTee Management existed, many of the celebrities she and Michael knew called to see if they would be interested in managing them. They turned most of them down because they didn't want to take on too much too soon, but when Blak called, there was no way Tee could deny him. He was her mentee, and she was honored that he wanted her to help manage his career. They finally had the details worked out, and Blak would be in town tomorrow to sign the contract. She was quite proud of the businessman he was becoming.

"Hey, Ma! I liked your name better when it was Tina Long," teased Blak.

"Boy, I told you I am nobody's mother. At least not yet, and I think my new name is beautiful and my new life is beautiful!" Tee looked down at her small, almost three-month baby bump. She was actually enjoying being pregnant. She got to eat as much as she wanted, and everyone pampered her. The breast swelling was annoyingly painful, but she was secretly excited about the notion of added cleavage. They seemed to be getting bigger every week. She hoped the added inches would stay once the baby was born. Although she didn't enjoy the morning sickness she first experienced after finding out she was with child, it seemed to have stopped. Odd eating habits were the newest phase in her pregnancy. She dipped a Cool Ranch Dorito in applesauce and chewed it loudly in Blak's ear.

"I hope it's a girl so I can continue to be your only son," said Blak.

Blak was one of several young people God placed in Tee's life to mentor. When she met Isaac Blakston, he was a 19-year-old secular artist tormented by the fast life he no longer enjoyed or wanted to be a part of. He was bedding multiple women, using excessive profanity, and spouting vulgar lyrics in an effort to live up to the image his record company created for him. Although it made him a million-aire, he was miserable. Tee convinced Blak to find peace by following his heart and his God. Doing so allowed him to repair his broken relationship with his parents, who didn't approve of his lifestyle, but ended his relationship with his record label and management company. He even had to sue them for the money they stole from him throughout his career. But the Lord worked it all out in Blak's favor, and he was now with a Christian music label and was getting ready to release his debut hip-hop gospel CD titled *Walking in the Light*. Blak prayed that his new CD would be well received. Even though he stood to lose thousands of his secular fans, he felt good about the positive messages in his songs that anyone of any age could enjoy. He was hoping to gain new fans and win souls for the Kingdom through his music. He couldn't wait for his first single, "Living the Good Life," to drop.

"Aw, Blak, that's so sweet. What can I do for you, baby boy? Is everything all right? You usually call my cell phone," said Tee.

"Yeah. I thought I'd catch you off guard. Nothing's wrong. I just had the urge to talk to you for a few minutes. I can't wait to see you," he said.

"Same here. Don't forget I want you to do a private meet and greet with the group I told you about, Behind the Bars. These little boys and girls have a mother or father who is locked up, and in some cases, both parents are in jail. I know seeing you would brighten their day. We're also going to swing by Mercy Children's Hospital and have you spend some time with the patients there too."

"No problem, Momma. I like doing stuff like that. I'll call you when my plane lands. You're picking me up, right?" he asked.

"Actually, I was going to send a car to get you."

"No deal. I haven't seen you since you convinced me to stop sleeping with a bunch of women just because I could. The only person I want picking me up is you."

Tee had a million things she needed to do, but she couldn't turn down the young man she had grown so fond of. "All right, Blak. You got it. Tee's escort service will be there waiting for you."

"That's the business! I gotta get to rehearsal now."

"Okay, Blak. I'm so proud of you."

"Thanks, Momma. I owe it all to you. I'm glad you'll be helping to guide my career. I trust you with my life. Holla."

He hung up before Tee could say good-bye. She smiled and looked around her spacious office. She and Michael had purchased the building right after she got fired from her old job. Upstairs was a luxurious loft they were renovating and hoped to move in within the next month or so. Soon, to go to work, all the couple would have to do is walk downstairs. So much had changed in only a few months, but the changes were for the better.

The holidays were especially good to her. She and Michael hosted Thanksgiving at their home. His family came into town from Ohio. It was a wonderful time as their two families fellowshipped together. They interacted very well, but there was a noticeable rift between the Stokes men. Michael, his younger brother Maxwell, and their father were cordial to one another but not warm and loving as they had been previously. The Stokes men had a very bad year of revealed painful secrets, sibling rivalry, and betrayal. They were all trying to get past it and become a close-knit family again, but it was going to take time. The bonds of trust had been severely damaged. Michael's mother, Vanessa, prayed day and night that God would restore her family. One member of the Stokes family was oblivious to problems of the adults in the room and had more fun than anyone in there. It was wonderful seeing Michelle play and laugh with Tee's niece and nephew. She truly was a beautiful little girl, and everyone hoped that her mother's past wouldn't have a negative impact on her future. No one would ever guess that her mother was a schizophrenic killer or that her life was the result of Michael's brother sleeping with his now deceased ex-girlfriend Becca.

Christmas held a special present that couldn't be placed under a tree. Tee's premature niece, Little Tina, was allowed to come home on Christmas Eve. After weeks in the NECU of the hospital, she was now able to sleep in her own nursery. It was hard to believe the chubby, gray-eyed baby was only four pounds when she was born. On Christmas Day she cooed, gurgled, and smiled to the delight of everyone in the room, especially her older brother and sister. They wore Sandy's nerves thin asking every day when Little Tina would come home. Now that she was home, they couldn't get enough of her. The two even stood watch over her crib and admired her while she slept.

Michael and Tee flew to Paris to ring in the New Year. They made some wonderful memories sharing kisses atop the Eiffel Tower and dining on French cuisine. They also took a train through the countryside and admired its beauty. Many romantic nights were spent under the starry skies of a foreign land living, laughing, and loving as happily married couples do. Their trip was short, but they promised themselves they would see much more of Europe in the future. It was now February, and the dynamic duo was hard at work launching their business.

Tee lovingly rubbed her stomach again. She could hardly wait for her and Michael's baby to arrive so they could also experience the joys of parenthood. She suddenly realized that Michael had not returned to the office yet. He said he was going to run some errands and come right back, but that was hours ago.

Chapter 2

It's Getting Hot in Here

Michael exited the mineral bathwater and wrapped himself in a large, thick, white towel. The room was hot and steamy, but the warmth felt good to him. He welcomed this opportunity to release some of the tension resulting from a busy week. Running a management business was hectic. All of the things he used to have other people do for him, he was now doing for himself as well as others. As he tied the towel around his waist, Tiffany entered the room. She loved looking at Michael shirtless. The two of them had grown quite close over the past few months. Michael, being a celebrity himself, took Tiffany under his wing and escorted her personally into the lives of the rich and famous. He, Tee, and Tiffany often went to industry parties to promote their business and help Tiffany get the connections she needed to make her mobile massage service a success. And it was working. Business was going so well she had to hire additional help. What began with only her and her twin classmates, Sierra and Siendy, now included a total staff of five extremely attractive masseuses—four women and one man. They traveled anywhere in the continental United States to see their clients.

Things were going so well that she and Michael were considering making her idea of opening a bathhouse a reality. Doing so would allow her to maintain a stationary location to work in. As the mother of an 11-year-old boy, she welcomed the opportunity to stay home as much as possible.

"Are you ready for me now, Michael?" she said while running her hand down his shirtless back. She loved the definition in his muscles. Even though he was retired, Michael still worked out regularly to maintain his solid NFL physique.

"I really need to go, Tiffany. I told Tee I would be back at the office at 1p.m. and it's now 3," he said.

"Well, you *are* working just not at the office. I need you to stay and get the entire bathhouse experience so you can tell me what would entice a man to patronize a bathhouse. Most men take showers, not baths," said Tiffany.

"So I'm you're guinea pig?" laughed Michael. "I could have kept my clothes on and told you that. Quality service and beautiful women. It's the same two things that have been driving them to Tiffany's Magic Touch from the very beginning."

Michael's cell phone rang. He walked over to the area where he laid his clothes and located his phone. The name Dr. Ida Foster was on the screen. He had barely spoken to her since she came to Memphis to tell him that she was unable to locate Becca's long lost brother. She thought he was living in Nashville, but when she arrived, no one she talked to ever heard of him or seen him. Michael told her to keep looking, but the trail was now cold and Dr. Foster had nothing to report. Michael didn't worry about it too much, though, because the disturbing phone calls he previously received from someone who sounded like Becca seemed to have stopped. For that he was grateful. Why would someone want to impersonate a dead woman anyway?

He looked at Tiffany and smiled. "Can you excuse me for a moment? I need to take this call in private."

"Sure, Sugah. Just call me when you need me." She exited the room, shutting the door behind her.

"Hey, Dr. Foster," he said.

"Hello, Michael. How are you? Have you heard from Becca lately?"

"First of all, it's not Becca. Secondly, I'm happy to report that for the last two months I haven't heard a peep from whoever was making those crazy calls," he said.

"I'm happy to hear that, but I thought you would like to know that I received a call from Tee Hee today," said Dr. Foster.

"You did? How's he doing, and what did he say?"

"He seems to be doing fine, but he told me Accent is planning a big celebration in honor of a new donor," said Dr. Foster.

"Oh, that's good. Did he invite you?"

"Not exactly. It seems that someone is giving them $20,000 to name the recreation room in honor of Rebecca DeFoy."

"You can't be serious!"

"I'm afraid so. I called the facility and talked to the director. She said Becca's little brother is behind it. He is trying to create a positive legacy for his big sister because one of the requirements of the donation is that the mural of you, Michelle, and Becca be preserved as long as the facility exists."

"No way! That's crazy!" shouted Michael. "I can't have a picture of me and another woman up for all eternity. I'm married now with my own child on the way. I've been meaning to call Accent and tell them to paint over it, but my life has been so busy I never got around to it. What if the media gets a hold of this? As soon as we get off the phone, I'm calling my lawyer to stop it." Michael slammed his fist on the bench he was sitting on.

"I understand how you feel, but I've been looking for Becca's brother for months with no success. This room dedication ceremony may be the only chance we have to speak to him. If you get the ceremony canceled, we may never find him. I suggest that you don't do that," she advised.

"I understand what you're saying, Dr. Foster, but I can't possibly allow them to keep up that mural. It's an untrue depiction of what happened between me and Becca. It makes it seem like me, Becca, and Michelle were a family. We weren't. She tried to kill me and my wife, and Michelle is not my child. She created that mural as a part of her delusional fantasy that we would one day be together. I don't have a problem with them naming the room after her, but that mural has got to come down. When is this dedication supposed to take place?"

"Friday."

"As in the day after tomorrow?"

"Yes."

"This can't be happening. Are you going?" asked Michael.

"I was planning to. That way, I can meet Becca's brother and find out if he knows anything about the strange phone calls you received."

Michael was curious to meet Becca's brother himself. He was Becca's only known relative, which made him Michelle's only surviving relative on her mother's side. Michelle would be five soon. Although she seemed content with the family she had now, he knew at some point she would want to know more about the other side of her family. It would probably be a good idea to find out what type of man her uncle is beforehand.

"I'll meet you there," said Michael. "I'll call you back in a little while to get more details about this dedication ceremony."

As he hung up, Michael wondered how he was going to explain all of this to his wife. How could he reveal that he needed to go home to Akron to the mental facility where Becca was previously treated to stop them from displaying a mural of him and another woman, that Tee didn't know existed? Tee was also completely in the dark about several other things. Michael hadn't told her about the Becca-like phone calls he received or his hiring of private detective Ida Foster to find out who was making the phone calls. He also hadn't told her that he and Dr. Foster paid a visit to the treatment facility and met Tee Hee, a patient there who befriended Becca while she was there. Michael didn't see how he could tell her where he was going without telling her everything. Maybe it was time to come clean, but she was in the first trimester of her pregnancy, and he didn't want to do anything to upset her. He had heard that the first trimester was the most critical stage of pregnancy and that many women miscarried during this stage. He also witnessed how stress and worry caused his sister-in-law to deliver Little Tina prematurely. Maybe it was best to keep her in the dark a little longer.

Tiffany knocked on the door. "Are you ready for some one-on-one time with me, Superstar?"

"Sorry, Tiffany, change of plans. I'm no longer in the mood for a massage; maybe some other time."

Tiffany's smile quickly morphed into a scowl. "What? I had something special planned for us, I mean you, today."

"I appreciate it, but something has come up and I need to go home. I have some business to attend to."

"But *I* am your business. I'm your number-one client," pouted Tiffany.

"Tee and I have an entire roster of clients to attend to. You know that."

The last thing Tiffany wanted to do was get on Michael's bad side. Because of him, her business was thriving and she was making more money than the rich, married man she used to sleep with.

"Okay. I'm sure there will be other times," she said softly.

"Of course there will be. Nobody does me like you," he said.

"And nobody ever will," she replied. She went over to give him a hug of thanks. As she pulled back from him, she inadvertently brushed against Michael's towel, and it tumbled to the floor. Unashamedly, she looked down and smiled. Michael had never been a shy man when it came to his body, but at that moment he wanted to run and hide. He was ashamed that one of Tee's best friends was ogling a part of his anatomy that should only be viewed by his wife. Rather than stoop and pick the towel up, he turned around and said, "Tiffany, I think you should leave now."

Tiffany had clearly knocked his towel off by accident, but she was not the least bit apologetic about it. She wished he hadn't turned around, but the back was a sight to behold as well. She stood there admiring the hard muscles that rippled through Michael's body from his ankles to his neck. He was a dark-skinned dream. She took careful survey of the definition in his thighs, gluts, and back. Still somewhat damp from the bath and sweating from the heat, beads of moisture slowly slid down his body adding to her enjoyment. She licked her lips. He looked delicious. Tiffany recently dedicated her life to Christ and was trying desperately to practice celibacy. She hadn't had sex in almost four months, and this visual feast in front of her wasn't helping her quest to keep her mind off sex. She realized Michael was embarrassed.

"I'm so sorry, Michael," she lied. "You have nothing to be embarrassed about. I've seen you nearly naked several times during your massages," she said.

"Nearly naked and naked are two different things, Tiffany. This is inappropriate. What if someone were to walk in? We are in a spa. Workers are in and out of here all the time. I asked you to leave. I need you to go now. As I said, I have some business to attend to," said Michael sternly.

Tiffany had done exactly what she was trying to avoid. Michael was upset. She wasn't quite sure if he was mad at himself or at her, but either way, it wasn't good.

"As you wish, sir," she said. She gave his backside another long glance before she turned around and exited the steamy room. *Tee is one lucky woman*, she thought to herself. She was trying very hard not to like her friend's husband, but how could she not? He was everything she ever wanted in a man: attractive, intelligent, sexy, charming, funny, and rich. She was now seeing someone, but he paled in comparison to the magnificent Michael Stokes.

Michael dressed hurriedly and left the spa. As he drove back to the office, he wondered if what just happened was yet another thing he needed to hide from his wife or if he needed to tell her before Tiffany did. He hated keeping so many secrets from the love of his life, but they were all things he felt Tee was better off not knowing until he had them under control.

Chapter 3

How Do You Like Me Now?

Lenora was enjoying her new job and her improved life. She was eating right, exercising, and feeling better than ever. Each morning she went to the gym and worked out for at least an hour before heading to work. She only worked part time, but she still came in almost every day. The private Montessori school where she worked was open year-round to students in kindergarten through sixth grade. She didn't care if she wasn't getting paid for the extra hours because she enjoyed planning her lessons in her art room.

The walls were lined with pictures and projects that her students created. The bright colors and lively designs helped bolster her creativity and transition her adult mind and eyes to seeing the projects she created the way the children would see them. She planned a different project for each grade level. Today, she was planning for sixth grade and was considering something with papier-mâché. The glue and water could get a little messy, but if done correctly, whatever they constructed could be quite beautiful.

Lenora tried every project herself before she presented it to the children. This provided an example of what the finished product would be like.

She cut several pages of a newspaper into long, wide strips to dip into the glue solution. Today, she wore her art apron and her shoulder-length haired was pulled into a ponytail to keep it from falling in her face while she worked.

Lenora smiled as she thought about her life. Her children were doing well. She found a summer music camp for

Herman to attend and he was enjoying exploring the different instruments. Lenora looked forward to the day he would decide which one he wanted to focus on. Her school had a preschool and the twins, Heather and Heston, enjoyed being in class and interacting with other children. She did a fine job of teaching them at home, and they were ahead of most of the other children.

She and her husband, Herman, were doing better as well. His attitude had improved, and he helped more around the house. He didn't insult her about her weight anymore, but he rarely gave her a compliment, either. They spent more time together, and he seemed to enjoy her company, but he was still very distant when it came to intimacy. Lenora prayed that would end soon. She was a married woman whose needs weren't being met.

She often found herself frustrated and wondered what she could do to entice Herman. If her weight was still the issue, she was losing it as fast as she could. She had lost 50 pounds in the last three months, which any weight-loss expert would tell you was great progress. And she did it with exercise and healthy eating. Lenora refused to take any more diet pills or try to rush the process with surgery.

There was something else about Herman that bothered her. She was almost positive that he was spending time at a bar. Yesterday, he came home smelling like beer and peanuts, again. She noticed it before but now it was becoming more frequent. The odd thing was that each day he came home around the same time he would normally come home from work. She was beginning to wonder if he was having an affair. He wasn't sticking his hand in her cookie jar, so he must be sticking it in some other woman's. She tried to not think about it too much and gave him the benefit of the doubt. Maybe he was meeting friends at a bar after work.

Lenora was so engrossed in her thoughts and the papier-mâché piggy bank she was making that she didn't hear the assistant principal, Mr. Rupert, enter her classroom. She almost knocked over her glue solution when he said her name.

"Oh, Mr. Rupert. I didn't know anyone else was here. You startled me."

"I'm sorry, Mrs. James. Your dedication to the students is heartwarming. You're here twice the amount of time you are required to be."

"Thanks, Mr. Rupert. I haven't taught in several years, and I'm trying to make sure my students are getting the best art education possible. I know they are only in elementary, but it was my elementary art teacher who sparked my curiosity and showed me that I had potential and talent. I would love to be able the help my students unleash that as well."

"I'm sure you will," said Mr. Rupert. He stepped closer to Lenora and smelled her hair. "I hope I'm not being too forward, but has anyone told you that you are a very beautiful woman?"

"Not lately," said Lenora. "Thank you. That was nice to hear. When you have a twin sister who looks like a model, you're usually not the one getting the compliments."

"My pleasure. Your sister is the woman you're in the picture with on your desk, right?"

"Yeah. That's Lenice."

"I see the resemblance, but I've always preferred a woman with some meat on her bones. You know, I'm a twin too. My brother, Richard, likes skinny women. Is your sister single?"

"Yeah, in the worst way. She hasn't had a man in forever."

"My brother doesn't have a girlfriend either. He got divorced last year. He took a break from dating, but he thinks he's ready to get back on the dating scene now."

"Well, that's understandable. It's not always easy to move on after a divorce."

"Believe me, I know. I'm divorced myself. You're married, right?"

"I sure am. My husband and I have been married for 10 wonderful years."

"Your husband is one lucky man. If I had a woman like you, there's no way you would be at work on your off days. You would be at home with me." Mr. Rupert let out a chuckle, gave Lenora a mischievous smirk, waved good bye and exited the room.

Lenora smiled. She couldn't remember the last time a man flirted with her. It felt nice. She was sure he didn't mean anything by it. A little harmless flirting never hurt anybody. She focused her attention back to her papier-mâché pig. She wanted to finish the glue portion of it before it was time to go. She needed to get home and do a few chores before fixing dinner for her family.

Chapter 4

Love Is Pain

Lenice looked up at the handsome gentleman smiling in her face. She was accustomed to having men smile at her, but it was obvious this one had motive behind his flashing teeth. He leaned in closely and looked deep into her eyes. He then gave her face a soft soothing touch before whispering in her ear, "It's too loud in here. Let's go someplace quiet where we can talk."

Lenice looked around the club. She was attending one of the more popular after-work sets in the city. It had a reputation for getting the party started early. Its motto, *Work Hard, Play Hard,* glowed brightly against the wall in blue neon lights. The bass was booming, and bodies were moving all around the room. Everyone appeared to be having a good time, and she was too—until this moment.

Here we go again, she thought to herself. Lenice struggled to remember what he said his name was. Was it David, Derek, Derwin? She could have asked him, but she really didn't care. She could have also asked him what they were going to talk about that required someplace quiet, but she already knew the answer. She smiled back at him.

"Where did you have in mind?" she asked.

"How about my place?"

"Your place? What's so special about your place?"

"I have a Jacuzzi, a California King bed, and a spacious patio. That gives you one of three places in which to let your hair down, get comfortable, and get to know me better. Or if you're up for it, we can try all three. How does that sound?"

"That sounds divine, but . . .," Lenice paused.

"But what, baby?" He touched her face again.

Her smile disappeared. "But no thanks, loser. I don't feel like being used for meaningless sex tonight."

The man was taken aback by her response. He looked at her in bewilderment, and then said, "What? What would make you say that?"

Lenice ran her hand through her freshly done coif. Her stylist Taneika designed another masterpiece that just so happened to be attached to her scalp. This one had curls that lay neatly across her forehead with the sides and back tapered.

"What made you think I'm the type of woman who would go home with a man I just met? Is it because I let you buy me a drink? Do you feel I owe you something for that? Perhaps it's because I smiled at you and laughed at all your corny jokes? Is it because I danced with you during a slow song? I'm not that easy, buddy. Now run along and find your next victim. I'm sure there's some clueless broad here you can give that hot-tub, king-bed, porch crap to."

The man clearly didn't know what to say in response to such blunt statements. He was quite attractive and wasn't used to being talked to that way. Most women were flattered by his advances.

"Wait, Doll. I didn't mean any harm, but I thought we had a good thing going. I was hoping we could keep it going outside this club. Don't be so cold." He attempted to grab Lenice by the arm. She snatched it away.

"I said get lost. My goodies stay in the jar. You are wasting your time with me."

The man mumbled something under his breath and walked away feeling embarrassed and dejected.

Lenice was now a serial dater. She had no idea how many men she'd been out with within the past three months. She entertained their company for an evening or more until she was bored or turned off by them. She usually left them alone when things began to get serious or they asked her for sex. She was a celibate, but she was also a commitment-phobe in the worst way. She seemed to have kicked her previous fear of dating, and she traded it in for another coping mechanism. In her mind, if she didn't get serious or develop feelings for a man, she wouldn't get hurt.

It was her refusal to commit that made her leave her church member, Deacon James, alone. She really missed him, but Lenice felt that if she wasn't able to give him what he deserved, it was in his best interest for her to remove herself from his life. He called to check on her occasionally, but whenever he asked her out, she always had an excuse handy for why she couldn't see him.

Chapter 5

Single, Saved & Celibate

Tiffany sat in church listening to William lead the Single and Saved Bible Study class. He was such a gifted teacher. He had a way of breaking down the Bible to where she and others could understand it perfectly. He didn't act like a know-it-all, and he wasn't condescending. All the class attendees talked openly and honestly about their struggles as single Christians and how hard it could be to resist temptation.

As a single man, William was going through the same things. He understood, but he also knew that the best thing Christians could do was to surround themselves with like-minded people and study God's word. The Single and Saved class had about 30 regular members. The majority were female with about five males. They met once a week.

Tonight William introduced them to a blog by an author named Jae Henderson. She had written a piece called "Celibacy 101: Keys to Keeping Your Legs Closed." Some of her advice could be found on her blog Saved & Celibate. Tiffany visited the site from time to time for advice and read what other celibates were going through. Jae was honest about her struggles as well and shared what she felt worked and what didn't work. In this particular piece she gave eight suggestions to help resist temptation. It was primarily geared toward women, but William found ways to make it applicable to anyone. Tiffany read each one carefully and highlighted them with her pink highlighter.

1. **Develop a strong relationship with God and with people of a like mind.**

Abstaining from sex is not easy. You cannot get through this without strong faith and friends who are traveling on the same road who can encourage you along the way. Read your Bible daily, pray, and spend time regularly with Christian friends who understand what you have chosen to do and won't waste your time telling you how crazy you are for abstaining. As iron sharpen iron, one man sharpens another (Proverbs 27:17).

2. Be mindful of your senses.

We live in a sex-laden society. It's in the music, the movies, our favorite TV shows, and the books we read. If you find that those things make you want to have sex, find other forms of entertainment that eliminate or lessen your likelihood to become aroused. Also, watch your speech. Having conversations about sex or sexting on the phone with someone you find desirable will only make you want to participate.

3. Get physical!

Physical activity is a great way to burn off energy. It can help your body get used to the adjustment of not getting any as well. Select an exercise regimen or sport you enjoy and do it regularly. Consider it trading one workout for another. Go hard!

4. Date wisely.

I don't recommend telling every man you meet you're celibate during your first conversation. You have to use your best judgment in this area. If his intentions are honorable, he won't try to have sex with you immediately after meeting you anyway. So it shouldn't be a big deal initially. If it's obvious that sex is what he wants, why entertain his advances? Stick to men who are interested in getting to know who you are, rather than what you look like naked. Try to find a man who is celibate as well. They do exist. If he's not, you will have to tell him as the courtship progresses. He will have to determine whether or not he can handle your decision. Dating men who constantly attempt to get you to have sex makes no sense, especially after you have told him where you stand on the subject. Typically this is a ploy to wear you down. If he can't respect your decision, tell him to kick rocks with no socks!

5. Don't prepare for dates or outings to entice.

We all want to look good when we go out, but if your goal is not to have sex, why entice the opposite sex by dressing provocatively? Plunging necklines, short skirts, and skintight material does not say "hands off." Many men see it as an invitation. You don't have to dress like a nun, but dressing like a video vixen is a no-no. It can also send mixed signals not only to your date but to yourself. Even wearing your sexiest lingerie "just in case" subconsciously says to your mind and body, let's get ready to get it on. Try wearing less-than-impressive underwear instead. They can serve as a mental stop sign. You won't be so quick to show him what you're working with if there's a chance you'll be embarrassed by those stained period panties or big bloomers. Let's not forget the panties with the missing elastic and the bra with the raggedy straps and worn-out cups. Some women choose not to groom their pubic area. I know it sounds crazy, but it works!

6. Put the brakes on affection.

We all want to feel wanted, but pushing the envelope will only frustrate you and your companion. Constant groping, long lasting kissing sessions, lying next to one another naked, and engaging in other forms of sex such as oral or phone sex will not help you achieve your goals. How is getting all hot and bothered, and then having to cool off quickly fun? You know what turns you on, and you also know what will send you over the edge. There is danger in testing the boundaries.

7. Plan outside dates and avoid late-night visits.

Sex usually occurs when two people are alone, so it's important to plan outside activities or activities that include others to help alleviate the temptation. You can double-date, go to the park, a concert, or a café and talk. Fun activities like those can allow you to really get to know a person, explore your common interests and lay a strong foundation of friendship. The best relationships are built on a solid friendship. Now, alone time and romantic evenings can be tricky, but if the two of you set some boundaries and don't cross them, you can have a great time enjoying each other with your clothes on. You may want to put an embargo on midnight movie nights at the house, though. Usually, the later it is the more tempted you will be to get physical. Avoiding alcohol also helps. Alcohol can also increase your desire to have sex.

8. Don't treat this like a prison sentence.

Not having sex isn't the end of the world. Enjoy this time or don't do it. You made this decision because you felt it was the right thing to do. If you're going to complain the entire time and stress about how horny you are, don't do it. Abstaining from sex is a time of self-reflection, spiritual enlightenment, and Godly purpose. You won't experience any of that if you are miserable and constantly brooding over the fact that you aren't getting any. If you are going to give yourself to God, be a cheerful giver.

Tiffany thought the one about wearing raggedy underwear was hilarious, but Jae had a point. She would think twice about shedding her clothes if she had on a pair of bloomers like her grandmother used to wear, but she didn't own a single piece of raggedy underwear. Everything in her drawers was view-worthy. Since she began attending William's church, she had gotten a greater understanding of what celibacy and Christianity was all about. God wanted her to save herself for the love she deserved. It wasn't about depriving her of physical pleasure. It was about preventing her from experiencing the physical and emotional pain that could come along with sexual relationships with the wrong man. She would have to work on being a cheerful giver of herself to God. There wasn't a day that passed that she didn't think about sex, but the good thing was that she wasn't acting on her desires. Tiffany wondered if Jae Henderson would be available for the I'm A Good Woman Empowerment Conference. She made a mental note to tell Tee about her.

Single and Saved Bible Study was her way of surrounding herself with like-minded people. They even went out on group outings once a month. Tiffany thought being a Christian would be boring, but she actually had fun when they were together. They went bowling, skating, to the movies, and out to eat. One night they held an old-school party at someone's home and danced the night away to many of the songs she grew up listening to. She was also surprised to find out that Christians were allowed to drink alcohol as long as it was in moderation. William explained to her that it wasn't a sin to drink. It was a sin to get drunk. He even backed it up with scriptures in the Bible to deepen her understanding.

One of her favorite parts of her Christian walk was William. Their friendship was blossoming into a beautiful courtship. He took a personal interest in her salvation as well as her son's and talked to her often about God, His unwavering love for her, and how she could depend on Him for anything.

This was the first Christian man Tiffany dated, and although he took some getting used to, she was thoroughly convinced that he was exactly what she and her son needed. He was handsome, hardworking, dependable, and kind. William was also a well respected associate pastor at his church with aspirations of one day heading his own church. Tiffany could see herself as a first lady sitting on the first row in a designer suit and big hat. All of those women who looked down at her and gossiped about her would have to eat their words when she emerged as a preacher's wife. She'd made some mistakes, but what woman in love hadn't? She was sure that now that she was a Christian, there was a major blessing in store for her. She just wished she could stop thinking about Michael. He was already taken.

Chapter 6

You Make Me Sick

Tee and Michael sat in their living room across from Solay Peterson of Ultimate Sports Network's popular show *Inside*. Tee promised Solay that when Michael was ready to talk to the media about what was going on in their lives she could have the first interview. Tee and Michael were both nervous. Interviews could be tricky because you never knew what a reporter was going to ask. There was only one topic that she told Solay she could not inquire about and that was Michelle. Michael refused to talk about his niece. He and his family did a good job of keeping her out of the limelight and from hearing negative messages about her mother. They wanted to keep it that way. They did not want to taint her memories of the first person who loved her. Besides, Michelle was still grieving Becca's death, and they didn't want to make it worse. Michelle often had dreams about her and would begin crying after she awoke and realized that her mother was not really there.

"Relax, you two. You look like you're going to the electric chair instead of doing a major television interview," joked Solay. "Besides, I'm your friend. I want you two presented in the best light possible. My reason for being here is not only to land an exclusive with Mr. and Mrs. Michael Stokes, but to dispel some of the awful rumors people have been saying because they know the two of you won't respond."

"Thanks. It's good to know that there are still journalists out there who are interested in the truth and not a sensationalized story," said Tee.

"Yes," agreed Michael. "I appreciate this opportunity to tell my side of the story."

Solay gave both of them a reassuring smile. "My director says we're about to begin. Are you ready?"

"As ready as we'll ever be," said Tee. She was happy that her friend was doing the interview and not someone she didn't know who didn't give a care about her or her family. She hoped this wouldn't take too long, though. She wasn't feeling well, and she needed to pick up Blak from the airport in a couple of hours.

Her assistant, Sheba, was there. Sheba looked at her and gave her a thumbs-up.

"Quiet on the set!" yelled the director. "Roll camera in five, four, three, two, one." He pointed at Solay to cue her that the cameras were rolling.

Solay looked directly in one of the cameras and said, "Hello, everyone. I am Solay Peterson, and this is Ultimate Sport's *Inside,* and right now, I am sitting inside the home of NFL Hall of Famer Michael Stokes and his beautiful wife, Tee. As you all know, the two of them encountered quite a bit of drama after they tied the knot last year. Michael was accused of accepting the gift of a corvette from boosters of the University of Miami during his senior year there, and the NCAA launched an investigation that could have tarnished his name, that of the school, and erased all his college achievements from their record books. The information was said to have come from Michael's manager and longtime friend Peter Parker. Peter later committed suicide, and the investigation was dropped for lack of evidence. The couple has remained very quiet about their ordeal, opting to only issue brief statements through their attorney until now." She then turned her head toward them.

"Hello to both of you and thank you for allowing *Inside* into your lovely home. How are you?"

"We're doing well," said Michael. "And we are happy to have you here."

"Now, there is so much that the public wants to know about you two so let's jump right into the interview, shall we?" asked Solay.

"That's fine with us," said Tee.

"Michael, I understand that initially the NCAA decided to continue its investigation of improper conduct even after your accuser, Peter Parker, was found dead. When you found out, how did you feel about that?"

"I wasn't bothered by it because I knew I was innocent. The NCAA has a job to do, and I respect their desire to do it properly."

Solay continued. "I also understand that it was your father who accepted money from boosters while you were in college, but you had no knowledge that he was doing so."

"Indirectly, yes. My father later explained to me that he was unemployed and Peter offered him money to persuade me to let him represent me after I graduated from college. My father is very sorry for his actions, but at the time he felt he had no choice. It was either accept the money or lose his house and watch his family starve. I'm sure anyone with a family could understand why he did it. However, that doesn't make it right. My father knew the rules. Once the NCAA realized that I had no knowledge about what he and Peter did, they closed their investigation. Also, Peter died before giving them his so called proof of me doing something wrong. But I really didn't do anything wrong."

"You have no idea how many people were happy to see that the man who has been heralded for being a great guy throughout his NFL career turned out to still be a really great guy."

"Thank you, Solay. I appreciate all of the people who stood behind me and continued to believe in me throughout that entire ordeal."

"We both do," chimed in Tee. "Michael and I had recently returned from our honeymoon when we received the news of the investigation. You have no idea how much of a strain that kind of news can put on a new marriage and a family as a whole. I'm proud to say that we survived. God is good."

Solay easily controlled the conversation but gave Tee and Michael each a turn to speak. "Yes, you did, and I understand, Tee, that you went through your own battle. You lost your job at a company you helped build because you took extra time off to be with your husband while he dealt with the situation."

Tee took a deep breath. It still hurt to think about the way she was fired. "Yes, I did. I've been an event planner for over 15 years and through my leadership and hard work the events division at the company I was previously with became one of the most successful marketing and event planning companies in this region. It was a job that I loved dearly and held for over a decade. When I returned to work, after taking some extra time off to support my husband, I was fired. But what others meant for bad God meant for my good. If I hadn't left that company, Michael and I never would have started MiTee Management. We're both really enjoying managing the careers of others."

"That's wonderful, and we'll get to your company soon," said Solay. "Before we change the subject, I want to talk a little more about Michael and Peter.

"Michael, can you tell us what happened with you two? You and Peter not only had a business relationship, but you were the best of friends. What made him turn on you? He was the one who alerted the NCAA to what your father did. Yet, instead of revealing his role in it, he made it look like you knew what was going on. He also went on a media blitz to tell anyone who would listen. He seemed to be trying really hard to smear your good name."

Michael looked at his wife. Tee nodded to let him know it was okay to let it all out. "I'm sorry to say it was about money. Because I'm no longer playing football, Peter could no longer claim a percentage of my multimillion-dollar salary. It didn't exist. What he was making off of my endorsements and speaking engagements wasn't enough for him. He wanted more, and he wanted to make it by hiring me out to host parties at strip clubs. I'm a Christian now. I don't do things like that anymore. When I wouldn't agree, he lashed out at me through the media."

"You must have been very hurt," said Solay.

"I was, but I was more hurt by his death. I'm sure in time Peter and I could have worked through our differences, but because he's no longer with us, we won't be able to."

"Is it true that even after what he did to you, you paid for his entire funeral and even spoke during the service?"

"It's true. I choose not to focus on the last few ugly months of his life. They pale in comparison to the years of good times we had together. Even though he had his own motives, Peter guided my career and helped to make me the NFL great I am today. He took a naive 21-year-old and showed him what to do to become a superstar. It was his negotiating skills, PR skills, and vision that helped to put my name on the lips of millions of people. I can't forget that. He was also my friend. We had some really good times together. Peter was my brother from another mother, and I miss him."

Michael turned his head away as he fought back tears. He was not about to cry on national television. He had to be strong.

"Do you think he killed himself because he felt guilty about what he was doing to you?"

Michael looked at Tee and asked a question with his eyes. She nodded her head yes again.

"I know what the coroner's report said, but I don't believe that Peter committed suicide. The one thing Peter loved more than money was himself. The Peter I know wouldn't have killed himself no matter what he did to someone else."

Solay sat back in her seat. "Whoa. You mean to tell me that you believe Peter was murdered."

"I sure do," said Michael.

"Do you have an idea who could have done it?"

"No, I don't," Michael lied. He knew that if he said on national TV that he believed his brother's dead baby momma killed Peter it would ruin him.

"Have you shared your theory with the police?"

"I did, but they said the coroner's report clearly showed that Peter committed suicide. I don't care what they say, though. I know in my heart that Peter was murdered."

"Tee, do you stand by your husband's theory?"

"What I know is my husband knew Peter very well. If he feels that strongly that Peter didn't kill himself, then who am I to question it? If he was murdered, I only hope that they find whoever did it and bring them to justice."

Solay turned her head back to the camera. "You heard it here first, folks. We'll be right back with more Ultimate Sports *Inside* after this quick break."

"And cut," said the director.

"Give us a second and we'll get right back into the interview," said Solay.

The portable studio lights were shining brightly on Michael and Tee, causing their temperatures to elevate. Michael's bald head was sweating, and the sweat was slowly making its way down the sides of his face. Sheba handed him some water and someone from makeup came with a towel and wiped away the beads of sweat. Tee squeezed his hand tightly.

The director said loudly, "And we're back in five, four, three, two, one . . ."

"We're back with more Ultimate Sports *Inside*. I'm Solay Peterson, and I'm here with one of my favorite couples, retired NFL player Michael Stokes and his wife, Tee. Michael, I can tell that the death of your former manager, Peter Parker, is a very emotional topic for you. However, I have another touchy topic I want to talk about. Last year, your ex-girlfriend Rebecca DeFoy was captured by the police and admitted to a mental institution. She was supposed to stay there until her trial. From my understanding, she abandoned her four-year-old daughter and followed you and Tee for weeks in an attempt to break you up. She even tried to injure you. Michael, she attempted to run you over with a car, and she threw Tee off a boat into the middle of the ocean while the two of you were vacationing in Jamaica. As if that weren't enough, she also stole large amounts of money, jewelry, and a car from your parents.

"I think it's safe to say she was obsessed with you, Michael. Rebecca later escaped from the mental facility in Akron, Ohio, where she was being treated and stabbed you and Tee during a benefit dinner here in Memphis. During the attack, she was shot to death by a private investigator who happened to be in the audience. Michael, your injuries were minor, but Tee ended up being admitted to the hospital for severe puncture wounds. She lost a lot of blood and could have died.

"I'm sure you both have a lot of anger and resentment toward Rebecca for that act. Please look at the screen over there." Solay pointed to her left. "On the screen is a mural that Rebecca painted on a wall in the facility where she was being treated. This Friday, the facility is planning to name the recreation room where she painted it after her. If you look at this picture I have here of the mural, you can clearly see the mural is of Rebecca, Michael, and her daughter Michelle. Now Michael, you and Rebecca broke up before Michelle was born; you didn't even know she existed until last year. Rebecca originally made you believe that Michelle was your daughter, but a DNA test proved that she wasn't. However, that didn't stop her from painting what some might call a 'family portrait' of all of you. Michael, I understand you've known about the mural for quite some time. What went through your mind the first time you saw it? And what about you, Tee?"

Michael looked at Tee and reached for his water. He gulped it down rapidly. Tee looked at the picture on the screen and blinked several times before she turned and looked at Michael in disbelief. She then turned her attention back to the mural and began to rub her stomach as she looked at the painted smiling faces of Michael, Michelle, and the woman who tried to kill her on a wall in a room she didn't recognize.

"Michael, you knew about this and you didn't tell me?" asked Tee. "There's a gigantic picture of you and the woman who tried to take my life and you didn't tell me?"

"Tee, I was going to tell you," said Michael.

"When?" she screamed. "After the dedication ceremony and it was all over the news? How could you keep this from me? You sicken me. This interview is over!"

Tee stood up to leave, but she suddenly grew dizzy and her body began to sway. The room felt like it was moving. In an attempt to steady herself she reached for the arm of her sofa. Michael noticed her discomfort and stood up to help her regain her balance. When she was standing, it was obvious that Tee was pregnant because she dressed like it. She wanted the world to know she was with child. She wore a lovely blue maternity dress with matching blue two-inch heels. She would have looked beautiful if it weren't for the scowl of disapproval mixed with nausea she wore across her face.

"Are you okay, Tee?" asked Solay.

Tee opened her mouth to answer, but instead of uttering a word, she bowed her head forward and vomited on all three of them. Solay received the bulk of her breakfast. Vomit splattered in her face and hair. She let out a high pitched screamed in disgust. Tee put her hand over her mouth in an attempt to try to catch some of it, but it was too late. Moans and comments could be heard around the room from members of the camera crew voicing how grotesque they believed her actions to be. Sheba laughed. Tee realized the cameras were still rolling and was overcome with embarrassment. "I'm sorry. Pregnancy can be hard," she sobbed and ran from the room.

Solay was mortified. She was still sitting down and held her arms away from her body as if she didn't want to touch herself. One of the crew members ran over with a towel and began trying to wipe away the vomit. Michael didn't know what to do to make the situation better, but he knew everyone needed to leave.

"Like my wife said, this interview is over. I suggest you and your camera crew get out of my house as fast as possible. Solay, you knew my wife knew nothing about this mural. This was a set-up. You pretended to be my wife's friend so you could get a story. Don't you people realize that this is our life, not some daytime drama to increase your ratings? As far as I'm concerned, you got exactly what you deserved." He looked down. Vomit was all over his pants and shoes. "How's this for shock value? Get out!"

"You heard the man, people. Party's over!" screamed Sheba. "Pack up your stuff and get ta steppin'! I got this, Michael. You go check on Tee." She turned to Solay. "Don't even think about trying to use one of their bathrooms. There's a gas station bathroom somewhere with your name on it. You smell about as foul as you are right about now."

Chapter 7

Blackmail

"I need more money," said Casper.

"No deals. I don't need your help, nor do I want it. Tee is happy. I've decided to leave her alone. I'm not going to help you mess up her life. I still love her, and it hurts to see her with someone else, but I'm not that selfish," said Mac.

"You will help me, or I will tell the entire city you are a pedophile!" screamed Casper.

"A pedophile? What are you talking about? You're crazy. I only date grown women."

"Oh really? Well, while you were on your little women spree, I arranged for you to meet a certain 16 year old who looks to be in her 20s. Do you remember Star?"

Mac laughed. "You're mistaken. Star is 24."

"Check your phone. I'm sending you something."

Mac referred to the woman on the other end as Casper because it was as if she were a ghost. He never saw her, and she wouldn't tell him her name. So he gave her one. He wondered what she was up to now. His phone chimed to announce the arrival of a text message. It contained four pictures. The first was of him and Star laughing and having drinks at the bar. The second was of them kissing each other near his car in the parking lot. The third was of Star holding the camera up and smiling next to Mac while he was asleep in his bed. They both appeared to be naked. The fourth was a smiling girl in a ponytail and a cheerleader's uniform who closely resembled a young Star.

"You can't fool me. That's an old picture. All this proves is that two consenting adults slept together. Get off my phone."

Casper laughed. "That picture was taken this year. Do yourself a favor and go to the basketball game tonight at Lester High School. Pay close attention to the cheerleaders and see if you recognize anyone. I now realize that the two of you were drinking, so add buying liquor for a minor to your list of sins," instructed Casper.

"Why would you do that to a child?" Mac demanded.

"I needed some insurance. I figured you would grow a conscience at some point. Honey, that girl has been turning tricks to help support her and her baby since she was 13. It's a sad situation. Her mother is a crack head and can't stay sober long enough to keep a job, let alone take care of her kids. All I did was offer her the opportunity to step up her game. You were a nice change from the grimy blue-collar workers she's used to doing. I encourage you to investigate this one for yourself. Go ahead and go to the school. See if I'm lying. I'll tell you in the morning where to leave my $10,000." Casper hung up the phone.

Mac didn't know what to think. Did he really have a sexual encounter with a minor? He remembered going out with Star. He remembered taking her to a restaurant, having dinner and way too many drinks. Everything else was a blur. They were both so drunk that night. The next morning he woke up next to her in his boxers. They both had a hangover and slept in. Later that afternoon, Mac gave her some money and dropped her off at the nail salon. She said she would find her own way home. He never contacted her again. He didn't like her that much, but she was cute.

He looked at his watch. It was 1:30 p.m. High school games normally started around 6 p.m. Mac was scheduled to play poker with some buddies that evening. He called to tell the host he wouldn't be there. He had the urge to watch high school hoops instead.

Chapter 8

My Achy-Breaky Heart

Tiffany sat in a restaurant anxiously waiting for William to arrive. He called her that morning and asked her to meet him for a late lunch. He said he had something very important to talk to her about. Tiffany was on pins and needles because she was sure that he was going to ask her to take their relationship to the next level and become a couple. They were already acting like boyfriend and girlfriend, and she felt that it was time for her to have the title. William spent time with her and Quincy 2 at least twice a week. They saw each other at Bible Study each Wednesday and church on Sunday. She truly enjoyed Bible Study, but she enjoyed seeing him in his Sunday best much more. She looked at the way other women in the church swooned over the handsome young pastor as he led the church in praise and worship.

In addition to being a pastor, William was a gifted psalmist. He often led the choir, using his soothing tenor voice to help usher in the Spirit of the Lord. She also loved to hear him pray. He prayed with such sincerity and fervor that Tiffany was sure all his prayers were heard by God. William suggested that she pray often, and she did. She tried to pray in the morning, around noon, and at night before she went to bed. She felt herself getting to know the Savior, and she was enjoying the feeling of comfort that came with it. She hoped it would always be this way. She and William looked good together. With a savvy sexy businesswoman like herself by his side, there was no telling how successful his ministry could become. William could be the next T. D. Jakes.

Tiffany drank her water and daydreamed about all the things they could accomplish together while she waited for him. They could head conferences that would be attended by thousands, write books, and produce movies. Tiffany put her thoughts away and gave a demure smile when she saw William stride into the restaurant looking as handsome as ever.

William enjoyed his time with Tiffany. She was a beautiful woman with a sweet personality. She wasn't a bad cook either. However, he never expected her to garner the type of attention she did. Whenever they walked into a room, it was all eyes on them. She was a flashy woman with a cutting-edge flair for fashions. She liked nice things, and other people seemed to notice. He had been praying for the last three months about their relationship. He even consulted his pastor and some of the elders of the church. He needed to be sure that she was the woman God wanted him to be with. He now felt he had his answer, and it was time for him to share it with her.

William spotted Tiffany as soon as he walked in the restaurant. She looked beautiful. She wore a red Capri jumpsuit and five-inch heels. She recently colored her hair a rich reddish brown. The hue seemed to bring more attention to her brown eyes he loved so much. William wiped his sweaty palms on his slacks. He was nervous. Tiffany stood and greeted him with a warm hug. He kissed her on the cheek and asked her to have a seat. He wanted to say the words before he lost the nerve to do so.

"You look lovely. Tiffany, I don't know how to say this delicately. It's not going to be pleasant no matter how I word it. I don't think we should continue dating."

Tiffany was almost sure her heart momentarily stopped, and then started beating double time to make up the beats missed.

"What? But why? I thought you liked me," she said.

"I do like you. I like you a lot, but I don't think you're the woman for me," explained William.

"This makes no sense. You mean to tell me that you've been wooing me for the past three months only to tell me that I'm not right for you?"

"I'm sorry. I never meant to hurt you or lead you on but God has revealed a few things to me over the past couple of weeks that I can't continue to ignore. He's showing me that we shouldn't be together."

"Do you mind sharing with me what the good Lord showed you," said Tiffany sarcastically.

"Tiffany, you are too sexy and distracting to be a preacher's wife. Don't get me wrong, you're beautiful. It's obvious that you take great care to look your best each day, but your selections aren't becoming of the kind of woman I need by my side."

Tiffany looked down at what she wore. Her fitted jumper was Evan Picone—expensive, stylish, and sexy—her favorite fashion combination. She was in New York last week working a private party and purchased it from one of the boutiques she saw on her way to the airport.

"What's wrong with what I wear?"

"Well, for starters, everything is form-fitting. You are a shapely, voluptuous woman. It's obvious you are proud of your assets. Almost every top you wear reveals cleavage and not to mention those hip and booty-hugging dresses, pants, and skirts you wear. You're just too beautiful for me and too glamorous. I need a woman who doesn't call so much attention to herself. I need someone a little more humble in attitude and appearance. Everything you wear screams *Look at me! I should be the center of attention.* I'm not the right man for you. People have begun to talk, and I don't like my woman being the topic of locker room sex jokes and lustful stares all the time. The provocative manner in which you dress makes men want to sleep with you.

"I thought about asking you to dress more conservatively, but I realized your attire is part of what makes you who you are. Besides, I didn't think you would do it. Perhaps you don't realize it, but you ooze sensuality. The way you bat your eyelashes, the way you sashay across a room, and the way you lean into a man, like you're doing now, so he can look down your shirt as you talk to him, is who you are. Tiffany Tate is this beautiful, sexy goddess who makes men want to jump her bones without even trying. If I asked you to change you wouldn't be you anymore, but I can't deal with it. It's not becoming of a preacher's wife, and that's what I'm looking for, a wife.

"I hope this doesn't deter you in your Christian walk. I've enjoyed watching you mature in Christ, and I'd like to think that I had a hand in it. Continue to let God use you. He wants to. I would like to be your friend, if you'll let me." William took a gulp of Tiffany's water when he finished. Breaking up with someone you aren't officially with was nerve-wracking.

Tiffany sat up straight and bit her bottom lip as she listened to William say some of the most ridiculous nonsense she ever heard. Not once did he mention a flaw in her personality. It was all based upon her outward appearance.

"Let me get this straight. You don't want to see me anymore because I'm beautiful and sexy. I make you look good wherever we go. You're the envy of every man in the room, but because I choose to accentuate the physical gifts

God gave me rather than hide them, I don't have preacher's wife potential. That is the most idiotic thing I've ever heard. I don't care what people say or think about me. I'm above such nonsense. I prefer to focus on things that could enhance the lives of me, my son, and my future husband. You are a hypocrite, Pastor William. You preach about coming as you are and how God loves each of us and looks at what's on the inside, and it's our job as Christians to emulate that. Evidently, you don't believe your own teachings because you're more concerned about what other people think than how I make you feel. You like me and you know it, but because I don't dress like a plain Jane, I'm too much for you. You don't want me to steal your shine. That's what this is about. You're upset because when we walk in a room people see me before they see you. You want a woman who wants to stand in her man's shadow and solely work behind the scenes to advance him. If that's what you want, then you're right; I'm not the woman for you.

"Furthermore, you want a woman who doesn't intimidate or seem like a threat to other women. Everyone knows that the backbone of the black church is its female members. I see the way those women at your church look at me. They look down their noses while they fan with those raggedy Martin Luther King fans. They're jealous! You know why I like you, William, and why I *wanted* to be with you? It's because I thought you were different. Until now, you hadn't mentioned or beat me up about my past once. You made me feel special and wonderful, but now I see you're just like everybody else. Well, you won't have to worry about me anymore. I won't bother you again with my flashy ways, and I won't be back to your church. You have wasted three precious months of my life. You should know that under these designer clothes and this flawless skin is a woman with a heart, and you, sir, have wounded it deeply. While you were finding reasons not to love me, I was finding reasons to love you more than I already do.

"I don't want your friendship. You don't deserve my friendship, and you are going to regret letting a woman like me go. I thought you were the man for me, but you're right; you are not the man for me. The man for me is smart enough to know that women like me help build empires. Do think Jay Z ever thought once that Beyoncé's looks would be a liability for him? She flaunts her bootyliciousness everywhere she goes. I was going to upgrade you, but I see you're too holier than thou to see how much of an asset I am to you. Goodbye, William." Tiffany rose to leave.

William sat there speechless and embarrassed. While Tiffany went off on him several of the other patrons turned and gave them their full attention and were clearly enjoying the show. Some of the ladies even clapped when she finished. Tiffany retrieved her purse from the chair next to her and sashayed away from him. He felt horrible. He did care for Tiffany, and at times he thought he might even love her. He was happier the past few months than he had been in a very long time. She was beautiful, smart, and funny, and she went out of her way to treat him like a king. Best of all, not once since the night she found out he was a preacher had she tried to sleep with him. That was rare for him. Usually women acted like they didn't have a problem with his celibacy and later tried to entice him, repeatedly.

He continued to watch Tiffany as almost every man in the restaurant turned his head as her shapely behind made its way to the door. William began to wonder if taking the advice of the men in his church was the right thing to do. She didn't look or act like the dozen or so women at the church who were vying for his attention. That's what attracted him to Tiffany. Those other women were throwing themselves at him while quoting Bible scriptures.

They tried to find any reason they could to be in his presence and talk about how much they loved the Lord. It got to be so bad that he began referring all his counseling sessions with female members to one of the female associate pastors. He saw the way members of his church looked at Tiffany with disdain, and he heard the way they gossiped about her past relationship with a married man. William knew she was a changed woman better than anyone. There was even a rumor that she and her masseuse team were selling more than massages, but he knew that was a lie too. William lowered his head and prayed a silent prayer that his actions didn't deter Tiffany from continuing to serve God and abstain from sex. She was a good woman, and he knew that. He prayed that she would find someone who was able to give her what he couldn't.

Tiffany brushed the tears that escaped her eyes as she walked swiftly to her car. This wasn't supposed to be happening. She was Tiffany Tate, and Tiffany Tate always came out on top.

Chapter 9

Mentorship Is Mandatory

As Tee drove to the airport to pick up Blak she thought about the picture of the mural she saw during the interview. She couldn't believe that Michael kept something so important from her. And Solay . . . the nerve of that woman! She pretended to be her friend only so she could ambush her on national television. She hadn't meant to throw up on her, but Tee wasn't a bit sorry that she did. This was a horrible time for Blak to come in town, but she couldn't jeopardize their most high-profile client because she was upset with her husband.

Tee was so angry with Michael that she refused speak to him. She locked him out of their bedroom while she cried and got cleaned up. After standing at the door and begging her to open it for 30 minutes, he finally realized the best thing for him to do was leave and wait for her to calm down. Michael left Sheba to handle the exit of the television crew and went for a drive.

Tee didn't want to be late to pick up Blak from the airport. She pulled herself together as quickly as she could and left. She turned on the radio and listened to some classical music as she drove. It always had a calming effect on her. Once she arrived at Memphis International Airport, she parked her truck and made her way to baggage claim to wait for Blak. Tee thought about the day she met him and her mentee Patrice. That reminded her Patrice called her earlier and she needed to return the call. Patrice had come a long way. It was almost a year ago that she found the teenager and her friends in Blak's dressing room doing things no self-respecting young lady should be doing. Patrice later reached out to Tee, and she had been mentoring her ever since.

She seemed to have a good head on her shoulders, but she didn't have the best home situation. Tee was also shocked to find out that she habitually lied about her age. The night they met, Patrice told her she was 20 when she was only 16. She definitely had the body of a 20-something-year-old, and it had gotten more svelte since she joined the cheerleading squad and the track team.

Tee wasn't surprised to find out she was a teenage mother. Her son was one year old, but she was surprised to find out that she was being raised by her 27-year-old sister who had a child of her own. Despite her situation, Patrice got pretty good grades and was active in school. With the right influences and opportunities Tee was sure she was going to be okay. She was willing to do whatever she could to help her out.

Chapter 10

Be Good

"Are you angry?" asked Star.

"Yes, but with myself. I should have taken the time to get to know you, rather than doing what I did," said Mac. "I'm sure if we talked more I would have realized that you were a child."

He and Star were sitting in his BMW talking. He was trying his best not to scare the child, but Mac shuddered to think of what could happen if the media got their hands on those pictures. Star looked like a grown woman the night he met her, but now in her cheerleading uniform, long weave ponytail, and hoop earrings, she resembled the teenager she was. Mac felt sorry for her. No teenager should have to endure what she was going through. As she talked, he remembered what attracted him to her. She had a deep, bassy voice he found sexy. He thought she would make a great phone sex operator. She would have to get rid of that Southern accent, though. It wasn't bad, but she could definitely do without it.

"Star, I need to ask you something, and I need an honest answer. Did we have sex?" asked Mac.

"Naw, you were way too drunk for that. We slept in the same bed, though. I took your clothes off and took those pictures," she answered.

"Are you having sex with men for money?"

"No, sir. I only agreed to go out with you because that lady promised me that if I got you drunk I wouldn't have to have sex with you."

He breathed a sigh of relief. Casper was lying. Thank God.

"Is your mother really on drugs, and you are taking care of your child and your sister?"

"Yes, my mother is on drugs, but I live with my older sister, Amy. She helps take care of me and my baby and her daughter. She works at Burgerville as a shift leader. She doesn't make a lot of money. It gets tight sometime, though. Sometimes she can't pay the light bill until her next check, and they cut the lights off for a few days. Or we run out of Pampers and can't get more right away and have to use cloth diapers. I try to bring in some extra money when I can, but Amy doesn't want me working. She said she wants me to try to enjoy being a teenager and get good grades so I can get a scholarship to go to college. She said she doesn't want me to be like her. She wants me to get a good job. We both get food stamps so we got plenty of food, but what good is that if you can't use the stove to cook it or it spoils in the refrigerator?"

Star felt bad about what she did. Mac seemed like a nice guy. She didn't mean to put him in a bad situation, but she needed the money. So she set him up. She wanted to try to make it up to him some way.

"You hungry? We got lights now, and my sister cooked yesterday. There's plenty of food left. You could come over for dinner. My sister's a really good cook." She looked at him with bright eyes, a smile, and a hopeful, *please* puppy-dog face.

"No. I think I should go home," said Mac.

Her face fell.

"I thought you said you wanted to get to know me, Mac."

The last thing Mac wanted to do was hurt her feelings, and he would need her on his side if those pictures actually leaked. He hadn't figured out how he was going to get Casper to leave him alone, but he knew he was going to need Star's help to do it.

"You know what? A home cooked meal would probably do me some good. Let's go," he said.

"Cool! I should probably tell you what my real name is then. It's not Star. It's Patrice."

"I figured it wasn't. Patrice. That's a pretty name." Mac started the car and followed her directions to her house. He wasn't quite sure why she wanted him to be her friend, but he needed to keep her close to him in case Casper tried to use her against him. It angered him that someone tried to use a child to hurt him.

Patrice was holding her cell phone in her hand, and it began to vibrate. She kept it there the entire time they were talking in case Mac became violent and she needed to call for help. She didn't deserve to be hit no matter what she had done. Mac looked over and noticed that the name on the screen read Tee Stokes.

How does she know Tee? he wondered.

Patrice's face lit up, and she answered. "Hey, Ms. Tee. Thanks for returning my call, but can I call you back? I'm talking to my new friend. No, ma'am. He's not my boyfriend, but I'm taking him home to meet my sister. Yeah, I'll tell Amy you said hello. I love you too. Bye."

Patrice hung up the phone and Mac asked the question in his head.

"I met her at a concert last year. She got all on me and my girls for going backstage with a rapper who was trying to sleep with us. She gave me her card and told me I could call anytime. One day I did, and she's been my girl ever since. I don't see her that often, but she sends me gifts in the mail, encouraging text messages, and she really listens when I need someone to talk to. I'm supposed to volunteer during her I'm A Good Woman Empowerment Conference. I think I'm gonna be a greeter. She said it would be a good experience for me and would help me to network. I'm excited!"

"Well, she should know. Tee is the queen of networking."

"You know her?"

"I sure do."

"Isn't she cool!" said Patrice.

"As a cucumber," Mac replied.

He wondered if there was a way to use Patrice to get back in Tee's good graces. He hadn't spoken to her since her sister, Sandy, threw him out of her house months ago because she thought he was trying to put the moves on Tee. All he was trying to do was feed Tee breakfast. Sandy didn't believe him. He didn't want that to be Tee's last memory of him. Mac was no longer trying to be her man, but he didn't want there to be any hard feelings between them. He somehow felt better having her in his life in some capacity.

Chapter 11

Shopper's Delight

Lenora looked at a can of tuna fish and put it in the shopping cart.

"See, this is why I hate going grocery shopping with you. You take all day," complained Lenice.

"That's because I'm shopping for five people, and you're only shopping for one. Of course it's going to take me longer than it takes you. Why are you in such a hurry? It's not like you have someplace to go."

Lenice held up her index finger. "First, that is irrelevant. No one in their right mind wants to spend their entire day at the grocery store. It's cold in here, and second, I shop for two. Did you forget about Webster?"

"Oh yeah. I'm sure that five-pound dog of yours has an extensive grocery list. If you put more on your list you could put some meat on those bones, and you won't be so cold."

"Don't start, Lenora. Don't talk about my size and I won't talk about yours."

Lenora knew when to stop. She had lost quite a bit of weight, but she was nowhere near as thin as her sister.

They were approached by a short, chubby woman in tight jeans and an oversized pink shirt with Girls Kick Butt written on it. "Lenora, it's so good to see you," exclaimed the woman in a loud, shrill voice. She gave her a hug from behind like they were old friends.

Lenora didn't need to turn around to know who was on her backside. She could recognize that annoying voice anywhere. It belonged to Bernice Mayweather. Herman's boss's wife. She was a sweet lady but incredibly loud and incredibly emotional. Lenora turned, but before she could completely face her, Bernice grabbed her and pulled her to her massive bosom.

"I am so sorry about what happened. Leroy hated to let Herman go, but the order came directly from the corporate office, and he had no choice. He felt just horrible. We love you guys like family, and we knew how much you needed that money. We have three children ourselves, and I couldn't imagine what we would do if Leroy lost his job. How are you all doing? I heard you got a job teaching. I'm sure that money is coming in handy."

Lenora and Lenice both tried to quickly hide the looks of confusion on their faces. What was Bernice talking about? Herman hadn't said anything about losing his job. He still got up every morning and got dressed as if he were going to work. Lenora had to get to the bottom of this.

"We're doing fine. It's a struggle, but we're taking it day by day. Herman tried to hide it from me at first. He's such a proud man," she said.

"Honey, most men are," said Bernice.

"I still don't think he's telling me everything. Just between me and you, when exactly did the company let my Herman go?"

"It was right after the beginning of the year. Corporate wanted him to do it earlier, but my Leroy put his foot down and told the head honcho that he was not about to fire anyone around the holidays. He tried to stretch it out until Valentine's, but they refused. He was able to negotiate a decent severance package, though. That's better than nothing, but I knew with a family your size it wouldn't last long. Your lives aren't as lavish as ours, but it stills take a pretty penny to make sure everyone's needs are met, I'm sure."

Lenora was dumbfounded. That meant Herman had been unemployed for at least six months, and he hadn't said a word to her about it. If he wasn't going to work, where was he going every day?

Lenice did not appreciate Bernice's last comment. Her sister lived better than most. "Well, Bernice, thank you for your concern, but my sister and her family are doing fine," she said. "We have to cut this short. We have some other errands to run. Tell Leroy Lenora said hello." She grabbed Lenora by the arm and wheeled their shopping cart toward the checkout counter.

Lenora stood silent while a pimply faced young man with red hair rang up her groceries. She didn't want to discuss what Bernice told her in a public place. They could talk in the car. She decided that confronting Herman wasn't the way to handle this situation. She would have to use her detective skills to figure out exactly what Herman was doing every day. She was now more positive than ever that he was having an affair. There were too many unaccounted for hours in the day.

Chapter 12

For the Love of Tee

    Michael drove around in his Porsche wondering what to do. Tee didn't say one word to him before he left. She opened the door once to hand him the wallet he asked her to give him. He tried to talk to her, but she shot a look at him that let him know that she had no intentions of holding a conversation with him at that moment. She let him leave without giving him a kiss or asking when he expected to be back. Those were two things Tee usually did when he departed. He hadn't meant to hurt her. He wanted to protect her. His plan was to take care of the mural after he had a chance to meet Becca's brother. But now, meeting Becca's brother would have to wait, and Dr. Foster would have to be upset with him. He knew what he had to do, and he had to do it now.

    Michael made a call to his lawyer, Edward, and ordered him to call Accent Behavioral Health and inform the director that if they didn't stop the dedication ceremony and paint over that mural he would sue them. Michael's name and likeness were trademarked, and no one could use it without his written permission. He had Peter to thank for that. Peter insisted that he do it to protect himself in the event anybody ever tried to make money off his fame. Accent was in clear violation of that trademark because he was not asked, nor did he consent to have his picture on their wall. He also told his lawyer to inform them that he would give them a $50,000 donation for complying with his request immediately. They could still dedicate the recreation room to Becca if they wanted to, but that mural had to be gone within 24 hours or he would start legal proceedings. Edward assured Michael that he would make the call, and then follow it up with an official letter.

Michael hoped that would make Tee feel better. It certainly made him feel better. He decided that as soon as she got home he would come clean about everything. He would even tell her that he thought Tiffany had a crush on him. "No more secrets," he told himself. "No more secrets."

Chapter 13

Sin and a Shame

Teresa sat in the recreational room staring at a humongous mural of her friend's husband, the woman who attacked her, and an adorable little girl. She was disappointed in herself. After working so hard to kick the habit, she found herself returning to her old pastime during the cruise she and her husband took. That probably wasn't the best place for a recovering alcoholic. Liquor was everywhere in abundance. What started as one sip turned into a binge, and before she knew it, she was asking her husband, Zachery, to take her back to rehab. She didn't have a choice. The head of her police precinct told her to get cleaned up once and for all or get kicked off the force. She didn't want anyone to know. All her friends and family were so happy when she stopped drinking that she couldn't bear to see the disappointment in their faces if they found out she relapsed. She took an extended leave from her job and checked herself into a treatment facility in Akron, Ohio. She didn't know anyone there and wasn't likely to bump into someone who would recognize her.

It was quiet at Accent Behavioral Health, and the staff was nice, but she couldn't understand for the life of her why that mural was there. It was her fourth day at Accent, and each day she stared at the mural wondering if Tee knew it existed.

While she sat there an elderly gentleman she heard people referring to as Tee Hee came and sat beside her. He smiled, and she smiled back, but Teresa really wasn't in the mood for conversation.

"Pretty, ain't it?" said Tee Hee. "My friend Becca painted it before she broke out and got killed. I remember her working from morning 'til night on that thing like it was yesterday. *Tee hee,*" he laughed again. "She was obsessed with it. It's a shame it might have to come down."

Teresa looked at him and asked, "Why?"

"I was volunteering in the office and heard the director saying that man in the picture's lawyer called and said if they don't take it down he was gone sue'em. *Tee hee,*" he laughed again, "she said she might just get a lawyer herself because Accent could make a lot of money giving tours of the facility to his fans. Him being a native of Akron and all. She was even thinking about calling a press conference to tell the world about how he was trying to bully them into taking it down. *Tee hee,* don't make sense to me, though. Why would somebody want to get rid of such a pretty picture? It ain't done nothing. It's the person who did it who did the wrong. Becca wasn't all that bad. Poor soul. She was in love with a man who didn't love her. Last time I checked, that weren't no crime either. *Tee hee.*"

Teresa listened silently, mentally processing the information she was being given. It seemed that Michael and Tee did know about the mural. Knowing Tee, she was highly upset, and Michael was taking it down to make her happy. The facility was trying to get a payday off her friends. She didn't appreciate it, and she wondered what she could do about it. She also wondered why Tee Hee laughed while he talked, when clearly there was nothing funny. She later learned that it was a part of his disorder, and he couldn't help himself.

Chapter 14

Be Careful What You Ask For

The next day after Herman left for "work," Lenora searched his clothes frantically for some small clue of where he might be going each day. He was infamous for leaving things in his pockets. She was always careful to check them whenever she washed. Once he had a tube of superglue in there. It burst in the dryer and ruined several items that belong to her as well as Herman. She stuck her hand into a pair of khakis and came out with a book of matches that read The Kitty Kat Club.

The matchbook wasn't much, but it was something she felt was worth an immediate investigation. She called her elderly neighbor, Mrs. Crenshaw, to see if she could come over and watch the twins for a couple of hours. She was going to go to The Kitty Kat Club and get to the bottom of this.

Lenora pulled into the club's parking lot and prayed for strength. She knew he was there because she circled the building and saw Herman's car parked in the back. She had never been into a strip club before, and she wasn't comfortable doing so now. She asked her sister to come with her, but Lenice was at work and couldn't leave. Lenora prayed that she wouldn't see anything that could end her marriage. It was lunchtime, and the parking lot was full. Evidently, The Kitty Kat Club sold $5 lunch specials in addition to eye candy. The meal deal drew a crowd of men and women to their establishment each day.

Lenora walked in and was greeted by a scantily clad woman wearing a small top with her cleavage spilling out and a pair of boy shorts that barely covered her behind. She escorted Lenora to the only empty seats in the establishment, which were located at the bar. All the tables were full of hungry people stuffing their faces. The room was dark with flashing lights everywhere. The brightest lights shone on the stage to draw the audience's attention to three women dancing seductively to a slow beat. They were topless and several men were standing by the stage holding up bills waiting impatiently for the brief moment when one or more of the dancers would show them some attention. There were also women at individual tables giving patrons lap dances.

Lenora felt extremely uncomfortable and out of place. She tried to avert her eyes from the dancers. She didn't want to see women being objectified in that manner, even if they were doing it willingly. She wished she had some holy oil with her to anoint the room and ask God to drive out the spirit of lust that permeated the place. Lenora hastily claimed her seat and began scanning the room for Herman. It was dark, and she couldn't see much of anything, making it impossible to see him. She decided it was probably best for her to leave before someone recognized her. She was a married Christian woman and didn't need her name used in the same sentence as the words strip club. As Lenora rose, she was startled to hear the bartender behind her say, "What can I get you, ma'am?" She turned around and stared into the face of her husband. Herman's eyes widened to twice their normal size.

"Lenora, what are you doing here?"

Lenora narrowed her eyes and glared at him for a few seconds before answering. She wanted to see Herman squirm. "I was about to ask you the same thing."

"I'm working," he said.

"I thought my husband worked as an IT analyst for Hi-Tech Industries," she stated.

Herman hung his head and said, "He does or at least he did until he got fired. Don't be mad, Lenora. I'm only working here until I can get another IT job. I couldn't watch everything we worked so hard for slip away while I sat at home looking on the computer for jobs. I tried for months to find another IT job. I promise I did but nobody's hiring. So I went back to the only other thing I know how to do, bartending. The pay is pretty good. It's not as much as what I was making, but for what I do it's not bad at all. I know it's not the kind of job you would want me to have, but it helps pay the bills."

Lenora softened the look on her face and put her hand over her husband's. "Baby, you should have told me you lost your job. I know this must be hard for you to deal with. I'm your wife. I could have helped you get through this. I'm not mad. I'm actually a little relieved. I thought you were spending your days here looking at women when you should be out looking for a job." Lenora looked around to see if anyone was listening to their conversation. Everyone seemed busy feeding their faces or looking at topless women. "Because we aren't doing you-know-what, I thought you were getting it someplace else. You aren't messing with any of these women, are you?"

Before Herman could answer, a busty woman in a cowgirl outfit approached the bar and rubbed her hand through his hair.

"Hey, Cowboy. What's a girl got to do to get a drink around here?"

Herman moved her hand and said, "I gotcha, Sundance. I'll bring it to you in a minute. I'm a little busy at the moment."

Sundance pouted. "Aw, I was hoping I would get to lasso you." She looked Lenora up and down, smiled, and lifted up her breasts as if she was adjusting them to show Herman and Lenora exactly what she was working with. She licked her lips and said, "I'll be waiting."

Lenora repeated her question. "Are you messing with any of these women, Herman?"

"Heck no, baby. You're the only one for me. None of these women in here can hold a candle to the classy woman I've got at home. The only reason I'm bartending in this club is because the pay here is twice as good as other places. We haven't done you-know-what because I'm stressed. I'm not in the mood. The money here is decent, but it's not what I'm used to making. I'm not even making ends meet."

Lenora breathed a sigh of relief. "Herman, you should have told me. I'm making a little money now, so I can help out."

"I wanted you to spend that money on yourself. After what I put you through, you deserve to be able to go out and use your check to buy whatever you want."

"Herman, that's sweet, but I don't mind. I don't want you stressed. What wife wouldn't help her husband if she has the means to? I don't like you working here. You know that God is not pleased with you serving liquor. Especially, in a place where women get paid to take their clothes off."

Herman's face turned red. "Then, you tell God to get me a better job so I can quit. Because last I checked, the twins were still growing like weeds and Hermie needed a special tutor to help with his dyslexia."

Herman, Jr. was diagnosed with dyslexia earlier in the year, and his teacher suggested they utilize a tutor who specialized in helping children with the disorder. They took her advice. Herman's grades were steadily improving, but his tutor wasn't cheap.

"Herman, don't say such things. Don't get angry with God. It wasn't His fault you lost your job."

Lenora was interrupted by a drunk man at the end of the bar yelling, "Hey, Herman, what's a man got to do to get a drink around here? I'm so thirsty I could drink that fat chick you're talking to down there."

"Russell, you shut that hole in your face! This is my wife you're talking about. I'll be there in a minute," Herman yelled back.

He returned his attention to his wife. "Baby, we'll have to talk about this more when I get home. I need to get back to work before I lose this job too."

"That's your wife?" yelled Russell. "No wonder you come to work early every day if that's what you got to come home to."

A few of the men at the bar laughed. Lenora's feelings were hurt. Even a drunk man in a strip club was making fun of her weight. She turned away from Herman and looked around the room at the women all those men had come to see. They were all pretty and smaller than her. Herman said he wasn't messing with any of them, but she didn't believe him. Compared to her, they all looked like supermodels, even the thick ones. Lenora grabbed her purse and walked toward the door without saying good-bye to her husband.

As she did, she heard Herman say, "That's all for you today, Russell. I happen to think my wife is gorgeous. If you ever insult her again I'll knock you out. By the time you wake up you'll be sober. I'm sure you have no idea when the last time was that you were sober."

Some guys at the bar laughed at that too.

"Yes, I do. Nixon was president," said Russell, and then burped loudly.

The men laughed again.

Lenora smiled. It had been a while since she heard Herman say she was gorgeous. She turned around and blew him a kiss. "Don't take too long coming home, Cowboy. You're gonna have a delicious dinner waiting on you when you do."

He pretended to catch it and place it in his shirt pocket.

"I can't wait. Baby, I love you," Herman said.

"I love you too," said Lenora.

"Aw, that's sweet," slurred Russell. "Now that you and your wife have ruined my high with that mushy crap, can I puhleaaase get a drink?" He moved his head from side to side vigorously to emphasize his desire for another drink and almost fell off his barstool.

"I said the well is dry, Russell. You've had too much already. Go home!" yelled Herman.

Sundance made her way back to the bar and bent over displaying her cleavage in Herman's face. The smile on Lenora's face faded when she noticed that Herman was no longer smiling at her. He was smiling at Sundance's chest.

Lenora didn't like this situation at all, but what could she do? Beating Herman up about it wasn't going to fix it. "Lord, show me what to do," she prayed. "I'm scared my husband is going to be like that singer T-Pain and fall in love with a stripper."

As she drove home, she thought about when she and Herman met. Bartending was how he paid his way through college. At the time, they were both living in Atlanta, and he worked at a popular sports bar in Buckhead called Hoops. She would often sit at the back table and watch him work until it was time for his shift to end. He was good at what he did. Female and male patrons seemed to like him, and even though he was working, he never seemed to forget that his girl was there. When a woman came up to him trying to flirt, he would shoot Lenora a reassuring smile or a wink to let her know she was the only woman on his mind. Every so often, he would even send her a drink. It was always her favorite, a Shirley Temple. Those were good times. Back then, they were two college students in love. There were no car notes, mortgages, or little people running around calling them Mommy and Daddy. They were just Lenora and Herman. Life was so much simpler then. She wished he was working someplace reputable like Hoops, but she knew if Herman was working in a strip club, the money must be really good because with a house of five, their monthly bills weren't small. Lenora decided right then and there she was going to love her man and pray him through this. She was also going to figure out a way to bring some more money into the house to help.

Chapter 15

The New & Improved Blak

Blak was extremely happy to see Tee. He hugged her so many times she had to tell him to stop. She arranged for him to speak to a group of students before his appearance at a talent show later that evening. Tee admired how much Blak had grown in the past year. Not just mentally and emotionally, but physically too. He gained weight, and it was obvious he was hitting the gym to keep it toned. Gone was the skinny little bird-chest boy she met last year. Blak had morphed into a muscular man. His chest was broader, and his neck was a little thicker. He was at least 30 pounds heavier. He still sagged his pants a little too much for her taste. There were other changes Tee noticed, as well. He no longer traveled with an entourage. Blak arrived by himself. He didn't even have private security, which Tee was a little concerned about, but he didn't seem to be in danger. There were a few fans that stopped him as he made his way to her car, but for the most part, he seemed to go unnoticed by the majority of the people in the airport. He smiled and joked with them while posing for pictures and signing autographs. He looked much happier, and his attitude was more humble than the day she met him. The change God was making in his life was obvious.

An hour later, Blak and Tee walked into Excellence Abounds Charter School to give the students a special visit. The school had won numerous awards for excellence in education, and part of it was attributed to its extended school day. Students there went to school from 9 a.m. to 5 p.m. and were exposed to a very rigorous curriculum. The school also had a special program for children with one or more parents in jail. It was called Behind the Bars. The program offered counseling and mentors to try to help fill the void left by their absent parent. They even had a support group for other family members as well.

The principal, Mrs. Odessa Marshall, greeted them warmly. She took one look at Blak and said, "Young man, we are honored that you came to see us, but you will have to adhere to our dress code while you are here. Please remove your hat and earrings and pull up your pants. We do not allow underwear to be shown at any time."

Blak answered, "Yes, ma'am," and did as he was asked with no questions or hesitation. Mrs. Marshall then escorted them to one of the 5th-grade classrooms. The children were participating in character-building exercises.

"We spend 30 minutes to an hour each day helping the students with their self-esteem and self-confidence. If you equip a child with the knowledge that he or she is special and fully capable of accomplishing great things while encouraging him or her to stay on the right path and work hard, he or she is less likely to engage in unhealthy behaviors like drugs, sex, gangs, or violence. If I had to summarize what we do, I would simply say we love on these children. We let them know that someone cares about them, and they can always come to us no matter what," Mrs. Marshall explained.

"We require hard work from each of our students. We also focus heavily on African American history and strong morals. Our school is not a religious institution, but the lessons taught are based on biblical principles. Many of our students come from low-income, single-parent homes, but they are bright, talented, and eager to learn. Unfortunately, some of them also come from homes where they don't receive much time and attention from their parents because they're always working or feel they have better things to do than spend time with their child. When they're at school, we try to give them as much attention as possible. None of our classes have over 20 students."

The children were settling into their seats and preparing to do their daily exercises as they walked in. They immediately recognized Blak, and you could tell they were eager to jump out of their seats and run toward him, but Mrs. Ogilvie gave them that "don't you dare!" look they'd all come to know and fear.

"Students, as you can see, we have a guest today. Many of you know him as the hip-hop artist Icy Blak, but I'm proud to say that he now does hip-hop gospel and has changed his named to Isaac Blak. Before he shares his story with you, I want you all to line up in front of the mirror and let's show Isaac how to do our daily affirmations."

The children jumped up from their seats and walked quickly to the far side of the room where the mirrors were located. "Isaac and Tee, please join us. You can stand next to Jeffrey. Jeffrey, please raise your hand."

A skinny boy with freckles raised his hand; Isaac and Tee walked over and stood next to him.

"Now, look in the mirror and repeat after me," said their teacher. "I am a beautiful African American. I am the descendant of kings and queens. I am made in the image of my Heavenly Father who reigns over all. And if God is my Father, I am destined for greatness because He is great.

"When I look in the mirror, I see potential. I see promise. I see success. I will not let my circumstances determine my outcome. If I can see it, I can achieve it. While achieving my greatness, I will not degrade others. I will not let negativity flow from my lips. I have a responsibility to myself, my family, and my community. I will not take without giving back. I will love my neighbors. I will be a beacon of light and the deliverer of truth wherever I go. I will always strive for greatness because mediocrity is never good enough!"

The children, Blak, and Tee repeated each word in unison. They each looked intently in the mirror and spoke to the reflection staring back at them. Each word was said with emphasis and feeling.

"Now, point at yourself and say 'I am special, I am special, I am special,'" instructed Mrs. Marshall.

After they finished, Mrs. Ogilvie instructed them to hug the person on their left and on their right. The students did as they were told and went back to their seats. Blak was asked to come to the front of the room and talk to them.

"I'm sure none of you will be able to concentrate on your lessons until you hear from Isaac," said Mrs. Marshall. "I won't prolong your anticipation. Please welcome Isaac to our classroom with a warm Excellence Abounds round of applause."

Blak stood in front of the teacher's desk and talked to the students. He told them where he came from, how he came to be a rapper and all the great things he's been able to accomplish throughout his career. He told them about why he no longer wanted to do secular hip hop and the financial ruin he almost experienced by not paying attention to how much he was making and who was handling his money. Before he closed he said, "I started rapping seriously when I was about the same age as many of you. If you have a dream, pursue it. Don't let anybody stop you. Use your haters as your motivators. Don't do what I did. I sold my soul to the devil to achieve worldly treasures, but God told Satan he couldn't have me. My parents were praying that I would be delivered, and God sent an angel name Tee Stokes into my life to help me see that I was messing up big time and leading others down the wrong road while I talked about things that were immoral and not of God. In your affirmation, you talked about how we all have a responsibility to our community, and we do. Now, I use my songs to give God the glory."

Tee was so proud of him. Blak was not only a talented rapper, but he was a good motivational speaker. He was using his testimony to help young people make the right decisions in their lives. When he finished, all of the students gave him a thunderous applause. Mrs. Marshall and the teacher thanked Blak for his time. They said good-bye to the students, and then went to the office so Blak could autograph a few items for the principal to give away to exceptional students during their end-of-the-year awards ceremony.

Chapter 16

Art Imitates Life

"What do you mean she refused to paint over the mural?" yelled Michael.

"The director said she was under contractual obligation to dedicate the recreation room and the mural to Becca, and she had no intentions of cancelling tomorrow's ceremony," explained Michael's lawyer, Edward. "It seems that the only way we can stop her is a court-ordered injunction. Seeing that it's Thursday evening and the courts are closed now, I won't be able to get one until tomorrow. I'll be in the judge's office first thing in the morning, but we'll be cutting it kind of close. I can also come to the treatment facility if I need to."

"You go to the courthouse first, and I'll go to the recovery facility to talk to her. That way, if my talk fails, we can still hit her with an injunction. Do whatever you have to do. I'll see you in the morning." Michael slammed the phone down.

He was fuming. Becca was still finding ways to interfere with his relationship with Tee. There was no way he was going to lose his wife over a mural. He chartered a jet to take him to Akron in the morning and began packing a bag. He wondered if Tee would want come with him. He tried to call and ask her several times, but she refused to answer. He planned to do everything in his power to make sure that the dedication service didn't happen tomorrow.

Chapter 17

Paint a Pretty Picture

"Momma, you know what this office needs?" Blak asked, and without waiting for her to answer he said, "Some art. The furniture is fly. I like what you have going on with the leather and glass, but you need some pieces on the wall to accentuate things."

"Look at you sounding all scholarly, using words like 'accentuate,'" laughed Tee.

"Just because I'm a rapper doesn't mean that I don't have a vast vocabulary."

"I know you were a straight-A student in high school. I was only teasing."

Tee and Blak left the school and went to Mercy Children's Hospital to visit with a few sick children. It was obvious that seeing a young man they considered a superstar made them feel better, at least for a little while. Afterward, they came by the office to go over his management contracts. Everything looked in order, and Blak readily signed. Their next stop was a local talent show where Blak agreed to serve as the celebrity judge. Tee hired a street team to pass out Blak's first single and a few other promotional items. She still needed to bring in another person to help with their clients soon. With her pregnancy, she would be unable to travel with him regularly. Blak was disappointed to hear that, but she promised him she would find someone capable and cute. She only added the "cute" because Blak insisted.

"I don't need no ugly woman around me. I do better when attractive women are around. I try harder because I don't want to look bad around them," he told her.

Tee was grateful that they had another event to attend. She wasn't ready to go home and see Michael. She was still extremely upset with him. The image of that mural was seared into her brain like a tattoo. It was Thursday, and the show was scheduled to air Sunday. Her life seemed to be one drama-filled scene after another. Since she became Michael's wife, privacy had become somewhat of a luxury. She loved her husband, but she didn't like her life being on display.

She looked around the office. Blak was right. She did need more artwork, and she knew the perfect Montessori art teacher to paint it. She quickly sent Lenora a text telling her that she wanted to commission her to paint a few pieces for the office. She was pleasantly surprised when she read the response.

Lenora: Tee, you are an answer to a prayer. I love you, girl. Do you mind paying me in advance? I'll explain why later.

Tee: No problem. Just tell me how much and I'll write you a check.

Lenora: God bless you!

Tee: God bless you too, Twin.

Chapter 18

Ask the Love Doctor

Tiffany and Lenice sat in Lenice's living room discussing their man problems. Webster lay curled at their feet. The two were closer than ever now. Lenice was grateful to still have a single woman to discuss her love life with now that her sister and Tee were both married. She didn't need someone to empathize with her life. She wanted someone to sympathize in real time. Lenice prepared spaghetti with no meat and garlic bread for her guest. They happily stuffed themselves and washed it down with Lenice's favorite beverage, Welch's White Grape Juice. Lenice swirled the pasta around on her fork with no intention of picking it up and placing it in her mouth. She wasn't hungry. However, she was perplexed by the fact that she had more men calling her than she knew what to do with, but she was still unhappy. None of them seemed to be anyone she could see herself with long term. They were fun, but that's all. There was no substance.

She listened while Tiffany explained how William dumped her because of her wardrobe, and although she knew he was wrong, she needed her girlfriend to cosign.

"Well, Tif, you do wear your clothes kind of tight and revealing, and he is a pastor," said Lenice.

"What? You can't possibly believe that there's any validity to his statements. Sugah, I look good in my clothes. Sometimes I look in the mirror and I almost slap myself on the behind because I look so good. God knows my heart.

He knows that this sexy dressing diva is a good Christian woman."

"I didn't say I agreed with him. I was merely stating a fact. Your clothes are gorgeous, but it's no secret you like to accentuate your bottom half and those gigantic milk jugs of yours. What do you wear, a size D cup? And don't you even start that 'God knows my heart' stuff. It does sound like church folk have gotten in his ear, though. Without talking to them, it's hard to say if they meant well or if they were jealous."

"These big babies are Es, thank you very much," Tiffany said bouncing her breasts up and down slightly. "And if I had to guess, I'd say they were jealous. I did the church announcements last week, and I'm almost positive I saw the pastor staring at my behind. He wishes he could touch all this sweet goodness."

"You make yourself sound like a honey bun. Of course he was looking at your booty. Only a blind man could miss that big ole thing."

Tiffany laughed. "She does stick out, doesn't she?"

"Stick out? Honey, if we ever go to a restaurant and they don't have enough tables, I'm going to ask them for a tablecloth to place over your behind. Then, I'm going to pull myself up a chair and eat off it," said Lenice.

"Girl, you don't have any sense. But seriously, if you were me, what would you do?"

"Well, if I had a man I was truly interested in and the only thing he had bad to say about me was that I dressed like a slut, I'd stop dressing like a slut," teased Lenice.

Tiffany playfully punched her in the shoulder. "That's not what he said."

"But that's what he meant. He's likes you, so he doesn't want to hurt your feelings. I can't stand you so I can say it like it is," Lenice said rolling her eyes and snapping her fingers for emphasis. Tiffany stuck out her bottom lip like her feelings were hurt.

"Real talk, Tiffany," continued Lenice, "I haven't seen you this happy in years. William is a good man with an amazing heart, and I can tell you really like him. Your face lights up every time you say his name. Can you fault him for not wanting a wife that calls attention to her sexuality all the time? Especially, when his main focus is supposed to be on ministry. He's looking for a help meet. You can't help him keep a boy from going wayward if the whole time you two are talking to him he's looking at those big ole titties that you have on display in some scoop-neck top. Cut the man some slack. I'll admit that he should have talked to you about it rather than just breaking up with you, but this is an easy fix."

"I guess you're right. It's only been two days, and I really miss him. I don't know how to dress conservative. I've never been that type of girl. I like being sexy."

"That's an easy fix too. Talk to Tee. She's the queen of 'God is watching so let's cover everything up'. I'm sure she would be more than happy to take you out to purchase a new Holy Ghost-approved wardrobe."

Tiffany laughed. "I'll call her tomorrow," she promised.

"And whatever you do, don't stop going to his church. You have to let a brother see what he's missing."

Tiffany gave her a high five and said, "*Sho, you right*" in her best Barry White imitation.

"Also, don't go out with other people in the church. The last thing you want is to get a reputation for being passed around like the collection plate. Plus, if William thinks you are seeing someone else, he won't approach you. No matter how many men ask, always tell them no. It doesn't matter if he's rich, either. I know you, Tiffany. Dollars will make you take a second look."

"What!" said Tiffany innocently. "Money isn't all I care about. William isn't rich, and I still like him. He's not broke, but he's far from rich. How do you know so much about church folk? You rarely even go."

"That doesn't mean I've never been. My grandfather was a pastor. I was raised in the church, but the older I got, the less important it became to me. After my grandfather died, I stopped going all together. The only reason I kept going as long as I did was because Papa made me feel so guilty when I didn't go." Lenice did her best imitation of him. It sounded like a cross between Bill Cosby and Lou Rawls. "You know, Leni, God wakes you up every morning with a fresh breath in your lungs. You're still in your right mind, and you got the movement of your limbs. Now, you mean to tell me it's too much trouble for you to get to church on Sunday to say thank you?"

"You're not as big a heathen as I thought," teased Tiffany.

"I went so I wouldn't have to hear his mouth. Trust me when I say I know church and I know church folks. Quite a few of them are hypocrites, if you ask me. Same saints I partied with in the club were at church bright and early the next morning shouting hallelujah with a hangover. I started going back because Tee convinced me to give it another try. I like her church. That's where I met James.

"If William is who you want, tell everyone else to step off with your presence. Others will either behave or get extremely sneaky when the girlfriend or wife is nearby," Lenice advised.

"I can do that. Now that we've come up with a solution to my problem, what about yours?"

"What problem? I don't have a man. So therefore, I have no problems," said Lenice matter-of-factly.

"Sugah, puhlease. You have become the most pathetic player I have ever seen. Most players have reasons for wanting multiple suitors. It's usually sex, money, companionship, or all three. You don't want any of the above. You aren't giving up the goods, and you won't let those men buy you anything. You seem to be dating multiple men just to be dating multiple men. I bet you don't even let them kiss you."

Lenice rolled her eyes. "The last thing I want to be is promiscuous. HIV and AIDS is at an all-time high among African Americans, not to mention all those other nasty little STDs people are passing around. Did you know that there is a new strain of gonorrhea that medical professionals are having a hard time curing? And what if I get pregnant? There's no way you're going to see me on an episode of *Maury* with two or three men on stage trying to find out who my baby daddy is. It is possible to enjoy the company of a man without sleeping with him."

"You know that and I know that, but do you bother to let these men who are wining and dining you know that you are celibate? Usually when a man picks up a woman in the club, his initial thoughts are on how fast he can get into her drawers. You let them take you out multiple times, get their hopes all up, and then when they go for the goods, you drop them like they stink. You need to stop bringing these men to your house, too. There are a lot of crazies out there," said Tiffany.

"My house, my rules. I can control the situation better if we're on my turf. If I have sex with a man, I want to LOVE him, not like him. It takes a lot out of me if I have sex with a man and it doesn't work out. I feel like I gave away the best parts of me to someone who didn't deserve it. When I love, I give it everything I've got, and then some. Before a man gets into these panties, he has to prove himself more than worthy. He has to put in a lot of time and effort getting to know me. You should try it."

"You don't know what you're talking about. You're wrong about me. William and I never had sex," defended Tiffany. "Sex has meaning for me too."

"You two haven't had sex because he isn't interested. Have you ever asked yourself why you two are rarely alone? You scared that man half to death the first time you invited him over. Trying to seduce him with candles, strawberries, and cheese. Ha!" Lenice laughed so loudly Webster woke up and started barking. She picked her Chihuahua up and kissed his brown furry face.

"Sorry, Webbie. Did Mommy scare you?" She sat him in her lap and stroked his short brown coat. Then, she lowered her voice. "After that act of desperation, he made sure you didn't get the opportunity again. All I ever remember you talking about is going out or having dinner at your house when Quincy 2 is there."

Tiffany bit her bottom lip thoughtfully. Lenice had a point. William did avoid being alone with her for extended periods of time, but she figured it was because he was extremely attracted to her, not because he was afraid of what she would do to him. "How do you know that? Did he tell you that?"

Lenice rolled her eyes again. "He didn't have to. I have a cousin who was a single pastor until he was 45. Before he got married, I saw the kinds of women he was interested in. They were generally the Christian conservative type. The ones that turned him off were the aggressive, I'm-so-holy-you-should-notice-me-because-I-will-look-good-in-a-suit-

and-an-enormous-hat-sitting-on-the-front-pew. The fast ones with seductress tendencies really turned him off. Think about it, Tif. You not only think about sex in the wrong context, but you wear it. All those tight, revealing clothes say to a man is 'open season.'"

"You wear your cleavage out!"

"Yes, *sometimes,* but you have yours out *all* the time. Do you even own a blouse that isn't tight, low-cut, or made with buttons that allow you to keep a few open so the girls can peep out and say hello to everybody? You're only hearing what William said when you need to listen to what he *didn't* say. William is asking you to wear more clothing that is appropriate for an aspiring pastor's wife without actually asking. He wants you to make the decision to do it on your own because you think the two of you are worth it. He doesn't want you to feel forced into doing it for him. I use that technique all the time at work. It's where you make a decision for someone, and then sit back and wait for them to get offended like you did and come up with an alternative solution that both of you can live with. In the end, they do exactly what you wanted them to do themselves and end up thinking it was their idea when it really wasn't."

"So he's playing head games with me?" asked Tiffany.

"It's more like he gave you a reason to go in the right direction because you want to. People react so much better to change if they do it because they see change as beneficial rather than if someone else rams it down their throat.

"You're actually lucky to have a man like William who is willing to see past your wardrobe to find the real you. He also respects you. He's a pastor. He not only needs a woman who other people respect but respects herself. You've got to learn how to walk that fine line between classy sexy and sex me sexy."

Tiffany was tired of people beating her up about the way she's always been and decided to change the subject. "When did this become about me? We were talking about you. Sugah, I'm worried about you. This isn't you, Lenice. You're a one-man woman. Stop wasting your time on all these men you have no future with and go back to James. He was good for you. He respected your views on celibacy, and all he wanted to do was love you."

"I'm not ready for James, yet. I need to have some fun. Is that so wrong? I'm tired of letting men control everything. It's my turn. *I* run this!" Lenice slammed her fist down on the table.

"The only thing you're running is your mouth, but you'll see. Pimpin' ain't easy, player." Tiffany laughed. "Lenice, will you do me one favor?"

"What's that?"

"Ask God for guidance. Read your Bible and pray. It has worked wonders for me. I'm a better person with a daily dose of scripture in my life."

"I can do that. I need to read more anyway," said Lenice.

"Tif, will you do me one favor?"

"Depends on what it is."

"I know I'm probably not the right person to give relationship advice or even advice on how to get and keep a man, but don't let a good thing get away over something as superficial as clothes."

"I'll think about it," said Tiffany. She actually didn't need to. She had already made up her mind to get her man back.

Chapter 19

Out of the Ordinary

Mac sat in his downtown office thinking about what a good time he had with Patrice and her family. Her baby, Nathan, was a handsome eight-month-old, and her niece Tabitha was a high-strung four-year-old. After dinner, she put on a complete show for him that included dancing, singing, and even a botched magic trick or two. Patrice's sister, Amy, really could throw down in the kitchen. Their dinner of fried chicken with green beans, macaroni and cheese, and candied yams was more than enough to make a man come back for seconds. Then, she topped it off with pecan pie and homemade ice cream. He was most surprised at how beautiful Amy was. Her skin was the same shade as sandalwood. Her pouty lips made him want to pucker up, and her smile was warm and inviting.

Amy graduated valedictorian of her class and attended Vanderbilt University in Nashville one semester but dropped out after their grandmother died. The state threatened to put Patrice in foster care because their mother was deemed an unfit parent because of her drug addiction. She couldn't let that happen and became her sister's guardian. She planned to go back to school, but she got pregnant and later Patrice did too. Her life then consisted of keeping Patrice out of trouble, taking care of babies and working a low-wage job to pay the bills. She desperately wanted to get out of fast food. Amy felt she would never get to accomplish her goal of acquiring a degree. She was currently a shift leader at Burgerville. She did the best she could with what she had. They lived in their deceased grandmother's house, but it was badly in need of repairs. Amy was trying to figure out how she was going to pay to get the roof and a few leaky faucets fixed.

After dinner, Amy told Patrice to put the children in bed, and then do her homework before she went out for a little while with her friends. She wanted to talk to Mac alone. Like any good guardian, she wanted to know what a grown man was doing hanging with her little sister. Mac was honest and told her that Patrice had initially presented herself to him as older than she was, but after finding out her actual age, he had no desire to be anything other than her friend. He omitted the part about Casper and the pictures. Amy confided in him how she feared for the child. The neighborhood they lived in wasn't a positive atmosphere for her, and she didn't want her to end up pregnant again before she got out of high school. Mac promised her that he would be a good influence in Patrice's life, and he meant every word he said.

Amy was appalled that Patrice lied about her age and that she had gone out with Mac for money. She planned to have a stern talk with her later. For now, she was enjoying the company of a rich, handsome, successful man, the type that rarely even noticed her until he wanted a burger and some fries. She wanted to savor this moment while it lasted.

After her interrogation, she and Mac spent the next hour laughing and talking over a game of Scrabble. Mac was quite the wordsmith, but Amy proved to be a worthy opponent. He was about to spell the word "misdemeanor" to win the game when they were interrupted by the ringing of his cell phone. He excused himself and took the call outside. It was Casper. She still wanted more money. She threatened to release the pictures of him and Patrice to the media if he didn't pay up. Mac made a nice living as a lawyer, but he wasn't filthy rich. He was valued at about $1.5 million, but most of that was tied up in his business and his house. He only had about $300,000 in the bank, and if Casper kept asking for large amounts of money it would be gone in no time. He had to figure out a plan to get her the money and get her out of his pockets once and for all. He promised to send her the money the next day.

. He went back in the house and finished the game. There was a wager on it. If he won, Amy would cook for him, again. He was looking forward to it.

Chapter 20

Good Morning, Heartache

Tee straggled home close to 2 a.m. She wasn't as young as she used to be, and hanging with Blak and the street team drained her completely. Patrice and two of her friends surprised her by coming to the talent show. Afterward, Blak stayed for at least an hour signing autographs and taking pictures. Then, they all went to get breakfast at IHOP and much to Tee's disbelief, Blak wanted to go catch a midnight movie. She tried to politely decline, but he wouldn't take no for an answer. Tee was one of his favorite people in the world, and he didn't want to waste a single moment with her. Jesus Christ was his number-one Savior, and Tee Long Stokes was definitely number two. He looked forward to working with her more closely because he knew she had his best interests at heart.

Patrice told her friends good-bye and tagged along as well. She and Blak had a good conversation as Tee drove her home. He apologized for the way he treated Patrice the last time he saw her and asked her to forgive him. He didn't sleep with her, but he intended to, and afterward, he would have forgotten she even existed. Patrice forgave him but acknowledged that she shouldn't have come to his dressing room trying to entice him to sleep with him. They were both wrong that night and thankfully, nothing happened that they would later regret. Tee sat quietly listening to their conversation. She was proud of both of them. They were each learning the importance of sexual responsibility. She hoped they were both practicing abstinence, but if they weren't, at least they knew that it was necessary to give careful thought to who they were sleeping with, how well they knew that individual, and why. One night could alter their lives forever.

Patrice always enjoyed her time with Tee and getting to spend some time with a platinum-selling rapper was an added bonus. She decided not to tell Tee that she knew Mac. He and her sister looked quite cozy when she left home. She wouldn't mind having a rich brother-in-law at all. It wasn't any of Tee's business who her sister spent time with anyway.

After taking Patrice home, Tee dropped Blak off at his hotel and drove home. She enjoyed their company, and she welcomed the distraction. The last thing she wanted to do was think about Michael and what happened during the interview. It hurt to think about how she was ambushed by someone she thought was a friend, and to top it all off, pertinent information was hidden from her by the love of her life. She was so busy she didn't have time to call Sandy and tell her what happened. She needed to talk to someone, but it was too late to call now. Everyone in Sandy's house was in bed by midnight. Sheba tried several times to get her to talk, but Tee tried not to share too many personal details with her assistant. Each time she inquired about Tee's well-being, Tee told her that she was fine and to focus on the task at hand.

Tee parked her truck in the garage, quietly entered the house through the kitchen door, and padded softly toward the bedrooms. On the way home, she decided that she would sleep in the guest room tonight. She didn't have the energy to discuss the day with Michael, and she knew if she went into the bedroom he would want to talk. She soon discovered that she would have no choice but to face him because Michael waited up for her. He was sitting in the living room reading a book. The soft light from a nearby lamp accentuated his hard features and muscular physique. Tee was angry with him but seeing him sitting there looking studious, sexy, and distraught softened her anger a little. He made her heart rate accelerate even when she was angry. Michael put his book down and walked toward her slowly. He noticed how tired she was. Without saying a word, he took her oversized purse from her shoulder and laid it on a chair. He then cupped her face in his hands and kissed her lips. A tear trickled down Tee's cheek.

"How could you?" she whimpered. He pulled her to him, and she buried her face in his chest.

Michael bowed his head toward her ear and whispered, "I'm sorry. I thought I was protecting you. I was going to handle it without you knowing. I knew how much it would hurt you to see that mural."

Tee held him tighter. She and Michael were total opposites when it came to how they reacted to difficult situations. Not only did he try to avoid emotional and distressful situations, but he tried to distance those he loved from them as well—with the exception of his parents. When Tee encountered tough times, she tackled the problem head-on while clinging to those she loved most. Especially, her current love interest. Their love and encouragement gave her added strength. Tee continued to hold his body close to hers. If it were biologically possible, she would have melted into him. She raised her face toward his and said, "No more secrets. Your keeping secrets from me is going to tear us apart. Good or bad, I can handle it. It's the things I find out later that I should have already known that upset me."

"I promise, Beautiful. No more secrets. I'll tell you anything you want to know. I love you and him more than life." Michael knelt and kissed her stomach. He couldn't wait to meet the person growing inside of her. He loved watching the process. He noticed Tee's weight gain. Her face was fuller, and her nose was getting wider. Her hips were getting thicker as were her thighs and butt. He knew she was self-conscious about it, but he didn't mind one bit.

"How do you know it's a him?"

"I just know," he said and kissed her stomach again.

Even on his knees, Michael's head almost touched her breasts. He nuzzled her stomach and rubbed her behind. Tee lovingly caressed the top of his bald head. His hands continued to travel, roaming her hips and thighs. He wanted to strip her naked and feel her soft skin against his, but he was afraid to attempt to undo her clothing because he couldn't tell if Tee was still angry. He looked into her eyes as tears continued to spill down her cheeks. It pained him to see her like this and to know he was the cause of it.

Tee didn't mean to cry. She had every intention of sleeping in another room and getting up the next morning with her attitude and tough-girl image still in place. She planned to let him have it over breakfast. Was being pregnant making her so emotional, or was loving and needing a man as much as she needed her next breath the culprit? Whatever the case, she didn't need to prove she was right at that moment. She didn't need to give him a piece of her mind. What she needed was to feel loved in a manner that only Michael was able to deliver.

"Tomorrow you are going to tell me everything. Okay?" she whispered.

"I promise," said Michael. He recognized that husky voice and knew exactly where she was going. "But what are we going to do tonight?" he asked as if he didn't already know the answer. His wife was such an amazing woman.

She forgave him without making him suffer. From the very beginning it was her heart that drew him to her. Tee's love for others and their well-being often superseded her love of herself. She wasn't vindictive or backbiting. She could have given him the silent treatment for days and no one would have blamed her for it. He took his cue and began to touch places only he had access to.

Tee smiled. "This morning," she corrected. "You are going to show me exactly how sorry you are."

"I'm really sorry," said Michael.

"Shhhh," Tee said and gently placed her index finger to his delicious lips. "Shut up and show me."

Michael stood up. He never once allowed his gaze to break from hers. The desire she held in her eyes caused every muscle in his body to respond. He carefully picked up his wife and carried her to their bedroom where he showed her that he knew how to follow instructions very, very well.

****

The next morning, Michael and Tee got ready to board a private flight to Akron. They would face this problem as a team. Blak's flight was leaving around the same time as theirs so they went by his hotel and picked him up on the way. The three of them discussed their ideas for his upcoming album release. Blak wanted something dynamic that truly showed he was a changed man. MiTee Management promised him they would deliver. At the airport, they said their good-byes. Blak clung to Tee like a child leaving his parent.

"Take good care of yourself, Tee. I'm not worried about a thing because I know you'll take care of me."

"Blak, I appreciate your confidence in me. Words can't express how proud I am of you. You're gonna do big things."

"That's the plan," said Blak. He smiled, gave Michael a fist bump, grabbed his carry-on luggage, and dashed into the airport to catch his flight.

Chapter 21

Tell Me a Secret

Michael and Tee made their way to the private runway where the jet Michael chartered was waiting for them. Once on board, Michael answered all of the questions that had been churning in Tee's head since yesterday. The first was how long had he known about the mural? Michael told her how Dr. Foster discovered it while trying to find clues that would lead them to Becca's brother. Tee was quite miffed that he kept something so important from her for so long. He attempted to diffuse her anger by making her laugh with an impersonation of Tee Hee and his inability to control his laughter.

Tee actually did laugh and was looking forward to meeting him.

When Michael finished, she asked, "Is there anything else I need to know? I went easy on you last night, but if I find out any more secrets, you'll have hell to pay." Michael knew she was serious and thought it best to tell her everything.

"Tiffany saw me naked," he said. Tee raised a perfectly arched eyebrow and turned her body toward him to let him get the full view of her *you better have a good excuse for this one* face.

"I promise you, it was purely innocent. I was trying out her bathhouse idea to give her some feedback and my towel fell. When the towel fell, I turned around and asked her to leave. Nothing happened, but it felt so awkward having her look at me. She's your friend. Well, actually, she and I became close while working together, so I guess she's my friend too, but it still felt weird and inappropriate. We haven't spoken since it happened. I don't quite know what to say."

Tee relaxed her eyebrow. "Yes, it sounds like the two of you have become a little too close. There is no reason for you to be around her only wearing a towel," she said. "How did she react when the towel fell?"

"She's my masseuse, Tee. I'm normally wearing my underwear or a towel during massages. After the towel fell, she told me not to worry or be embarrassed. It was an accident and everything would be cool. But honestly, Tee, I think Tiffany has a bit of a crush on me."

"I always wondered about that as well. I noticed how she likes to touch you playfully when you two are together. I'm going to have a talk with her. It's best we nip this in the bud now. Also, it might be a good idea if I handle her account from now on. And no more massages from her. As a matter of fact, no more massages from women, period. I'll find you a man to rub that body down."

Michael gave her a dirty look but held his tongue. His massage therapists in the NFL were usually men. He was used to them, but he didn't necessarily like them. He would rather have a woman rubbing on him any day.

Tee thought about what she would say to Tiffany. She needed her to know who the woman of this castle was and there was no room for another. She was pretty sure that Tiffany wouldn't make a move on Michael, but she was 100 percent sure that Michael was the type of man Tiffany was attracted to, and just in case she had even an ounce of inclination that she had a chance, Tee planned to let her know she didn't.

"Whatever you say," said Michael. "You know more about this girl crush thing than I do. I don't want there to be any more problems between us."

"As long as you're honest, there won't be," Tee assured him. "Anything else?"

Michael took a long, hard breath. He had to tell her about the calls he received from someone who sounded like Becca. He hadn't received any in a while, but it was best she know. "I think Becca is possibly still alive, or someone is doing a really good job of impersonating her."

Tee laughed. "Michael, stop playing! I'm serious."

"I'm not kidding, Tee. I am serious." He took out his cell phone and found the voice mail she left him the morning after he found out Tee was pregnant.

Tee felt like all the oxygen was leaving her head as she listened to that message. It also sent a chill through her body that felt like she outside naked in 30 degrees below zero wintery weather.

She stared at Michael in horror and reached for the white paper barf bag in the compartment next to her. Tee held her mouth over the bag as she lost the contents of her breakfast for the second time in two days. Her baby didn't like the sound of that voice either.

Chapter 22

My Name Is Mrs. James

Lenora was in her room preparing for her next class. She figured out a great way for the younger children to create the papier-mâché piggy bank without making a huge mess. She laid out the strips of newspaper and the glue solution. She was now in the process of blowing up the balloons they were going to use for the body of the bank. She decided it would be faster if she blew the balloons up herself rather than letting the children do it.

A soft touch on her shoulders startled her. She spit the balloon out of her mouth and watched it sail around the room as it deflated.

"I'm sorry I startled you, again," said Mr. Rupert. "I need to do a better job of announcing my arrival. Most women enjoy my touch."

Lenora blushed. "It felt nice but was totally unexpected." She continued to sit with her back to him, and Mr. Rupert resumed touching her shoulders. He gently kneaded the flesh between his fingers.

"Let's try this again. You're very tense, Mrs. James. Is everything all right?"

"Everything is fine. I've been staying up late to complete some paintings for a friend of mine. I'm taking the kids to my mother-in-law's house for the weekend so I can try to get some rest."

Everything was not fine. Things were very strained between her and Herman since she found out he was bartending at The Kitty Kat Club.

"That sounds like a novel idea. I'm sure your husband will enjoy having you all to himself."

"I don't know about that. My husband works late."

Now that Lenora knew Herman's secret, he no longer tried to be home by 7 p.m. to make Lenora believe he still had his old job. He even agreed to work additional hours at the club to earn some extra money. The night before, he didn't get home until 11 p.m. After he arrived, he ate his dinner and went straight to bed. He didn't say more than five sentences to Lenora before he fell asleep. Herman no longer got up early either. He slept late, which meant he couldn't help her get their three children ready for school. Lenora did it all by herself, and the twins could be a handful.

Lenora closed her eyes and enjoyed the moment. Mr. Rupert continued to press his hands in her flesh. "That feels really good," she cooed.

"I'm glad you like it. There's more where this came from if you want it. Is that a new perfume you're wearing? It's delightfully intoxicating." He put his face near her neck and inhaled deeply. His nose gently grazed her skin.

Lenora was instantly aroused by the gesture. The spot he touched grew hot, and the heat quickly spread throughout her entire body. She could feel beads of perspiration forming at her temples, and a smile formed at the corner of her lips. She was enjoying this too much. She opened her eyes and squirmed in her seat. Mr. Rupert had noticed something her own husband hadn't noticed. She was at Wolfchase Mall last week and purchased herself some new clothes and a bottle of perfume. It was Someday by Justin

Bieber. When the saleslady in the aisle handed her a sample and said the name, she knew she wouldn't like a perfume developed by a young pop singer, but surprisingly, she enjoyed the scent and took a small bottle home with her.

"Why, yes, I am," she stammered, and then stood up. She used the palms of her now sweaty hands to smooth the front of her smock. The name Mrs. James was embroidered on the front of it, reminding her of her husband and how much she loved him.

"The children will be entering soon so I need to finish preparing for them." She picked up another balloon and started blowing it up. Mr. Rupert got the hint and began walking toward the door.

"Enjoy the rest of your day, Lenora James. My hands are available if you need them." He smiled and exited the room.

Chapter 23

Love of Money Is the Root of Evil

Michael and Tee's plane arrived in Akron where a limo was waiting to take them to Accent Behavioral Health. During the flight, Edward called to inform them that their injunction was denied. The judge refused to give them permission to stop the dedication ceremony, and Edward couldn't understand why. Michael told him to meet them at Accent. He hoped they would be able to reason with the director of the recovery center. They arrived two hours before the dedication ceremony was scheduled to begin. The building looked quite festive. Balloons and colorful streamers were hanging throughout the lobby. Workers were setting up several tables for the food and media. Michael and Tee made their way to the office and asked to speak to the director.

She was a short, round woman with fire-engine red hair. As soon as Tee saw her she thought, *Rihanna has all these women running around looking like Bozo the clown. This short butterball is nobody's pop princess. I'm glad Ri-Ri stopped wearing that color, but why hasn't this woman?*

"Hello. I am Rachel Hillman," she said, extending her plump hand. Her round face was smiling, but there was no joviality in her eyes. They were stone cold. "How may I help you? Mr. Stokes, my, you look much better in person than in our mural. It will be a delight to have you here during the dedication ceremony, but you're a bit early."

Michael shook her hand and got right down to business. "Thank you, Ms. Hillman. The mural is exactly what my wife, my lawyer, Edward Palmer, and I are here to see you about. We want you to take it down."

Edward stepped in. "As I told you on the phone, Ms. Hillman, Michael's name and likeness are copyrighted, and you are in full violation of that copyright. He has not given you verbal nor written permission to keep that mural on display. We are prepared to use the full extent of the law to have it removed."

The smile instantly faded from her face. The stone coldness it displayed now matched the iciness in her eyes. "And as I told you, Mr. Palmer, we are under contractual obligation to keep that mural on display. We already accepted the money to name our recreational food hall in honor of Ms. DeFoy. Your suing us is not my top concern at this moment. However, the donor is scheduled to be here today, and perhaps we can reach some type of agreement."

Ms. Hillman actually had no intention of helping the Stokes' remove the mural. She stood to make a lot of money giving tours in Michael's hometown. She secretly hoped that while they were tied up in court she would make as much money as possible before she was forced to paint over it.

Tee was growing tired of this conversation that was going nowhere. She had no desire to negotiate for the respect of her marriage. This mural was in direct violation of it. Her husband being on display with the woman who tried to kill her was totally unacceptable. "Mrs. Hillman, do you know who I am?" said Tee.

Ms. Hillman turned her head to look at her. "Of course. You're Mrs. Stokes."

"That's true, but I'm more than Michael's wife. I'm the woman Rebecca DeFoy tried to kill with a butcher knife. That woman almost claimed my life in cold blood, and I am sickened that you and your company are willing to build a shrine to her. I am the victim, and every day that mural is up I am victimized again."

"Mrs. Stokes, I understand your stance, but Ms. DeFoy was ill, and I'm sure that if she were of sound mind, she wouldn't have attempted to harm you. I see the beauty in that mural. The fact that a woman of her instability was able to create something so wonderful is worthy of recognition. When you look into the eyes of the three people on our wall, it's almost as if you can see into their souls. They are so expressive. I can take you to it, and you can see if for yourself, if you'd like," she said.

"See it? See it? I want you to see what you are doing is wrong but *you* don't. I'll have to show you!" exclaimed Tee. She pulled her shirt over her head in one sweeping gesture and held it in her hand. She used her other hand to point to her stomach. Now, protruding with pregnancy, the keloid scar on the right side of her abdomen was more noticeable than ever. It covered almost one-fourth of her stomach. The raised mass of skin and scar tissue was an ugly dark brownish black. It looked so out of place on her otherwise smooth brown skin. Ms. Hillman and everyone else looked at her in surprise, and no one uttered a word.

"Do *you see* what she did to me?" Tee turned to the side and pulled down the left side of her black French lace and satin brassiere so the director could see the matching scar on the side of her left breast. It wasn't keloid like the one on her stomach, but it was still quite noticeable and ghastly looking. Her small, perky breast was fully exposed in the presence of a man other than her husband. Normally, Tee would have been horrified at the thought of being viewed nude by others, but at this moment, she could care less. Ms. Hillman had to understand the severity of her actions.

Hot tears began streaming down Tee's face. "How could you possibly make a martyr out of someone who could inflict such pain on another human being? I lost so much blood that I required a blood transfusion. This isn't a scratch. It's a deep, painful puncture wound. What if it was your child who had to endure such pain at the hands of another? Would you be so quick to dismiss it as the unintentional act of a mentally ill woman? Would you call her sick depiction of the family she imagined in her head—that included *your* husband—a thing of beauty?"

Ms. Hillman was not moved. As a caretaker of the mentally ill, she had seen some of the most grotesque and obscene sights life had to offer. She once had a patient put out his own eye with a pair of scissors and another defecate on her desk. An irate woman screaming at her with her breast exposed was nothing to her. She wasn't mean, nor was she heartless, but to work at a treatment facility you had to possess the ability to see others as better than they actually were in order to help them become so. She didn't see Becca as the monster so many others did. She never had. "Mrs. Stokes, please put your clothes on. This is a place of business," she said turning away.

"I will not put my clothes on. I am going to parade around this facility just like this so everyone can see what the woman you are honoring today did to me. I want the world to know!"

Michael didn't know what to do. He and his lawyer stood there looking at his wife's boob. Her nipple was erect, and she was exhibiting the brassiness he knew and loved. Michael was somewhat turned on by her actions, but he also recognized their inappropriateness. One of the workers at the recovery center stuck his head in the office and was about to say something until his eyes focused on Tee's nakedness. He looked at his boss in bewilderment. Ms. Hillman tried to act as if having a pregnant woman with her breast exposed was the most natural thing in the world.

"Yes, Stanley, how may I help you?" she asked.

Stanley continued to stare at Tee's breast while speaking. "The TV people are here to interview you. Should I show them to the boob? I mean, room."

Tee turned to face him "Yes! Please see them in so I can show them what that monster you call a patient did to me." Stanley now had a full frontal view of her exposed areola. He continued to fix his eyes on it and didn't move them once toward Tee's face as she was talking. He was a 55-year-old bachelor, and it wasn't every day that an attractive woman showed him her breast unless you count the issues of *Playboy* magazines he kept stashed in his office drawer.

"No!" Ms. Hillman screamed, and positioned her body between Tee and the door. "Stanley, escort them to the recreational area and let them get some footage of the mural. Tell them I'll be there shortly." She directed her attention toward Michael. "Mr. Stokes, I suggest you get your wife to cover up before I have her committed. Her behavior right now is certainly not that of a sane person. I will call the police and have her arrested for indecent exposure, request a psychiatric evaluation and then ask them to bring her here for treatment. I'm sorry that our decision causes you so much pain, but I am not moved by her little display."

"Is that a threat?" said Edward. "I'm sure no judge would take it lightly that you are using your position to threaten a mentally stable individual into submission."

"Especially, to enact your plan of using the mural for selfish gain," said Dr. Foster.

They all turned around to see her standing in the door. "Oh yes, Ms. Hillman, I know all about how you plan to make this facility a tourist attraction aimed at Michael Stokes fans around the globe. Will Michael be getting a cut of that? He's certainly entitled to it."

"That does it!" screamed Tee. "I'm tired of people trying to exploit me and my family. I don't need your permission to tell the truth. She headed for the door. You're gonna pay. I'll have your job when I'm through!"

Michael grabbed her as she attempted to pass him. "No, baby, this is not the way. We'll have our lawyer sue her. Let's not give the news a reason to censor you tonight." He grabbed his wife's bra strap and brought it back over her shoulder. He then gently wiped the tears from her face. "Let Edward do his job. We'll file a lawsuit, and we'll get that mural down. I promise."

"No!" Tee screamed. "That will take too long. I want this mural gone now!" She struggled to get to the door as Michael attempted to put her shirt back on. As they tussled, they heard a loud commotion coming from down the hall. Another staff member ran up behind Dr. Foster panting and pushed his way into the room.

"Ms. Hillman, come quick. They destroying the mural!" he shouted.

Chapter 24

Computer Love

Lenice logged onto her computer. She was increasingly becoming bored with the selection of men in the clubs and was now migrating to online dating. She signed up for several matchmaking web sites. She even found one geared toward those practicing celibacy. It was called thecelibatemate.com.

Each day she checked her account to see if anyone new contacted her. She had her preferences, and if the man who in-boxed her didn't meet them, she didn't respond. That was the best part about online dating; it was easy to get rid of a guy if you didn't like him. She had about three different men she chatted with regularly. She enjoyed having instant message conversations with them that had nothing to do with sex. It was already understood that wasn't happening so there was no need to discuss it. She was almost ready to meet them in person.

A coworker suggested that she look at a site that catered to wealthy men as well. She was signing up for that one tonight.

Chapter 25

Good Food

Teresa stared at the mural in front of her with contempt. She didn't see what the big deal was. It was ugly to her. What it represented was even uglier. Her husband, Zachary, called her yesterday and filled her in on the commercials that were running about Tee and Michael's interview on *Inside*. He couldn't tell exactly how the mural played a part in it, but he was sure it wasn't good.

Teresa knew that today it would be front and center on news outlets all over the country. Camera crews with attractive reporters were already arriving to shoot footage. Several residents were asked to serve as greeters during the dedication ceremony, and she agreed to volunteer as well. She looked around the room. It was filled with people with various mental problems and addictions. They usually separated the substance abuse patients from the mental patients, but since they were having the dedication ceremony today, they had them eat breakfast together to save time.

Some of the patients had the mental capacity of children and seemed to want to play all day long. Others welcomed playtime just to relieve the boredom of being in a treatment facility. Teresa could use this to her benefit. She pulled the baseball cap she wore daily down as low on her head as it would go. Then she whirled around and hit a resident they called Cutie Judy with a biscuit. Judy had the mental capacity of a seven year old and dressed like it too. She loved to put her hair in ponytails; she often wore baby-doll dresses and black Mary Jane shoes. She took Teresa's gesture as an invitation to play. Judy laughed and threw her fruit cup back at her. Unfortunately, she had horrible aim and hit Angry Andrew.

Andrew was dealing with aggression issues. He was normally fine until provoked, but once someone gave him a reason to lash out, all hell broke loose. He often tired of having to bridle what came naturally to him, but he was more tired of being sent to solitary confinement and being served meals of peanut butter and jelly when he allowed his anger to surface. This was a particularly hard morning for him because the cafeteria ran out of strawberry jelly, and he was forced to use grape jelly, which he disliked. He knew how much his parents paid for him to stay there, and for that kind of money, he felt they could at least keep some strawberry jelly in stock. He was happy to have a way to release his pent-up aggression in a manner that didn't include drawing a picture of what was bothering him as he was often asked to do during his counseling sessions.

Angry Andrew picked up a spoonful of oatmeal and hurled it at Judy, hitting her on the shoulder and the young man sitting next to her in the face, smearing his glasses. His name was Vern. Like Teresa, he was there for alcoholism. Judy laughed. Vern didn't find it amusing and tossed his entire glass of cranberry juice in Angry Andrew's direction. Someone yelled out "food fight" and suddenly, bacon, sausage, oatmeal, fruit, juice, and milk were flung from several directions across the room. Teresa ran and stood in front of the mural and yelled, "Hey, everybody, I bet you can't hit me!" Several residents took her up on that dare and hurled food in her direction. Even docile Tee Hee joined in the fun.

Ms. Hillman ran in the rec room with Tee, Michael, Edward, Dr. Foster, and Stanley close behind her. She screamed for order. Men in white coats ran in and began restraining patients, but it wasn't easy. The residents were doing something they wanted to do for a change, not what someone told them they should be doing, and they were having a good time doing it. By the time the staff was able to get the situation under control, Teresa was covered with food, juice, and milk, and so was the mural. She was restrained by two men and escorted from the room. Ms. Hillman looked at the mural and let out a bloodcurdling scream that could have possibly awaken the dead.

"It's ruined! Do you have any idea what you've have done? I was gonna be rich!" She began yelling obscenities at the residents. She called them everything from crazy to dumb to four-letter words that don't belong in a Christian novel. It was all caught on tape because the news cameras, although covered with food and juice, never stopped rolling.

Teresa laughed as she was hauled from the room and placed into solitary confinement. She watched the colors from the mural slowly run their way down the wall while clumps of breakfast food rested on the painting. Rehab wasn't so bad after all.

Tee gave Michael a hug of victory and a big kiss. She realized that she was still half-naked and put her top on before the cameras zoomed in on the pregnant woman in her bra. This wasn't over. She still had to diffuse the situation with the *Inside* interview, and she knew exactly how to do it. She would fight fire with fire.

"Everybody out!" screamed Ms. Hillman. "Get out of my facility, and I mean get out right now! Turn that camera off and leave."

In all the confusion, no one noticed the lone figure in the back that came for the specific purpose of dedicating that mural to his only sister. He watched in agony as the food destroyed what was supposed to be his way of making amends for the years he refused to speak to her.

Michael and Tee declined interviews by the media as they left. They held each other lovingly and answered every question with "no comment." They headed back to the airport, and went home. Michael wanted to go home and make love to his wife again, but Tee had other plans. As they left, Tiffany texted her and asked her to go shopping that afternoon. Tee readily accepted.

Chapter 26

Findinglove.com

Lenice read the book of Proverbs that morning and one section in particular stuck out in her mind. "Trust in the Lord with all your heart and lean not on your own understanding; in all your ways submit to him, and he will make your paths straight. Do not be wise in your own eyes; fear the Lord and shun evil. This will bring health to your body and nourishment to your bones." Proverbs 3:5-8

She tried to listen for instructions from the Lord, but sometimes His words didn't seem clear to her. She hoped that clarity wouldn't escape her when it came to her dating selections. The last thing she needed was another catastrophic mistake like her ex.

Today, she agreed to meet one of her cyber suitors for lunch. Her online name was SOFTASSILK, which she thought fit her perfectly. Her date used the name LUVURIGHT74. He didn't have a picture posted on his page, but Lenice decided to meet him anyway. Based on their instant message conversations, they had a lot in common and she hoped he was cute. In her daydreams, she imagined that he would be 6'2" with a head full of black curly hair and a strong resemblance to one of her favorite actors, Shemar Moore. The compatibility software the online dating site provided said the probability of them being compatible was 95 percent. She liked those odds.

As she sat in the restaurant sipping a Cherry Coke and waiting for her date to arrive, Lenice was approached by

James. She hadn't seen him since he kicked her to the curb for being unwilling to make a commitment. She missed him dearly but really didn't think this was good time for her to settle down. She was happy to see him, but she didn't want him to be at her table when her date arrived. She had to get rid of him.

"Hello, James. What are you doing here?"

"This is one of my favorite restaurants. I come here often for lunch. How are you?"

"I'm doing pretty good, and yourself?"

"I can't complain. I saw you at church this week and noticed your new haircut. It really looks good on you."

"I appreciate that, James. I don't mean to be rude, but I'm kind of waiting on a blind date, and I don't want him to be unable to recognize me because I have someone at my table."

"I understand," he said, "but I don't think that will be a problem."

"Why is that?"

"SOFTASSILK, I'm LUVURIGHT74, and it's a pleasure to finally meet you face-to-face."

Lenice paused. She didn't know whether to laugh or release a sigh of relief. James tricked her into going out on a date with him. She thought she was about to go out with someone new and exciting, but it was James. Not that she had anything against James. She did care for him, and they always had a good time, but he wasn't the man of her dreams. She decided to make the best of it.

"Then, have a seat. I hope you brought your wallet because I'm starving," she said and burst into a fit of laughter.

"Sorry, darling, but we're going to have to go Dutch. I don't get paid until next week."

Lenice stopped laughing.

"Gotcha!" said James and pulled out a chair. "I've missed you, Lenice."

"I've missed you too, James."

They sat there smiling at each other until the waitress interrupted to take their drink order.

Chapter 27

Woman to Woman

Michael decided to go check on the progress of the renovations of their new home while Tee went shopping. She was yearning for a little girl-time. Since she got married and started the business, she rarely had time to hang out with her friends. This outing would also provide the perfect opportunity to discuss with Tiffany what may or may not be happening with her husband.

While on the plane, Tee called her favorite publicist, Karen Robertson. Karen held the contract for all of MiTee Management's public relations activities. She was knowledgeable and possessed a media rolodex that included contacts from one end of the country to the other and even overseas. She told Tee exactly what to do. By the time they landed, Tee had crafted a letter, taken pictures of her scars, and e-mailed her the video Sheba took of them being interviewed by Solay.

When they landed in Memphis, Tee kissed Michael good-bye and took a cab to meet Tiffany. Michael drove downtown to their condo/office. Tee met Tiffany at Made Woman, one of her favorite boutiques. It catered to the professional woman and was sure to have several conservative pieces Tiffany would like. Tiffany waited for her in the parking lot until she arrived. Before they went in, Tiffany informed her of what was going on with William and why she wanted new clothes. They entered the boutique together, and the two saleswomen behind the counter greeted them with hearty smiles.

"Hello, Anastasia and Alice," said Tee.

"Oh, how nice to see you," said one woman and rushed to give Tee a hug.

"I've been holding some pieces in the back I knew you would love. Let me get them for you," said the woman.

Anastasia and Alice Smith were cousins and business partners. They opened the boutique together three years ago after leaving their jobs in corporate America. Alice was the eldest and looked to be about 55 years old, and Anastasia looked about 40. They were each quite successful in their respective fields but grew bored with the demands and lack of creativity their jobs provided. They decided to put their fetish for fashion to work. As managers of Fortune 500 companies, they both saw their fair share of office fashion faux pas: too much makeup, too much cleavage, too short skirts, sheer blouses with brassieres showing underneath, and flip-flops. They held monthly workshops to educate women on the proper way to dress and behave in corporate America. It was not unusual for companies who felt their executives could use a little polishing to recommend they visit Made Woman.

"Thank you so much for thinking of me, Anastasia, but I'm not here for myself today," said Tee. "Please meet my friend, Tiffany. We are trying to find some conservative but trendy pieces for her to wear to church. I knew this would be the perfect place for us to begin our shopping venture."

Anastasia extended her hand to Tiffany. "Please to meet you. I'm sure we have something here you'll like."

Alice wasn't as friendly. She peered over her glasses at Tiffany and silently assessed her outfit. She was quite casual today. Tiffany saw no need to get dressed up to try on clothes. She wore a pair of tight jeans and a tank top with a pushup bra. Her large breasts were up high and firmly in place. Her pants fit snugly at the waist causing a row of her midsection to rise above her belt and bulge. In Alice's opinion, that was a major fashion no-no. Tiffany stared back at her but didn't say a word. Both Tee and Anastasia noticed the optical standoff and tried to steer Tiffany's attention elsewhere.

"We received these beauties yesterday," said Anastasia while pointing to a rack of navy blue pants suits in the back of the room. Tiffany continued to stare at Alice wondering what her problem was.

"Oh, those are gorgeous," said Tee. She grabbed Tiffany by the arm and led her toward the suits.

When their backs were turned Anastasia shot her cousin a look meant to encourage her to be nice. They both knew Tee was a millionaire, and it wasn't uncommon for her to come into the boutique and spend $3,000 to $5,000 at a time. They hoped that her friend was on the same financial level. For the next hour, Tiffany tried on clothes for Tee and Anastasia. She fought to resist the urge to ask for everything in a smaller size, unbutton her blouse, or find a low-cut top for each outfit. She settled on two pieces she believed William would like but still allowed her to showcase her personal style. The entire time they were there, Tiffany noticed how Anastasia and Alice catered to Tee. They gushed about how good her hair and her outfit looked. They even told her about their recent excursions to New York and Los Angeles looking for new pieces to showcase in their store.

It was obvious these women felt that they had a relationship with Tee. She wondered why Tee was socializing with the help. Tiffany purchased her items and took Tee's suggestion to visit another boutique Tee thought she might like. It was called Design 1. Tee also knew the salespeople there by name, and they too went out of their way to make the two of them feel comfortable and valued as customers.

Tiffany wondered what Tee did to make people love her so. She purchased two more outfits complete with accessories and shoes.

As she drove Tee home Tiffany asked, "How do you mesmerize people like that? The salespeople broke their necks to make sure you were having a pleasant shopping experience. At times, I think they forgot I was there."

"No, they didn't. You were the one spending the money, not me. People are nice to me because I am nice to them. When I met Alice and Anastasia, they barely had any customers. They were going to close the store the next month if business didn't pick up. I invited them to a tea I coordinated for some of the wealthiest women in Memphis. I even wore a beautiful dress I bought from them. Under normal circumstances, they never would have been invited into that circle. Every time someone commented on my dress, I introduced them. Alice and Anastasia maximized the opportunity and invited everyone present to their store. Those women spent so much money that Alice and her sister were able to keep their business open, and many of them still shop there. Therefore, they look out for me.

"If you want friends, Tiffany, you have to show yourself to be friendly. I know in the past you were guarded because you didn't want people to know about your affair with Quincy. Well, once the tabloids got a hold of the information, the cat was out of the bag and you started putting up more walls to protect you and your son from people with negative opinions. I understood that, but what's your excuse now? You're not seeing Quincy anymore. There's no reason to keep people out, Tiffany. It doesn't cost you a thing to be nice to others or to strike up a conversation or give them a compliment. This ability you have to mesmerize men can be used on women too, you know."

"Women are different, Tee. Many of them feel threatened by me," said Tiffany.

"That's because you had a reputation for bedding married men. They thought you were a home wrecker and needed to keep you as far away from them and their husbands as possible. I know it won't be easy, but now you have to show people the new and improved Tiffany. The one who is only interested in *single* men.

"One of the keys to being friendly is taking a genuine interest in the well-being of others. You can do that rather easily. It's as simple as calling to check on people. The worst thing you can do is call someone only when you want something. I hate when people do that, don't you?"

Tiffany nodded her head up and down in agreement.

"Call to say hello or wish them a happy birthday. Actually, these days you don't have to call. Send them an e-mail or a message on Facebook or Twitter. It's a small gesture, but you'd be surprised how many people appreciate it."

Tiffany continued to listen to Tee's advice on how to make friends as she drove. She was starting to see why Michael was so in love with her. Even though her appearance was somewhat plain, the woman was wise beyond her years.

"I'm glad you're not willing to let William go without a fight. Sometimes men don't know what's good for them, and it's up to us women to tell them. He's going to love the outfits you picked out today. I know they're not what you usually go for, but change can be good."

"I agree," said Tiffany.

"If you need more pointers on how to be a woman of virtue worthy of a pastor read Proverbs 31. By the way, did you enjoy seeing my husband naked?"

Tiffany wasn't expecting that question, and she had no idea how to answer. She panicked, slammed her foot down on the brake, and was almost rear-ended by the car behind them.

Chapter 28

Home Not So Sweet Home

Lenora took the children to the park so they could play on the playground while she ran around the track. She kept her eyes on them as she pushed herself to complete at least 3 miles. Losing weight was hard work, but she enjoyed seeing the results more than she hated the workout.

Her babies looked so happy. She loved them dearly. Her family meant the world to her, and it was agonizing to think of Herman working at that strip club. As far as she knew, he never cheated on her, but she knew in a place with hot bodies everywhere it could happen. She prayed every day that Herman would find another job. She even started submitting his résumé to companies herself. Lenora tried not to nag Herman about finding another job. She knew he was doing the best he could, but she couldn't help mentioning from time to time that he shouldn't be there. He was a brilliant man, and she believed his brilliance was going to waste in a place like that. Besides, if people asked her what her husband did, she didn't want to have to lie. Yet, there was no way she was going to say a bartender at a house of ill repute.

Lenora also hated his work hours. She and the kids barely saw him anymore. He seemed to come home later and later each day. His reason was that they needed more money. She didn't know how much debt they were in, but she noticed that Herman always looked stressed and overworked. He asked her not to worry about it but how could she not? She had no idea how much their monthly bills were because Herman always took care of that. The only bill she was aware of was the grocery bill, and that's because she did all of the shopping. She wanted to help so he wouldn't have to be away from home so much.

Lenora was grateful that Tee paid her in advance for the paintings. She used the money to buy groceries and anything the children needed without having to ask Herman for it. One of the twins needed glasses, and Hermie was making such good progress that his tutor wanted to work with him more often. She said he was beginning to catch on to his lessons more quickly, and if he continued to do so, he would have no problems keeping up with the other children in his class. That was wonderful news, but they really couldn't afford it right now.

Chapter 29

Unintentional

"Tee, Sugah, I wouldn't exactly say I enjoyed looking at Michael naked. I mean, it was totally unintentional. He's got a nice body, as you know, but nothing I haven't seen before. I mean, not on him; other men with nice bodies," Tiffany struggled to find the right words. Her Southern drawl was more prominent than ever when she was nervous.

Tiffany maneuvered her car over to the side of the road. There was no way she could have this conversation and drive. She was sweating. Of course she enjoyed seeing Michael naked. He had the body of a Greek god and a behind so tight she was sure he could use it to crack nuts, if necessary. Yet, she was fully aware that he was her best friend's husband.

Tee enjoyed watching her squirm. She wanted Tiffany to feel as uncomfortable as her husband felt being placed in that situation. She didn't want to ruin their friendship, but Tee knew he couldn't continue to spend time alone with Tiffany.

"Neither Michael nor I meant for it to happen. You're not mad, are you? I'm sure it won't ever happen again. I'm sorry. I really didn't mean to knock Michael's towel off. Tee, Sugah, say something."

Tee smiled. "Tiffany, daaaarhling," she said imitating her accent, "exactly what do you want me to say? What would you do if you were me?"

"I would trust my friend and my husband, and remember that the love they both have for me is genuine, and they would never do anything to intentionally hurt me."

The car wasn't moving but Tiffany gripped the steering wheel tightly as if she needed to be ready to maneuver the car at a moment's notice. She loosened a hand, reached over and turned up the dial for the flow of the air conditioner. Cool air began to blow harder from the vents of her car.

"Then, that's what I'll do," said Tee. "Apology accepted."

"That's it?" said Tiffany.

"That's it," said Tee. "Unless there is something else about you and my husband you need to share with me."

"No. There's nothing." Tiffany breathed a sigh of relief. She was thankful that Tee was such a nice person.

"Good. I hope you don't mind, but Michael has turned your account over to me, and he will no longer be joining you for any massages."

"Do you really think that's necessary, Tee? Michael and I have developed a good work rhythm that benefits MiTee Management as well as me. He told me I was your highest-grossing client."

"You *were* our highest-grossing client. I signed Blak yesterday. And yes, I do think it's necessary. As your managers, it's important that we keep business and friendship separate and your friendship and the professionalism of this company has been compromised by that little private showing of my husband's penis. As his wife, it is my job to step in and make sure that the integrity of this company is upheld. As a new business, the last thing we need is ugly rumors flying around about you or my husband," said Tee.

Tiffany was not happy about this decision. Tee was able to land her clients in the corporate world, but it was Michael who used his connections to attract her entertainment clients. She and her team had flown all around the country giving massages to the same faces seen in *Essence, Jet,* and *Ebony.*

"How would that happen?" she asked. "No one saw us, and I left immediately after his wardrobe malfunction happened."

"No one saw you *this* time, Tiffany, but I can't take a chance on it happening again. I hate to go all bossy on you, but this isn't up for discussion. This decision has been made by the principals of MiTee Management. If you want us to continue to represent you, you'll deal with it."

"I see," said Tiffany. "Let's get you home to that husband of yours," she said and maneuvered her car back onto the road.

"If you don't mind, could you drop me off at Lenora's? I want to see how the paintings I asked her to do are coming along."

"Sure, Sugah."

Conversation between them was strained from that point on. Tiffany was relieved when they pulled in the driveway of Lenora's house. Under normal circumstances, she would have exited the car and gone in with Tee to see her paintings, but these weren't normal circumstances. She was a bit rattled that decisions concerning her and her company were made without her input.

Tee gathered her things, and as she prepared to exit the car she said to Tiffany, "How would you like to begin paying back the money you owe me and Michael?"

"What money?" asked Tiffany.

"You know, the $30,000 we lent you after you left Quincy. Do you want us to take installments out of your checks, or do you want to give it to us yourself? Either way is fine with us. Now that you are making a decent salary and receiving child support from Quincy there's no reason you can't start making payments. Can you do at least $1,000 a month?"

Tiffany forgot Tee was in the courtroom when the judge ordered Quincy to pay a hefty child support payment each month, plus their son's private school tuition. Tee had been toying with the idea of giving Tiffany the money and almost reached the conclusion to let her have it. Now, she realized she needed to make sure that Tiffany understood that you shouldn't abuse her kindness.

Once again, Tiffany was caught off guard. She never expected Tee to ask her to repay that money. She and Michael were multimillionaires. It wasn't as if they needed it, but she couldn't dispute that it was a loan. She did agree to pay them back.

"I don't know," said Tiffany. "Quincy 2's tuition is due next week. Quincy is usually late with the payment. I pay it and then wait for him to pay me back. Can I look at my bills for the month and get back with you?"

"That's fine," said Tee. " But we'd like to finalize payment arrangements sometime this week. Let me get inside now. I'm dying to see what kinds of ideas Lenora has for my décor. See you later. Oh, you are still coming to the viewing party at my house tomorrow, right? Michael and I want to be surrounded by those who love us when Ultimate Sports airs that horrid interview with Solay. This is a kid-friendly event so bring Quincy 2."

"He'll still be with his father, but I wouldn't miss it for the world. Give Lenora my love," said Tiffany.

"Will do. Thanks for the ride." Tee gave Tiffany a hug and exited her car. After Tee closed her car door, Tiffany used her cell phone to dial Michael's number. She had to get him to agree to continue managing her. As far as she was concerned, Michael was the reason she was so successful. Her call went straight to his voice mail. Perhaps she could get a few minutes alone with him during the viewing party. There was no way Tee could help her land the same high-paying clients as the magnificent Michael Stokes.

Chapter 30

Pay It Forward

Mac awoke to the scent of lilacs and lavender and a slight heaviness on his chest. He opened his eyes to find Amy's sleeping head resting on him. Her long black tresses were in his face. He didn't mind. He rather liked it, but he wondered how she got there since they fell asleep on opposite ends of the couch. He looked down at her. *Here I go again,* he thought. *Falling for another unrefined woman who comes from the hood.* He realized that this one was different, though. She had attended a prestigious four year college. She didn't care that he had money. She hadn't asked him to do anything other than spend time with her and her family. They all went out that night. Mac offered to pay, but Amy refused. She said he was their guest. She took him to the $2 movie. There were several second run movies he hadn't seen. After she purchased the tickets, Mac thought it was odd that they bypassed the concession stand. In his opinion, it was almost criminal to go to the movies and not order popcorn, gummy bears, or some other tasty treat. He soon realized that Amy and Patrice carried a concession stand in their purses. Once they found their seats in the theater, they distributed cheese and crackers and fruit juice to wash it down.

"I try to limit the amount of junk I give them," Amy explained. "I'm also taking everyone out to eat after the movie so they don't need much." Mac smiled and ate his cheese and crackers. That was his favorite snack as a child.

Mac always wanted children, and Patrice and Amy's children were so sweet and adorable you had to love them. Patrice's son, Nathan, sat in his lap during the movie and didn't want to move. He figured it was because the child wasn't used to having a man around. He must get lonely being the only boy in the house.

That evening he got a glimpse of how they survived on Amy's meager means. After the movie, they went to Burgerville, where Amy worked. Each person ordered items off the dollar value menu and used her discount. The children didn't even complain that they couldn't get a Smile Meal with the toys, but Amy's manager was nice enough to give them the toy anyway. They were only allowed to order water with their meal. Once they finished eating, they went to a discount grocery store and got a gallon of ice cream and some cones for dessert and took them to Mac's house to eat.

After the children finished their ice cream, Patrice and Amy took them to his spare bedroom and put them to sleep. Patrice went to sleep as well. Mac and Amy retreated to the den to watch TV and talk. During a commercial break, he told her that he almost slept with her sister. He thought she needed to know.

"I know. Patrice told me everything," said Amy. "I have even been trying to find out who the woman is who tried to set you up, but she really doesn't know. What she does know doesn't provide enough clues to figure it out."

"You don't have a problem with the fact that I took out your little sister and almost slept with her?"

"Naw, you didn't know she was underage, and you didn't sleep with her. I had a long talk with Patrice about misleading people and doing dishonest things for money. She knows better. She has a baby, but she's a good kid. I'm trying to teach her to be a young lady, but those hoochie friends of hers seem to be a bigger influence on her than me. I gotta get her away from them. I'm really glad you took an interest in her, Mac, and it was nice of you to offer to let her work in your office. She'll get to see how successful folks live. I try to expose her to as much as possible. I don't want her to end up like me."

"Your circumstances did this to you. You didn't do it to yourself. It was admirable of you to come home and take care of your family. You could have let Patrice go to foster care," said Mac.

Amy shook her head. "I couldn't do that. I never would have forgiven myself, and Big Momma would have turned over in her grave. She probably would have returned from the dead to haunt me. For her, family was everything. She sacrificed a lot for us. She should have been enjoying her retirement instead of raising her crackhead daughter's kids."

Mac could hear the pain in Amy's voice. He was growing to care about all of them in a short amount of time.

"What's your story?" asked Amy.

"What do you mean?"

"Why are you single? You're handsome, successful, and charming. Why are you hanging out on a Friday night with two single mothers from South Memphis and their kids? Shouldn't you be at some black tie function or something?" she teased.

"I'm single because I haven't met the right woman, and I'm with you because you invited me. I enjoy your company, Amy."

"Likewise, Mac." She moved her face toward his and kissed him.

Mac sucked her in slowly. Amy was petite but curvy. Her medium-sized breasts grazed against his chest while they kissed. He knew a needy body when it was near him. He could tell that Amy hadn't been touched by a man in quite some time. She took his hands and placed them on her hips. He responded by caressing the rounded flesh through her jeans. He removed his mouth from hers and placed it on her neck. He kissed and gently nibbled right below her ear. Amy moaned with pleasure. Their temperatures grew warm. Mac toyed with the thought of taking her to his bedroom. Amy must have read his mind.

"You can have me if you want. I promise I won't take it for more than it is and start getting all clingy and stuff. No strings attached. We can still be friends. I know how to keep my emotions in check," she said.

Mac was surprised. Amy was either used to being used only for sex, or she didn't want to scare him away by making him think she wanted a relationship. He sat up and gently pushed her shoulders back to put some space between their heated bodies. He looked deeply into her eyes and said, "Thanks for the offer, Amy. I think I'll pass."

"But why?" She looked down at her body, and then back at him. "Don't you think I'm pretty? Do you think I'm not good enough for you? I know I'm not a high-society lady or nuthin' like that. But I bet I look as good as they do, minus the designer clothes."

Mac shook his head. "No, I think you're gorgeous." He gave her full lips a quick kiss. "Don't misunderstand me. I find you very attractive, but some things are worth waiting for. I'm having a good time getting to know you. I don't want to ruin it by rushing."

Amy's chest heaved, and she raised her hand. Mac braced himself for what he thought was going to be a slap. He hoped she wouldn't start yelling. He didn't want her to wake Patrice and the children. She brought her hand down against his face with the one of the gentlest touches he ever felt and kissed his cheek.

"That's the sweetest thing any man has ever said to me. I'm glad we met," she said and kissed him again before settling her body onto the other end of the couch. They both laid there and watched television.

Just as Mac was about to enter a brand-new dream he heard Amy ask in a drowsy voice, "You like pancakes?"

"I love pancakes," answered Mac.

Amy yawned. "Good. I'ma fix us all some for breakfast before we go home in the morning."

Mac yawned. "Can you add strawberries?"

"Anything you want, baby."

Mac smiled. He liked the sound of that . . . anything he wanted. He decided that Casper's luck had run out. He was no longer interested in helping her ruin Tee's marriage, and he had to find a way to stop giving her money. He didn't care what she threatened him with. He needed to tell Tee that someone was after her, and he needed to tell her soon. He owed Tee more than he could repay. Because of her, he now knew what real love was supposed to look and feel like. It wasn't selfish or manipulative. It was kind and meant putting someone else's needs above your own. He was sorry that he didn't appreciate it when Tee tried to give it to him. Their time together was over. She was someone else's woman now, and he had to move on as well. Amy had the same giving spirit as Tee.

Mac was becoming a better man, and he genuinely wanted to help Amy and her family more than anything. He was so wrong for even agreeing to help Casper. He was going to repay Tee's gift to him by showing Amy what he learned. She wasn't very educated and she had baggage, but he didn't care. She deserved a helping hand in life. He knew his efforts wouldn't be wasted on her.

Chapter 31

Paint Me a Pretty Picture

Lenora and Tee sat in Lenora's studio and talked about her ideas for the MiTee Management paintings. Tee was amazed at her friend's weight loss. She looked great, but her eyes were sad, giving Tee an outward indication that there was something bothering her.

Lenora showed Tee two paintings she was working on and sketches for the other two she wanted to do. They were all colorful, with bright images of men, women, or nature. One even reminded her of works by Tee's favorite artist, Morissette. She looked at each one thoughtfully and tried to imagine what they would look like when mounted on the walls of the office. She tried to remember the colors of the walls and the style and color of the furniture. She really didn't need four paintings, but she was sure she could find space for one or two of them upstairs in the condo. If not, she could always give one away as a gift. She wanted to support Lenora's efforts so that she would continue to do things that made her happy. She enjoyed seeing her smile.

"I like all of them. I haven't seen your work in so long I almost forgot how talented you are," said Tee. "How soon do you think you can have them ready?"

"I'm hoping to have at least two of them completed next week," said Lenora. "I have an art show next weekend. Do you mind if I showcase them? I'll be sure to let people know that they are not for sale."

"I'll do you one better. Be sure to put a sign next to each one that they are part of Michael and Tee Stokes' private collection. Hopefully, that will entice people to buy from you if they know someone rich and famous has already made a purchase from you," said Tee.

"Tee, what a wonderful idea. You really are a marketing guru!" exclaimed Lenora.

"Comes from years of experience," said Tee. "I can even have my publicist send out a press release about your art show. Send me the info."

"Thank you so much! Maybe after I lose all this weight you and Michael can manage me."

"We'll look into it, but you probably need someone who specializes in art. Why do you have to lose weight to get a manager?" asked Tee.

Lenora looked down. "I'd feel more confident taking pictures and talking to people if I were smaller. I've lost weight, but I still feel huge."

"Nonsense. You should be proud of what you've accomplished so far. You look great. I'm sure Herman thinks so too."

Lenora changed the subject. "I love my family, my work, and painting, but juggling all of it is hard. I barely have any free time. I don't see how these single mothers do it. I couldn't imagine having to work a full-time job and take care of my babies. Even after my father died, my mother had my grandmother to help her out."

"When you're a mother you do what you have to do. If that means putting in long hours, then going home to cook dinner, help with homework, wash clothes, and put children to bed you'll do it," said Tee. "How's Herman?"

"He's fine. He's at work." Lenora let out a deep sigh. She cringed every time she thought about Herman at that place.

Tee smiled. "I heard he was unemployed. I'm so happy that he got a new job. Praise God! Where is he working?"

"At The Kitty Kat Club," she said in a low voice.

Tee got up from the stool she was sitting on, walked over to Lenora, and stood behind her. "The strip club? What's he doing there?"

"He a bartender. I should be happy that my husband is willing to support us by any means necessary, but how can any woman be thrilled about her husband working around naked women with big ta-tas? Here I am looking like a two-liter soda, and he's there with those coke bottle-shaped women who think he's the best bartender in the world."

"I can understand your frustration. I wouldn't like it either, but if that's the only work he can find right now, try not to be too hard on him. He's trying, Lenora, and that's got to count for something. Don't feel threatened by those women. You've got big ta-tas too."

Lenora ignored her attempt to make her laugh. "I've also got a big stomach, a big booty, and big hips. Yeah, he's trying. That's what I keep telling myself, but then I remember that he works around naked women all day," she said.

Tee gave Lenora a hug. "Is he cheating on you?"

"I don't know, but he's never home anymore. He's always working. So, even if he isn't, it feels like he is. I miss my husband, Tee."

"Have you told him?"

"Yes, but evidently our bills take priority over my feelings right now."

Tee held her friend and whispered in her ear. "It's going to be all right," she soothed. "I feel it in my spirit. Everything is going to be fine."

"I hope so," Lenora whispered back.

Chapter 32

Slaying the Media Monsters

Tee spent Saturday working with Karen on their plan to play defense against Solay and Ultimate Sports. That evening their new blog MrandMrsStokes.com would launch, and she couldn't wait. Solay wasn't the only one who would have a world premier story that weekend. Karen convinced Tee that it was time to show her scars. They were the perfect representation of what she and Michael went through and what they are still going through. Tee was a little apprehensive about having her breast on the Internet, but they took a close side shot to keep it from appearing pornographic. They also posted any articles and news stories they could find about the hell Becca put them through. The site also contained a heartfelt letter from Tee addressing the mural.

Michael and I find it incorrigible that a news network and a residential treatment facility would use our pain for their own personal gain. Below you will find photos of the scars that were left on my body by the blade of Rebecca DeFoy. You will also find a picture of the mural she painted. It's a delusional portrait of the life she wished she'd held with my husband. What is even more frightening is that a facility that has been certified by the state of Ohio to treat her disorder allowed her to illustrate this delusion and intended to use it for financial again. We, as concerned citizens, must stop this madness. I will no longer allow the media to attack my family without fighting back. Being a celebrity shouldn't mean having to constantly defend yourself. It shouldn't mean being bombarded with accusatory questions, ambushed by success-hungry journalists, and robbed of any semblance of normalcy.

These wounds don't only represent an attack on my body but an attack on my very being, as well as my marriage. I made the decision to love a wonderful man, and I was stabbed for doing so. My physical wounds have healed, but the emotional ones are still wide open and bleeding. People won't let them heal because they continue to stick knives of insensitivity, greed, and personal gain in them. I recognize that Rebecca DeFoy was mentally ill and she was not fully capable of preventing her attack. But I have to ask the Ultimate Sports Network and Solay Peterson, what's your excuse? And I ask the administration and executive board of Accent Behavioral Health, what's your excuse? My husband and I started this blog as a means of fighting back on our own terms. We will no longer play the victim, and we will emerge the victor. Check back after the show airs. There's more to come.

Tee's scars were on display for the world to see. Until yesterday, she kept them carefully hidden beneath her clothes. The only person who was allowed to see them was Michael. She needed every man and woman to feel her pain and understand exactly what was being unmercifully stripped from her each day by people who appeared to have no conscience. She prayed that public outcry and support would make them stop.

Chapter 33

Blessed & Highly Favored

The next day was Sunday. Tiffany strolled into church in the new tangerine suit she purchased. It was modest, but the color made it pop. The skirt stopped slightly above her knees and her blouse exposed no cleavage. She also wore a large white hat with several ostrich feathers stemming from it. She wasn't used to wearing hats, but she pretended that it was a crown. She thought she looked like a regal first lady. She arrived late so that William would have no choice but to see her. She knew exactly what time he would be in the pulpit leading praise and worship.

As Tiffany walked down the aisle toward a semi-empty pew near the front of the church, she smiled at him. William nodded his head and smiled back in acknowledgment while continuing to lead the praise team in Donnie McClurkin's song "We Fall Down."

"We fall down, but we get up. We fall down, but we get up. We fall down, but we get up. And a saint is just a sinner who fell down, and got up," he sang.

She sat down and began to meditate on the words. She knew exactly what Donnie meant. She wasn't perfect, but she wasn't the same woman she used to be. She knew that she and her child were better for it. It warmed her heart to see Quincy 2 happy again. She realized that she and her son were searching for the same thing. They wanted to feel wanted. He now felt wanted and accepted by his father and his siblings. Tiffany, on the other hand, felt an intense emptiness without William. He made her feel wanted. She was sure he still wanted her. Church folk were telling him that she wasn't good enough. Who were they? They didn't know her. They didn't know her struggles. They didn't know that she got on her knees and prayed to God each day. They didn't know that she read her Bible every morning. She was also living a life free from sexual sin. Tiffany began to get angry, but she quietly whispered to herself, "Greater is He that is within me than he that is in the world."

She stood up and raised her hands to the heavens in praise. God was so good, and she wouldn't disappoint Him again. As the song ended, she had tears in her eyes. The ushers passed a box of tissues down to her. She took a few and dabbed her eyes, being careful not to smear her mascara. The change that had come over her life was one of peace. She was living right, and it felt good.

Tiffany sat back down. It was time for the pastor's sermon. It came from Hebrews 12:7-11. Pastor Lancelot Gaston rose from his seat in the pulpit and asked the congregation to open their Bibles to Hebrews. He was an elderly gentleman with a young spirit. He walked with a slight limp. It was a reminder of his days in the military. He was injured while on a special assignment in Korea.

"Endure hardship as discipline; God is treating you as His children. For what children are not disciplined by their father? If you are not disciplined—and everyone undergoes discipline—then you are not legitimate, not true sons and daughters at all. Moreover, we have all had human fathers who disciplined us, and we respected them for it. How much more should we submit to the Father of spirits and live! Our earthly fathers disciplined us for a little while as they thought best; but God disciplines us for our good, in order that we may share in His holiness. No discipline seems pleasant at the time, but painful. Later on, however, it produces a harvest of righteousness and peace for those who have been trained by it."

Tiffany knew that sermon was meant for her. God was definitely disciplining her. She thought about all the "whippings" she received for messing with married men. She shook her head. It seemed as if she was still being disciplined. If she hadn't allowed herself to develop feelings for Michael he would still be her manager. Tee was right. They needed to put some distance between them. The scripture said that the discipline was to prepare her, but what was God preparing her for?

As the service ended, Tiffany hugged several people around her and told them to be blessed like the pastor instructed as he dismissed them each Sunday. Several men in the church approached her for a hug. She gave them the friendly one-arm church hug she witnessed her mother give to men when she was a child. Her mother was quite beautiful in her youth, and several men tried to lure her away from her father with promises of treating her better. Although her father was unfaithful, her mother was dedicated to her family and let them all know they were wasting their time.

One of the men who approached Tiffany was Brother Ezekiel Franklin. Brother Franklin was a widower and the owner of Franklin Construction. They were known for building beautiful megachurches and large office complexes. There was recently an article in the paper about how his company was awarded a $300 million contract to build a new arena in Denver, Colorado. Not only was he rich, but he was also attractive. The tailored suit he wore was brown. His shirt was the same color as Tiffany's dress and his wing tipped shoes were brown as well. He was a bit old school but always stylish.

"Sister Tiffany," he said, "you look lovely today. That color brings out the rosiness in your cheeks." He leaned in closer. "I'm sorry to hear that things between you and Pastor William didn't work out. I hope you don't mind me saying so, but I always thought he was too young for you. You need an older, more established man. A man like me has connections. I could help take you and your business to the next level. Why don't we go to dinner this week and discuss it?" Brother Franklin looked down at her ample bosom and to his dismay her breasts were fully covered. He delighted in the vision of her cleavage every Sunday. It was one of the reasons he came to church regularly. Before Tiffany started attending, he only came every once in a while. Disappointed, he moved his eyes back up to her face. "I'm glad to see that you didn't let Cupid's mistake keep you from church. I so enjoy having you here."

Tiffany had no intentions of discussing what did or didn't happen regarding William with Brother Franklin. The invitation to dinner was tempting. She had heard about his lavish spending, but he also had a reputation for being a bit of a playboy. He was generous with the women he dated but after he finished with his female toys he easily discarded them. She had heard more than one story about women in the church he wined, dined, and bedded. Those poor women ended up falling in love with him and believed they were going to be the next Mrs. Franklin. They later found themselves ejected from his life when he found a new better-looking plaything. Although Tiffany was sure she had more than enough tricks up her sleeves to keep him interested for a very long time she knew not to mess with him. Lenice gave her sound advice about not dating any other men in the church, and she was going to listen.

"Thank you for your kind words, Brother Franklin. I am doing well, but dinner won't be possible. I'm quite busy these days. I appreciate your willingness to assist with my business, but me and my associates can handle it."

Brother Franklin was not one to give up easily. Years of being in business taught him the power of persistence. "I understand if you want to take a hiatus from dating after a breakup. That's very wise of you. However, I could use a massage." He rubbed his hands together and winked at her.

"That I can do," said Tiffany. "May I have your business card?"

Brother Franklin fished inside his coat pocket and pulled out a money clip. It was full of one hundred dollar bills, and then he pulled out a 14 karat gold diamond-encrusted business card case. Instead of putting his money back, he kept it out in full view of Tiffany. She wondered why anyone would carry around so much cash. There must have been at least $2,000 there. She pretended not to notice and took the business card he extended to her.

"Thanks, Brother Franklin, I'll have someone from my office call and set something up with you. One of my staff members would be happy to come to your home or office and work those kinks out. I've got to go now." She began walking off before he could tell her that he wanted her to administer the services.

There were other men milling around waiting to talk to Tiffany, and she was not going to tie up her Sunday afternoon with unwanted advances. If they all behaved like Brother Franklin she was going to lose her mind. In her haste to get away, she didn't look where she was going and almost tripped over William. He was standing in the back of the sanctuary spying on her.

"Oh, excuse me, William," said Tiffany.

"It's all right. I was headed your way. It looked like you could use a little help escaping the church's selection of eager eligible bachelors. By the way, you look great." He smiled at Tiffany warmly. Her heart fluttered. She was no damsel in distress, but she was not about to let this golden opportunity pass her by.

"Please get me as far away from them as possible. Especially, Brother Franklin," she pleaded. "If he continues to undress me with his eyeballs the way he is I'll be standing in my panties in front of the pulpit before you know it."

William laughed, gently took her by arm, and led her through the sanctuary and into the vestibule. Tiffany glanced behind her and noticed the dejected look on Brother Franklin's face as well as the four other men standing in close vicinity to him. They tried to act as if they weren't watching the two of them walk away. Tiffany chuckled and planted a small kiss on William's cheek.

"My hero," she said.

"My pleasure," he responded. "I know we're not together, but would you mind if I took you and Q to dinner? Did I tell you that I love this suit? It's very becoming but lose the hat. It's not you at all, and it covers your beautiful face."

Tiffany blushed. She really did want to accept William's invitation to dinner, but she knew what she wanted and how to get it. If William wanted her back in his life, he had to make a commitment. They were past the "just dating" phase. Either he wanted her, or he didn't.

"I still want to be with you, but I need to know that you want the same thing. An occasional dinner won't do. Quincy 2 is with his father, but I already told him we aren't together anymore. He wasn't happy about it. He likes you a lot. I don't think it's a good idea for us to spend time together. It will only make him think we're back together, and we're not. I need to be able to make that distinction myself."

William said he understood and escorted her to her car.

"I won't force the issue, but I think you're making a big mistake. We're good together, William," said Tiffany as she hugged him good-bye. She hoped she had made the right decision by not going to dinner with him. Her stomach growled as if to tell her she hadn't.

Chapter 34

Blessings unto You

"Oh, the devil don't like it 'cause I'm blessed like that. The devil don't like it 'cause I'm blessed like that!" Tee sat in church next to her husband listening to the choir sing one of her favorite songs by Elder Jimmy Hicks and The Voices of Integrity. Faith Persists Missionary Baptist Church was on fire today. There was no denying that the Holy Ghost was in the house. The lead singer was giving the song his all, and the choir was behind him rocking in their purple and white choir robes. "Like that, like that, I'm blessed, like that" they sang. That was exactly the way Tee and Michael were starting to feel. It was as if the devil had launched an all-out assault against them but they recognized that they were still blessed.

Pastor Alexander Mason III stood and greeted the congregation. The beautiful woman with a man's name was head of the largest female-led congregation in the state of Tennessee. She was the only child of a man who desperately wanted a son. Her parents had so much trouble conceiving and carrying her to term they knew that if they were going to give her father a namesake it had to be her. She was as tough as any man but with a face and body that no one in their right mind would mistake for a man.

At first, Michael was skeptical about joining a church with a female pastor, but after he attended several times, he became hooked on Pastor Alex's real-world applicable preaching and the atmosphere of love that flowed throughout the church. Michael squeezed his wife's hand as Pastor Alex gave the scriptures for her sermon.

"God put it on my heart to talk to the married couples today. Turn in your Bibles to the book of Mark, chapter 10 verse 9. It reads, 'What therefore God hath joined together, let no man put asunder.' That's the King James Version. Now, the New American Standard Bible reads, 'What therefore God has joined together, let no man separate.'"

Tee squeezed Michael's hand. Their marriage was not challenge-free, but there was no one she would rather go through a storm with. She looked at her husband in his dark blue Giorgio Armani suit. He was so handsome. Michael looked over at Tee. That morning she chose to wear a simple A-line red dress. She looked beautiful, and pregnancy was giving her a glow she didn't have before. Her hair was growing rapidly and her skin looked flawless. The dress fit her snugly around her waist and displayed her growing baby bump.

He knew everyone thought she hit the jackpot when she and Michael started dating, but Michael believed it was he who was the lucky one. Each day with Tee was pure bliss. He leaned over and kissed her on the cheek. Tee reached for his hand and placed it firmly in hers before she returned the favor. The woman behind them cleared her throat to signal them to stop their display of affection. Michael turned around and looked at her. She returned the glare with that a look that seemed to say, *Is there a problem*? Tee and Michael laughed. "Hater," Michael muttered under his breath.

"Be nice. God don't like ugly," whispered Tee.

"Then, I know He doesn't like her, her hat, or her dress," Michael whispered back.

"Hush! You're going to hell, and I'm not going with you," Tee said, then buried her head in his shoulder to keep from laughing out loud and disrupting the entire eservice. She had to admit Michael was telling the truth. The woman's outfit resembled something you might see on Aunt Esther from the television show *Sanford and Son.*

The woman cleared her throat again. This time louder. They both ignored her and looked straight-ahead to enjoy the sermon.

"Before I forget," said Pastor Alex, "Our very own Michael and Tee Stokes will be on TV tonight in an exclusive interview for Ultimate Sports. Let's all tune in and show our support for them. This beautiful couple is an example that good marriages do exist."

Lenora and Lenice were sitting on the pews in front of them. Lenice turned around and gave them a thumbs-up. Several amens resounded within the congregation. Michael and Tee both responded with nervous smiles. Tee gripped Michael's hand a little tighter. They both wished Pastor Alex hadn't done that. They had no idea what Ultimate Sports had in store for them, but they had a feeling they wouldn't like it. Tee prayed that whatever the devil was doing God would turn it around and use it for their good. Her plan of counterattack was firmly in place, but she hoped she wouldn't have to use it.

Chapter 35

I've Got a Secret

Momma Pearl sat in the Benjamin Hooks Library waiting for her daughter's ex-boyfriend to arrive. Mac sounded quite distraught when he called her earlier that morning. She agreed to meet him after church. Even though Tee was married to Michael, Mac continued to call and check on her every so often. She gladly took his phone calls. Momma Pearl grew fond of Mac when he and Tee were dating. Back then, she hoped he would marry her daughter, but even Momma Pearl had to admit that Michael was better suited for her.

Mac entered the Benjamin Hooks Library and made his way to the study rooms on the second level where Momma Pearl sat waiting for him. He entered the small enclosed room and kissed her on the cheek. It was eerily quiet to him, but it was perfect for people who needed complete silence to study. Mac wasn't there to study; he was there to confess.

"Hello, Mac," said Momma Pearl.

"Hello, Mom. You look lovely," he said.

Momma Pearl didn't mind if he still called her Mom, and she did look nice. She was dressed in a sleeveless cotton summer dress the color of the blue sea. She appreciated his compliment but she was extremely curious to know what was so important that they needed to hide away in a private room of the library on Sunday.

"Mom, I can't stay long, but I needed to tell you what I have to say in person. I've done something terrible, and

Michael is in trouble. Someone wants him dead, and I'm afraid Tee may get hurt in the process."

Momma Pearl gasped. "Mac, what would make you say such a thing?"

"I'm ashamed to admit this, but for a short while I helped someone to carry out a horrible plan to break Michael and Tee up so I could have another chance to make her mine. I thought with Michael out of the picture she would come running back to me. I now see that I was wrong, and I am deeply sorry. But I can't go talk to Michael and Tee about what I've done, so I'm telling you. I'm willing to tell you everything if you promise not to tell them what I did."

"I promise, son. Now spill it. Who is after my baby and why?"

"That's the problem, Mom. I don't know who, and I don't know why."

He sat down next to Momma Pearl and told her about his various dealings with Casper. Momma Pearl listened attentively asking a question here and there for clarity. It quickly became clear that loving Michael could be the end of her Tee if she didn't act fast. For the first time since she met Michael, she wondered if he was really the best thing to ever happen to her daughter.

Chapter 36

Sunday Supper

Lenora was happy it was Sunday because on Sundays Herman didn't go to The Kitty Kat Club. It was his only day off. She tried to get him to come to church, but he refused. Instead of going to church with his family, Herman stayed at home to catch up on his sleep. He was working 12-hour days, six days a week, but it still wasn't enough to catch up on all their bills. He hadn't paid the mortgage in three months. He was currently working with their lender to try to negotiate a lower mortgage, but it wasn't looking good. He was told that they needed some type of payment soon and his inability to pay was ruining their credit score. He knew Lenora was working and hoped she could help out. Herman planned to talk to her about it that day, but he didn't know how she would take it. Herman had never asked her for money before, but that's because she didn't have any. After Hermie was born, he became the sole breadwinner. It hurt his pride to have to ask her for some now.

Herman was in the kitchen fixing a cup of coffee when Lenora and the children entered the house. His children looked so adorable in their Sunday best. The boys wore matching outfits: khaki pants with white shirts and black shoes. Heather wore a pink dress with red roses all over it. She also wore pink ribbons in her hair, but it was Lenora who took his breath away. She was losing weight at a steady pace. Her face was thinning out. The double chin and pudgy cheeks that made her resemble a Cabbage Patch doll were hardly noticeable anymore. Herman could now see a semblance of the figure he used to know and love within her clothes. She wore a pink dress with a black belt. She recently added some reddish highlights to her hair and the color complimented her skin beautifully. In her arms, she carried food from Kentucky Fried Chicken for their dinner. Herman put down his coffee and walked over to her. He took the bag from her, placed it on the counter, and kissed her lovingly on the lips.

Lenora was pleasantly surprised. Herman wasn't very affectionate these days. Three sets of little eyes were on them. The twins giggled. Hermie yelled out, "Gross! Get a room."

Lenora turned around in shock. "Hermie, where did you get that from?"

"The television," he said as if he hadn't said a thing wrong. "Can I have a cookie?"

"No, you may *not*. I don't want to hear you ever say that again. Go take off your church clothes and get ready for dinner. Wash your hands and take the twins with you."

"Yes, ma'am," said Hermie. He grabbed his siblings by the hands and led them from the room.

"I have to do a better job of monitoring what he watches," said Lenora.

"I thought it was pretty funny myself. That isn't such a bad idea," Herman said mischievously. Lenora laughed. He leaned over and kissed her again long and lovingly. The time seemed to roll by slowly as he caressed the inside of her mouth with his tongue. She couldn't remember the last time Herman behaved like he desired her, but the kids needed to eat. It was almost 2 p.m, and they hadn't eaten anything since they left for Sunday School at 8:30 a.m. The pitter-patter of little feet let her know they were headed back.

There was no way they could have taken off their clothes and washed their hands that fast. She was right. They hadn't changed their clothes, but there was evidence that they washed their hands. Heston's white shirt was soaked, and so was the front of Heather's dress. She broke her mouth away from Herman's and said, "Hold that thought."

Lenora went to the cookie jar and pulled out three large, low-fat oatmeal raisin cookies. She handed one to each of the children and told them to follow her into the living room where she put on a DVD of the popular children's show *Blues Clues*. After they were settled in front of the TV with their snack, she returned to the kitchen. Herman was standing there with his shirt open and a *let's get it on* gleam in his eye. That mischievous smile was still plastered across his face.

"Where were we?" she asked as she slid her arms around his neck.

"I was hoping to make love to my beautiful wife," answered Herman.

"We got about 30 minutes before the kids get bored with that video and start tearing the house apart."

"That's about 15 more minutes than I need. Right this way, Madame." Herman took Lenora by the hand and led her to their bedroom.

As her husband removed her dress she said a silent prayer of thanks. During altar call, Pastor Alex instructed them to pray for two things they really wanted and when they were done walk away from the altar praising God like it was already accomplished. Lenora asked the Lord to give Herman a new job that was even better than the one he had before and restore his physical desire for her. She was working so hard to lose weight, and she needed some small indication that he was pleased. Part of her prayer was being answered right now.

Lenora was on cloud nine. She was thirsty, and Herman was her thirst-buster. He was better than one of those 44 oz drinks for only 49 cents at the gas station. He gave her everything she desired and more. She only wished they had more time. Twenty minutes later, her head lay nestled in the crook of her husband's arm and her exposed bottom sat snuggly against his torso. She was basking in the afterglow of what happens when two married people enjoy each other. By her calculations, they had about five minutes before Hermie came and knocked on the door.

"Lenora, how's your job going, baby?" asked Herman.

"Fine. No, better than fine. I love it. The school is nice, the faculty is nice, and the children want to learn."

"Are you saving your paychecks?"

"I've done a little shopping for myself and the kids, but other than that, I really haven't spent much. I buy some groceries and get gas as I need it. Why do you ask?"

"Baby, I need your help. We're behind on the mortgage, and the bank is threatening to foreclose on us if we don't get them at least $3,000 by next week."

She moved her body away from Herman's and sat up. "Why are you just telling me this?"

"I didn't want to bother you. I thought I could handle it."

"You didn't think the fact that your wife and kids could end up on the street was something you needed to talk to me about?"

Herman's milky white skin turned red. This wasn't going to be easy. "I really thought I could handle it, but the bills kept coming so fast. The payments on our cars, the utilities, health insurance, Hermie's summer activities, school tuition and tutoring. I knew it would be a few months before the bank actually foreclosed on our house so I paid the more time-sensitive bills and sent in what I could on the mortgage, but it's not enough. Do you have any money you could send to them?"

Lenora glared at Herman. At that moment she hated him for what he was doing. She felt like a $2 trick and he was her pimp. "Is that why you had sex with me? To butter me up so you could ask me for money? I thought you were finally finding me desirable again, but this was all a part of your plan to find out if I had a few thousand dollars lying around you could have."

Angrily, she got out of bed and put on her robe.

"Baby, it's not like that. You looked so sexy when you came in from church I couldn't help myself. I was going to ask you for the money regardless, but we were lying here with none of the kids around to disturb us. So I thought this would be the perfect time to ask."

Herman's cell phone chimed indicating he had a text. He reached for his pants to read it. It was his boss asking if he could come in today.

"I don't believe you, Herman. I've got exactly $2,000 in the bank, and you can have it, but the next time you want some money there's no need for you to screw me to get it."

"Lenora, it's not like that. Thanks, that helps a lot, but we're still $1,000 short. My boss has asked me to come in. If I'm lucky I can make at least $300 in tips tonight. I've got to go, but we'll talk about it some more when I get back."

There was a knock at the door. "Mommy, *Blues Clues* is boring. I seen that one," said Hermie.

"It's 'I saw that one' or 'I have seen that one.' I'll be there in a minute. It's time for dinner. You and your brother and sister go change your clothes like I asked you to earlier and wash your hands again."

"Yes, ma'am," said Hermie.

Herman put his pants on while Lenora stared at him in disgust.

"So, on the only day you have to spend with your children, you're going to work. We're supposed to eat dinner as a family on Sunday, Herman. You can neglect me, but you will *not* neglect your children."

"You're talking crazy, Lenora. Didn't I just tell you that we're behind on the bills? I'm going to work. I love you, woman, but sometimes your priorities are all messed up."

"No, you're the one that's messed up. You are not leaving until you eat dinner with your children. You expect me to be okay with you leaving your family to go serve drinks to a bunch of horny men and lesbians standing around watching women take off their clothes and shake their behinds. God is not pleased with you working at a strip club, Herman."

"Okay," said Herman. "I'll stay for dinner. Then I'm gone, and when God starts paying our mortgage, then I'll worry about whether He's pleased or not."

"Never mind, Herman. Go ahead and leave because when God strikes you dead with lightning for saying idiotic things like that, I don't want me or my children anywhere around."

Herman knew he was getting under Lenora's skin, but he didn't care. "For your information, I like my job. The owners are good people, and they appreciate the fact that I'm a hard worker. I never felt appreciated at that IT job you loved so much. At the club, I'm the man. I forgot how good I was at fixing drinks until I jumped back in the saddle. It's almost like it was when we were in college. People love them some Big Herman!"

"We're not in college anymore. We're 30-something-year-olds with three small children. It's time for you to put whatever *Cocktails*-Tom Cruise-wannabe dreams you have away. Get a *real* job, Herman. I know you're not even looking for another job because you're always at that one!" screamed Lenora.

Herman shook his head. His wife was comparing him and his enjoyment of his job to a 1988 film he never liked. His old job wasn't the only place he didn't feel appreciated anymore. He finished getting dressed and left. Herman was sure to kiss all of his children and his wife on the cheek before he left. He wondered if Lenora would ever understand what it was like to be a man. For most of their marriage she hadn't worked and all his family's needs were provided for by him and no one else. Being able to do that made him feel good about himself. He wasn't feeling so good about himself these days because he was barely holding it together. Lenora used to make him feel good about himself. Since she started losing weight and working she seemed to have developed a sense of pride and importance about herself that he hadn't seen since college. In college, she was popular and very active in extracurricular activities. She was an officer in this club, member in that club, and a stellar student showcasing her art all over campus. She had so many big dreams that she put on hold for her family. He realized that family had limited her ability to shine, and his wife deserved to feel special because she was, but was her success diminishing his worth? He wanted to be supportive. She supported him in everything he did, until now. Why couldn't she be proud that his bartending skills were giving them something to fall back on when times got tough? Why did it matter where he worked? It was paying the bills. Most of them, anyway.

Chapter 37

Dear Journal

> He makes love to me without taking my clothes off
> Undressing me mentally with every word
> Carefully peeling back the layers to reveal what I didn't
> want anyone to see but me
> I hesitate at first, but he's so gentle
> His eyes beg me to let him in
> Hold still, don't be scared, I won't hurt you he says
> Then, when I am standing there naked as a newborn
> and vulnerable
> He laughs and walks away
> I feel like a fool
> A fool for love

Tiffany poured out her heart to her journal in the form of a poem. After Quincy 2 was diagnosed with depression, his therapist suggested that he start journaling to help him express what he was feeling. To help him understand that writing can be good for you, Tiffany began journaling with him. Each day they sat down for 30 minutes and wrote. She was surprised at how much she enjoyed it too. It was therapeutic. Lately, she was inspired to write poetry.

She was still upset that William ended their courtship, and she really did want to go to dinner with him after church, but she knew that if she let him straddle the fence in their relationship he would. He had to make a decision.

Tiffany heard a knock at the door. She wasn't expecting company. Quincy 2 was still with his father for the weekend and wouldn't be home until later that evening. She agreed to let his father get him every other weekend. On those weekends, she missed her only child terribly. For most of his life, she had him all to herself and being forced to share him was a big adjustment for her, but it needed to happen. She now had other people to show him he was loved and important on days she was out of town or busy working.

Tiffany got up to answer the door wearing leggings and a tank top with no bra underneath. This was her normal attire around the house. She saw no need to feel constricted when no one was around. She was surprised to find William standing on her porch with a brown paper bag.

"I know you said you didn't want to go out to dinner, but I was hoping you wouldn't mind me bringing dinner to you. I tried to go to dinner at Mae Lillie's by myself, but it wasn't the same without you and Q. Sandy even threw in peach cobbler and red velvet cake for dessert when I told her my second plate was for you. May I come in?"

Tiffany breathed a heavy sigh. There was no way she could resist macaroni and cheese from Mae Lillie's. Sandy always melted big chunks of cheddar cheese on top and throughout the dish, making it an ooey-gooey, cheesy delight. Although, it probably wouldn't look as good as William in his Sunday best. He shed his suit coat, and even with his clothes on, his bulging biceps were fully visible through his white dress shirt. How could she turn down a delicious dinner from a delicious man? She opened the door and escorted him to the kitchen. Then she went to her bedroom to put on some looser-fitting pants and a bra. She was learning the art of sexy modesty, and she didn't want to do anything to tempt him. She also realized that this was the first time the two of them would be in her house alone since she tried to seduce him.

When she returned, William blessed the food and they dug in. Tiffany wholeheartedly agreed with his dinner selection. The deep-fried boneless catfish with macaroni and cheese, collard greens, and sweet potato casserole smelled delicious. He even brought their signature lemonade/sweet tea drink, Sweet Thang, to wash it down. As usual, the two of them had great conversation over dinner. Tiffany talked about her business.

William talked about the ministry. They made fun of Brother Franklin's attempt to get her number after church. She thanked him again for rescuing her.

"Tiffany, I must be honest. I don't like that other men think they have a chance with you now. I was glad you didn't give him your number. How could I compete with a millionaire who can buy you anything you want and fly you all around the world? I know how much you like the glamorous life," said William.

Tiffany was flattered that he was jealous, but she played it cool. "William, it takes more than money to impress me. Besides, his game was weak, but you have to realize that we are not a couple. Actually, we never have been. You ended our courtship, and if that's the way you want it, you have to accept the fact that I have the option to date anyone I please. I'm not going to sit around the house pining for you." Tiffany laughed within because she knew that was exactly what she was doing when he arrived.

"I'm not sure if what I did was the right thing to do, Tiffany. I know I have no right to ask you this, but will you give me a little time to pray some more about if we really belong together? I won't lie to you. I always had this image of what a wife and first lady should be, and you don't fit any of it. I've developed some strong feelings for you, and I know you have them for me. I knew that it wouldn't be fair of me to continue seeing you if I don't think we have a future together. I'd like time to reconsider my decision," said William.

"No, William. I will not promise you that I won't see someone else while you sort out your feelings for me. However, what I am willing to do is make this a no-pressure evening and enjoy your company. This visit has gone from fun to serious, and I don't like it. I have stuffed myself silly, and I need to work some of this off. Come to the living room so I can beat your butt on my Wii."

William was a former athlete, and competition was like a drug for him. He had to have it. "Is that a challenge? Choose your weapon—bowling, tennis, golf, whatever. I guarantee you'll lose. How about I play you in all three, Ms. Overconfident?"

"My weapon of choice is *Just Dance*." Tiffany loved to dance and that game gave her a great way to do it while working out in the privacy of her home. She could shake it as hard and as fast as her heart desired without others peering at her.

"You got it!" said William.

He loved to dance as well, but he didn't get to do a whole lot of it these days. Some of it stemmed from him not wanting to give church folk something to talk about if they saw him getting down on the dance floor.

He was actually pretty good, and with the right partner he could go all night long. "You better beware. Big Daddy's got moves, baby!"

"Bring it," said Tiffany rolling her neck at William. "And you are nobody's Big Daddy up in here. Care to make a wager?"

"Sure. Why not? What do you have in mind?"

"The winner has to massage the loser's feet. I have no doubt I'll be victorious. So I hope you rub feet as well as you preach, Pastor," Tiffany teased. She stuck her finger in William's chest for emphasis.

"Lead the way, Tiffany Tate, and we'll see who's rubbin' who."

They both talked a lot of competitive mess while playing—taunting, teasing, and making jokes about each other's moves. Tiffany was surprised at how coordinated William was, and they both had a ball trying to follow the directions of the game. Tiffany's son thought the game was for girls and rarely played with her, and when he did he wasn't much competition. William, on the other hand, was a worthy opponent. They played four games, and it was a tie. Neither one of them had the energy to play a tie breaker. They both sat on the couch exhausted. It seemed that neither of them would get a massage.

"Give me your feet," William instructed.

Tiffany started to object but decided not to deny herself that simple pleasure. She slowly swung her legs around and placed them in his lap.

"You can tell a lot about a woman by looking at her feet."

"Oh really?" she said.

"Really." William took her right foot in his hands and began massaging it gently.

"Manicures and pedicures date back to ancient Chinese and Egyptian times," he continued. "Back in 3000 BC, the Ming Dynasty used polish to denote your social status. Royalty painted their nails black and red. In Egypt, it was said that Cleopatra painted her nails a deep red while Queen Nefertiti preferred a ruby color." Tiffany sat and listened intently as he gently caressed her foot, being sure to give each toe individual attention. It felt wonderful. "Yours are red so that means you're royalty, baby."

Tiffany smiled. She sure felt like it. She loved having a man around to make her feel good.

"That's interesting. How do you know that?" she asked.

"I was a history major in college," he said.

"You never told me you went to college."

"Yeah, I went two years before I got bold enough to tell my mother I didn't want to be there. She never went to college so her children going to college was part of her dreams. I went to make her happy. Plus, I had a wrestling scholarship, and I loved to wrestle, but I hated attending class. I knew it meant a lot to her for me to further my education, but school wasn't for me. Moms was a little disappointed when I dropped out, but I promised her I would be successful with or without a degree. I'm proud that I have been able to make good on that promise. I've been the top salesperson at the car dealership for the past three years. I plan on going back to school, though. I want to go to seminary. I guess I had to find something I really wanted to study. I enjoyed history, but I didn't want to spend my life doing something involving it. I enjoy sales, and I love ministry. I also love giving massages to special people in my life."

Tiffany was impressed. "Well, you're very good at this, William. Some woman taught you well."

"I'll tell my mother you said so."

"Your mother?" *What man rubs his mother's feet?* thought Tiffany.

"Yeah, my mother was a single parent, like you. She often worked two jobs and one of them was always manual labor. When she got home, she was beat and she would complain about how much her feet hurt. I was around 12 at the time when I started doing research to figure out what I could do to help her, and one day, I ran across a book about reflexology and massages. After my mother got home, cooked dinner, ate, and sat down in front of the TV to relax, I would massage her feet before she went to bed. I did that to make her feel better and to let her know that I appreciated the sacrifices she was making for me and my little brother."

"William, that was a thoughtful thing for a little boy to do. I think if I asked my son to touch my feet he would puke," joked Tiffany.

William moved his hands to the other foot. As a massage therapist, Tiffany wasn't used to being given massages. She was usually the one giving them. She had a little downtime coming up and was thinking about flying to California to check on Sierra and Siendy's progress. She was getting so much work in that area that she moved them there a couple of months ago. They were booking plenty of jobs, but the twins weren't answering her calls as promptly as they should be. Sometimes, they would go 72 hours before they returned her call.

"We need some music. May I play DJ?" asked William.

"Be my guest," said Tiffany. William got up from the couch and walked over to Tiffany's stereo system. He pulled a small iPod from his pocket and connected it to her stereo using her iPod dock. The next thing coming from her speakers were the sweet soulful sounds of Marvin Gaye's "Trouble Man."

"Marvin? What do you know about Marvin?" she asked.

William began to dance slowly back to the couch with her stereo remote in hand. "What do you mean what do I know about Marvin? I know that no one sings a ballad like Marvin and he died way before his time."

He sat down next to her. Tiffany's mind wandered back to the last time they were alone on her couch. She embarrassed herself by throwing her goodies at him. She would not make that same mistake twice. If this visit was a test to see if she could keep her hormones at bay, she was going to pass with flying colors.

"Yeah, I'm with you on that, and to think Marvin's own father did it," she said. "So tragic. The man who brought him into this world actually took him out." They sat and listened in silence while William resumed massaging her feet. As "Trouble Man" ended, "Sexual Healing" came on. William hastily used the remote to change it.

"I don't want to give you the wrong impression," he said shyly.

"I appreciate it, but I wasn't thinking that at all. We're two saved and celibate people enjoying each other's company. Right?"

William gave her a smile and nodded in agreement.

The two of them continued to talk until Tiffany announced she needed to start getting ready for Tee's watch party. William had been at her house since 3:00 p.m and it was almost 5:45.The show was supposed begin at 7 p.m. and she didn't want to miss a thing. She asked William to accompany her. He agreed.

"I'll clean the kitchen while you get ready."

This man is almost too good to be true. She was glad William was going. Having him there would keep her from staring at Tee's husband all night. She had to admit, though, that she was a little excited about seeing him. She hadn't seen Michael since his towel fell down in front of her. She remembered that moment as easily as she remembered her own name.

Chapter 38

What Goes Around Comes Around

By 6:45, the Stokes' house was full of people who all came to watch the *Inside* interview. Sandy, Patrick, and their children; Momma Pearl; Tiffany and William; Lenora and Herman and their children; Lenice and Webster; Tee's former coworker and best male friend Edgar and his wife Vera; and Sheba were all present. Everyone was pleasantly surprised when Zachary and Teresa showed up. They thought Teresa was still out of town on a special assignment and didn't expect to see her again for weeks. Tee and Michael prepared plenty of food and drinks for their guests to enjoy. Everyone fixed themselves a plate and settled down to see the interview.

They all watched with disgust as Solay pretended to be Tee's friend, and then turned on her in a matter of minutes. She looked so sinister as she introduced the video, and she did a terrible job of behaving as if her actions were unintentionally malicious. She was fully aware that she was causing problems in their marriage. The network edited out all footage of the beautiful, pristine Solay being vomited on. They made it seem as if Tee's breakfast landed on the floor, and then the interview cut to the part where Tee and Michael told everyone to get out. They also ran footage from the food fight at Accent. Everyone in the house clapped and shouted with glee as the mural was destroyed.

Zachary beamed with pride while watching what his wife did for her friends. He always admired her spunk and her loyalty to those she loved. He wanted to tell everyone that Teresa destroyed the mural, but he knew how important it was to her that her friends not know she returned to rehab. In the baggy clothes she wore and with her hat pulled low it was virtually impossible for others to recognize her, but he could recognize his wife in any attire. However, his smile disappeared when he saw how she was restrained by the staff. He clenched his teeth and fists tightly as she was hauled unceremoniously from the room. Teresa saw her husband's reaction and put her arm around him. She was so happy to be home with the love of her life. She never planned on having to leave him again because of alcoholism.

Before the show ended, Karen uploaded the unedited video onto MrandMrsStokes.com as well as YouTube. It went viral in a matter of minutes, and the world watched as one of America's journalistic darlings sat with vomit on her face and hair. They all laughed heartily while reading the hilarious comments several people posted after viewing the video.

Tee, Michael, and friends celebrated the destruction of the mural and Tee's foresight to create this avenue for them to always release their side of the story without worry of censorship or misleading editing.

The mood was festive, but Momma Pearl needed to have a serious talk to Michael in private. She pulled him to the side and asked for a few minutes of his time. Michael adored his mother-in-law and was more than happy to oblige her. She promised Mac that she wouldn't tell what he told her or where it came from so she employed a little creativity regarding her warning to Michael and Tee that someone was after them.

"What's up, Momma Pearl? Is everything okay?" he asked.

"No. I'm worried about my baby. I've had horrible nightmares of Tee being captured and tortured. I can't shake this weird feeling that someone is after you two. Is everything all right?"

Michael was not going to tell Momma Pearl about the phone calls from Becca without making sure Tee wanted her to know. The last thing he wanted to do was make her worry.

"Everything is fine. Maybe you should stop eating before you go to bed," he joked.

"This is not a case of indigestion, Michael. This is a mother's intuition that her child and her husband are in trouble. Have you noticed anything strange lately?"

"No," Michael lied. "But if it makes you feel better I'll be on the lookout for something that may be out of place."

"That would make me feel better, but what would really make me feel better is if you get some extra security around here. You and Tee are celebrities, and you walk around all day like you don't need protection."

"Momma Pearl, the only time I ever needed protection was from Becca, and she's dead. Tee and I are fine."

"Michael, heed my warning. My dreams usually mean something. I love you, son, but there are only two things in my life that I can't live without. That's Tee and Sandy, and two times now Tee has had her life in jeopardy because of you. Loving you has been a bittersweet experience for my daughter from the beginning. You're like delicious poison. You need to do a better job of taking care of her."

Momma Pearl's words hit him like 100 pound weights. He knew loving him wasn't easy. Michael felt a horrible nausea build up in the pit of his stomach. He thought back to their Jamaican vacation and when Becca threw Tee off a boat and left her to drown with the fishes. He thought about the day she stabbed them both, but Tee was the one who ended up in the hospital for days, and now this. Could Momma Pearl be right? Was loving him going to be the death of her?

Momma Pearl left Michael so he could be alone with his thoughts. She hated to be so mean to him, but she hoped her words would strike a nerve that prompted him to be more careful and hire more security before it was too late.

Michael returned to the den with the rest of the family with a look on his face Tee had never seen before. After everyone left, it was still there. That look was a result of Michael's increased sense of admiration for his wife and fear for her well-being. Once again, she exceeded his expectations. He was proud of her decision not to let the media continue to invade their lives.

After all their guests were gone, he wrapped his arms around her and said, "You call yourself a good woman, but I think you're a great woman. I know that loving me isn't easy simply because of who I am, but I promise to always look after you and love you to the best of my abilities. You almost got killed because of me, and you keep getting attacked because of me. Your life would be so much simpler if I weren't in it."

Tee looked at him lovingly. "My life would be empty if you weren't in it. I have many regrets, but loving you and marrying you have never been on that list. I'm still adjusting to a lot of things, but waking up to you each morning makes it all worthwhile. The happiness you bring to my life is indescribable," she said.

"I'm glad you feel that way, Beautiful. You do more than complement me; you complete me. I'm not whole when I'm not with you. You're like food to me. You nourish my heart, body, and soul. If anything were to ever happen to you I don't know how I would go on. That's why it's so important that we find out who has been impersonating Becca. I have to keep you safe. If she killed Peter, she will kill someone else. I have to make sure that you are not on the target list."

"I know, Handsome," said Tee. "We'll get her. She is going to slip up somewhere, and we'll get her."

Tee and Michael went to their bedroom, got on their knees, and issued a prayer of thanks to God as a couple. He had been so good to them and was keeping them every step of the way. They also prayed that the unknown caller would be discovered and peace could return to their lives.

Afterward, they climbed in bed and Tee fell soundly asleep. Michael's slumber wasn't so peaceful. Someone cloaked in black invaded his sleep. Unlike previous nightmares, the person wasn't trying to stab him. They were trying to stab Tee and a baby she carried in her arms. Michael woke up the next morning more disturbed than he was when he went to bed. Momma Pearl was right. He needed to do a better job of looking out for his wife.

Chapter 39

Momma's Baby

Tiffany couldn't wait to see her son. Immediately after the interview ended, she and William left the Stokes' house so that she would be home when her child arrived. This weekend was the first trip out of town Quincy 2 had taken with his father and his entire family and Tiffany wanted to be prepared for whatever emotional state he was in when he walked through her door. Quincy called her a week ago to ask if he could take Quincy 2 camping in Arkansas. She almost told him no, but she realized that it was a step that needed to be taken. For so many years Quincy 2 was left out of his father's family vacations and this was a reason to celebrate, not be overly protective.

Since working out their court-ordered visitation arrangement, Tiffany and Quincy were taking baby steps when it came to including Quincy 2 as part of his family. At first, they were very careful to keep him away from Quincy's wife because she made it clear that she didn't want anything to do with her husband's illegitimate son. Tiffany didn't really care. She would rather that witch stay away from her baby if she wasn't going to treat him right. Instead, Quincy 2 would go on outings with his father and his three sisters only.

Quincy 2 adored his big sisters. Especially the middle one, Priscilla, and she was equally drawn to him. She was now driving, and Tiffany allowed her to come over once or twice a week to see him and help him with his math. Math was Quincy 2's weakest subject, and Priscilla was a wiz at it.

Tiffany often stood silently and watched the two of them together. Priscilla was good for him. She doted on him like a mother instead of an older sister, and her youthful sense of humor kept him laughing. Her little boy was almost his old self again. Even his therapist, Dr. Fleming, admitted that Quincy 2 was recovering quite well from his depression. Feeling the love of his father and his siblings was a big part of that.

After a few months, Quincy told Tiffany that his wife didn't like feeling left out and was ready to spend some time with her husband's son. She was actually the one who suggested that they take Quincy 2 on vacation with them. Tiffany waited anxiously for him to return. She was ready to call and cuss that woman out if she said or did anything to hurt her baby. She heard a car pull up outside her house and without looking to see who it was, she made her way to the front door. Tiffany let out a sigh of relief when she saw the big grin across Quincy 2's face as he ran from the car to greet her. He gave her a huge bear hug that almost knocked her over. He was so excited about his trip that he barely took a breath while he told her about it.

"Ma, I had so much fun!" he shouted. "We went hiking and fishing, and I caught a fish almost as long as my arm. We also went swimming in the lake. Daddy fried the fish we caught outdoors and Momma Marilyn—"

"Momma Marilyn?" interrupted Tiffany. She gave Quincy's father a sidelong glance. He acted as if he didn't notice.

"Yeah, that's what my stepmom told me to call her. She sang songs as we sat around the fire and roasted marshmallows. Ma, she can really saaang," said Quincy 2.

"She can?"

"Yep, and she was really nice. She made me smiley face pancakes for breakfast. But you know what was missing?"

"What, baby?"

"You! The whole time I was wishing my real ma was there. My sisters had theirs. I wanted mine."

Tiffany smiled at her only child. Even though he was growing up so fast, Quincy 2 was still her baby. His father stood nearby listening to the conversation. She looked at him and mouthed the words thank you. He winked, handed her their son's backpack, and started to walk back to his car.

Quincy 2 noticed him leaving and said, "Hey, Dad. Wait a minute." He then ran over and gave his father a great big hug too and said, "I love you. Thanks for giving me my sisters. Momma Marilyn's kinda cool too."

"I love you too, son. Thanks for being such a great kid."

Quincy 2 gave his father a huge grin and another hug and ran back to Tiffany. They watched Quincy drive off, and then went in the house so he could finish telling her about his family camping trip.

Tiffany sat and listened to her son excitedly relay his tale. She realized that she had no reason to feel like her life would be ruined if she and William didn't reconcile. Without a man, she had a full life, but she had to admit, life with William was better than life without him.

Chapter 40

A Season for All Things

The next morning, Michael and Tee woke up feeling good. Sheba called to say that there were several messages on the office voice mail from media outlets requesting an interview to talk about what happened with Solay. There was also one from someone who preferred to remain anonymous but wanted them to know that Solay asked to take an extended leave of absence after the video of her with vomit all over her went public. Michael and Tee both agreed to only do one interview and booked an interview with *The Today Show* for the next morning. They made plans to fly out later that afternoon. Tee was in the kitchen cooking breakfast when Michael's cell phone rang. The number looked vaguely familiar so he answered it.

"Hello, Michael. You sound like you're in a good mood. Does your wife throwing up on journalists put a smile on your face?"

Michael had to do something to flush this person out. This was getting old. Momma Pearl's warning and the return of his nightmares weren't good signs. He decided to press a few of her buttons.

"Becca or whoever you are, I've grown very tired of this game of cat and mouse we're playing. So, if you're going to kill me, I suggest you do it and get it over with. Every day I'm alive is a day I'm searching for clues and getting closer to finding you. Every day I'm alive is another day I have to think about all the things I'm going to do to you when I find you."

"Is that so?" asked the voice. "What happened to the good little Christian? Aren't you supposed to wait for God to give you vengeance? Turn the other cheek or something like that?"

"You should read Ecclesiastes 3. 'To everything there is a season, and a time to every purpose under the heaven: a time to be born, and a time to die; a time to plant, and a time to pluck up that which is planted; and a time to kill.' There's more, but that's the only part you need to worry about," said Michael.

"I admire your ambition, but there's one flaw in your plan. You're not the one I want. This isn't like one of your football games. You won't be the go-to man in a pinch. You won't win this one. This will be the epic loss of a lifetime," the voice said and hung up.

True to his promise to stop keeping secrets, Michael went downstairs and told Tee about the phone call. She stood silent for several minutes before making a comment.

"I'm tired too, Michael," said Tee. "Do you trust me?"

"With my life," he said.

"Good. I think it's time we asked someone other than Dr. Foster to help us with this."

"You want me to hire another PI?"

"No, I was thinking bigger," said Tee.

"What do you mean?"

"Tomorrow, on *The Today Show*, we are going to ask their entire viewing audience to help us locate Becca. We are going to tell them everything in hopes that someone knows who this is and is willing to tell us."

"Are you sure you're ready for that kind of attention? We could have people from everywhere calling us."

"Yes. This is a perfect way to try to get to the bottom of this. We'll use the office as a phone bank. I'll get Sheba and a couple of temps to take the calls. They can take the information and give the leads that sound legitimate to Dr. Foster to investigate further."

"I'm game, Mrs. Stokes. I'm so lucky I married a smart woman."

"Yes, you are. I can also cook. Come and get your breakfast."

Michael decided to wait to get additional security. Momma Pearl was overreacting. He and Tee had everything under control.

Chapter 41

The Colors of Love

    Lenora moved her brush across the canvas in wide, broad strokes. To her, painting was as rhythmic as dancing or singing. She didn't have to go to the school today, but she decided to drop the twins off at day care anyway. She wanted to get home and work on her paintings in peace without having to worry about the whereabouts and doings of two incredibly curious three year olds.

    Her art show was this weekend, and she wanted to create at least two more pieces to present. So far, she had ten. She also needed to get two of Tee's paintings completed. The twins weren't home, but Herman was, and his presence was just as distracting. She hadn't said two words to him since Sunday. He had another thing coming if he thought she was going to support him working at a strip club selling liquor. Neither one of them even drank! Instead of being asleep in bed he needed to be pounding the pavement looking for a job.

    Lenora continued to make her brush dance across the canvas. Painting was not only enjoyable but therapeutic for her. She could magically transport herself into whatever world she was painting. In her special world, her children behaved all the time and she was married to a man who knew the value of behaving as a unit and not making employment decisions without consulting his spouse. Lenora was so engrossed in painting in her euphoric atmosphere that she almost didn't hear Herman enter her sacred domain. As far as she was concerned, her studio was off limits to everyone. No one could enter unless invited by the master artist. She didn't issue an invite to Herman. She tried to ignore him.

"Lenora, I know you're not happy with me right now, but I need you to support me on this. You were going to a job you loved while I was going to one I sorta kinda liked. You love your job so much you go on your off-days. I couldn't imagine going to my job on the weekend. Me being fired is a blessing in disguise. I enjoy being a bartender, and The Kitty Kat Club pays more than other bartending places. I need you in my corner, Lenora. I don't have a problem working another IT job, but it has to be at a company I like, doing something I enjoy. I promise to find one so I can quit working at the club but until I do, that's where I'll be."

Lenora continued to ignore him. She couldn't and wouldn't understand how a man could think it was acceptable to do what he was doing.

"Lenora, say something," pleaded Herman.

"Since you're home, can you pick the kids up from day care at 3:00? If I sell a couple of my paintings we should have enough money to pay the mortgage for the next three months. One of us has to keep some money coming into this house since you have evidently forgotten that as the head of this household you need to be the primary bread-winner."

"I haven't forgotten anything. Is it too much to ask that I be able to come home with a smile on my face at the end of the day instead of a frown?"

"I don't know what look you have on your face, Herman, because you come home in the wee hours of the morning when everyone else in this house is asleep. You're not home for dinner, and you're asleep during breakfast.

Even if I did approve of that farce of a job, which I don't, I would still have a problem because the hours aren't conducive to a family with three small children. I used to get your help in the morning before work and in the evenings when you came home. Now, I'm left to deal with them alone all day. You're being selfish, Herman. You couldn't possibly be thinking about us right now. Doesn't it bother you that you don't see your children? Why did we spend all that time in counseling learning to function better as a unit if you aren't going to be here to do it?"

Herman let out a loud sigh. He wasn't in the mood to argue. "I see the conversation isn't going to end well so I'm going to leave you to your painting. By the way, whatever you're painting, it's looking real pretty. I've always been proud of you, Lenora. I'm sorry you began to feel like taking care of me and the kids wasn't enough because you're really good at it. For what it's worth, I miss being home with you and the kids, but right now, this is the way it's got to be."

The entire time they spoke Lenora didn't turn around once to look at him. Herman had no idea how disappointed in him she was or how afraid she was that one of the girls at the club would offer him something that looked better than what he had at home and he might take it. Perhaps, he already had.

Chapter 42

Daddy Big Bucks

Lenice didn't know why she felt that James wasn't a good enough reason for her to stop seeing other men. He was a good man, and they got along very well, but every time she thought about giving her heart to him, a feeling of dread took over her entire body. She enjoyed going out meeting new people. She enjoyed having men fawn all over her, take her out, and pay for the evening. Sure, most of them had no idea they had no chance of having a future with her, but she wasn't hurting anybody. It was a little harmless dating fun.

Tonight, Lenice had a date with a millionaire. Brighton Stone was one of the richest men in Memphis. He was older than the men she usually dated, but there was no need to throw out her options. Besides, if she wasn't having any luck with men her own age, maybe she should try someone more seasoned. Maybe he could respect her decision not to have sex at this point in her life. He asked her to meet him at a sushi restaurant. Lenice loved sushi, so if the date didn't go well, at least she would enjoy the food.

Brighton was also white. Unlike her sister, Lenice usually didn't date outside her race, but she liked Brighton the moment she saw him. His face was tan and ruddy. His skin was home to several wrinkles, but his eyes had a youthful quality about them. He greeted her with a warm smile and a soft kiss on the cheek.

During dinner, she peppered him with questions about his life. She soon learned that Brighton was very athletic for a 66-year-old. He played golf, tennis, and swam regularly. He was a widower with no children. He had multiple houses, and every year, he rented a yacht and took a cruise along the Mediterranean. He was also very aware of what was going on with her generation. As an employer of over 500 people, it was important for him to be able to relate to all of them on some level. She was impressed. Brighton tried to answer each of her questions openly and honestly, but he eventually tired of Lenice's version of 21 Questions.

"Enough about me. Tell me about you," he said.

Lenice smiled and told him about her job, her family, and her hobbies. Brighton sat and listened attentively and asked questions at the appropriate spots. She hadn't had anyone show this much interest in her since James. There was only one problem. He didn't make her heart flutter like James.

Chapter 43

Help!

The interview on *The Today Show* went well. The hosts were very interested in Tee and Michael's story and read excerpts from the letter Tee posted on their web site and replayed the video of Tee vomiting on Solay.

Before the interview ended, Tee and Michael revealed that they were being harassed by someone who sounded like the woman who tried to kill them. They made a passionate plea for anyone who had any information to call their office. They also asked for help in locating Becca's brother. The hosts sympathized with Tee and Michael's situation and expressed concern for their well-being and also encouraged the audience to help them.

Before the interview ended, phone calls came pouring into the office. Sheba and the two temporary workers they hired took as many calls as they could. Most of the calls made no sense, but there were a few that seemed to be legitimate leads. Those were carefully documented and passed along to Dr. Foster to follow up on. She was now back in Akron, Ohio, trying to get more information out of Becca's brother's wife.

After they left the studio, Karen Robertson posted a video of the interview on their site as a way to continue to ask the public for their assistance.

Chapter 44

Model Teacher

Lenora sat in her classroom waiting for her next class to begin. She really didn't feel like being bothered with other people's children today. She would rather be at home in her studio painting. The bell rang, and she waited for her students to arrive. To her surprise, no one entered her room except her vice principal.

"Mrs. James, I have cancelled the rest of your classes for today. You and I are going to lunch to have a conference instead."

"But why? With all due respect, Mr. Rupert, I would rather teach my class," responded Lenora.

"It's not up for discussion. I need to speak with you, and I prefer to do it away from the school. Please gather your things and meet me at Mario's in 30 minutes." Mario's was a four-star restaurant in close vicinity to the school. Lenora thought that was little swanky for a conference with her boss, but she could use an expensive meal for a change. She and Herman rarely went out anymore. They couldn't afford it. When she arrived, Mr. Rupert was already seated and had taken the liberty of ordering them both a Caesar salad and water with lemon to begin with. Lenora ate her salad and waited patiently for him to tell her why he cancelled her classes.

Mr. Rupert was a very attractive man. He was tall with skin the color of vanilla beans and smoky eyes. Lenora caught him staring at her several times, and it made her uncomfortable.

Mr. Rupert made small talk, asking her how she liked her job and about the well-being of her husband and her children. He didn't address her job until after the waitress took their entrée orders.

"I like you, Mrs. James, but I've received several complaints about you. I've recently been told by other teachers and students that you have been moody and rude and you've been snapping at the children. You don't seem to have your usual patience. Is something wrong?"

Lenora hadn't realized that her situation at home was affecting her work. "I haven't been feeling like myself lately, but I don't think it's that bad."

"I run a private school. What the parents think about your behavior overrides what you or I think. We added an art program because the parents requested it. However, I must have someone who is a good fit for our school. Until recently, I thought you were perfect. I decided to take you to lunch to let you know my concerns."

Lenora looked up and caught a glimpse of her sister entering the restaurant with an elderly white gentleman. *What is she doing here with some white man that could be old enough to be my husband's father?* she thought. Mr. Rupert was waiting for her response.

"I have been having a few problems at home, but I really didn't realize that they were affecting my relationship with my coworkers and students. Now that you have made me aware of it, I promise to amend my behavior and it won't happen again." She gave him a reassuring smile.

"Lenora. May I call you Lenora?"

She nodded her head yes.

"I know I'm you're superior, but I'd like to be your friend as well." Mr. Rupert placed his hand over hers. "I'm here if you need someone to talk to. I have great listening ears and strong shoulders to cry on." He reached into the front inner pocket of his suit and pulled out a business card. "Here's my personal cell phone number. Call me anytime."

Lenora smiled. Mr. Rupert's hand was soft, but they were also large. The way his hand covered hers made her think of comfort, stability, and security—three things Herman wasn't giving her right now. A covering, as her Papa, used to say. Every woman wants to feel as if her man has got her covered. If anything goes wrong, he can protect and keep her. Mr. Rupert was very successful and considered a pillar in the community. He had a Ph.D. in education, but he preferred to be addressed as "Mr." instead of "Dr."

He felt the title was too formal. He helped start the Montessori school where she worked to give inner-city children from low-income families the same education as children at other private schools for a fraction of the cost. Tuition at the school was high, but the children's parents paid very little and the rest was covered by grants and private donors. He actually placed himself in the position of vice principal so he could spend less time doing paperwork and more time with the students. He even began a program specifically to help boys learn how to be responsible men called, "Man of the House."

Lenora was impressed by his success at such a young age. She guessed he was around 35. He was also single with one child from his previous marriage. An eligible bachelor if there ever was one. He was always a topic of discussion with the other female teachers. Several of them were trying to sway his interest. She was attracted to him. There was no denying that. Each day she looked forward to his impromptu visit to her classroom. She actually began preparing for them, taking extra time with her wardrobe and her makeup. There was nothing wrong with a little harmless flirting. She actually needed it. It made her feel like a real woman. It was as if he were serving as a small substitute for what was missing at home.

"Thank you, Mr. Rupert. I appreciate that. I'm not ready to pour out my soul right now, but if I get to that point, it's nice to know you care," said Lenora.

Out of the corner or her eye she could see Lenice coming her way. She quickly removed her hand from underneath his and slid his card in her purse. Lenice stopped at their table and gave her a hug.

"Hey, sis! I'm surprised to see you. I thought you were at school today."

Lenora observed the way Mr. Rupert looked her sister up and down. He held his composure, but she could tell he was pleased with what he saw. A tinge of jealousy tugged at her.

"I am, but I'm on my lunch break with the school's vice principal. Mr. Rupert, please meet my twin sister, Lenice."

He extended his hand. "It's a pleasure to meet you. Your sister is doing a fine job as the new art teacher at our school. I wanted to take her to lunch as a small token of our gratitude. We know what an asset we've got."

"Yes, my sister is amazingly talented. I think she deserves a raise," joked Lenice.

He winked. "I'll see what I can do."

"I will let you two enjoy your lunch. I'm going to powder my nose and get back to my own little luncheon. Call me later, sis."

"I will. Enjoy your lunch as well," said Lenora.

Lenice left their table and headed to the restroom. There was something very wrong with that picture. They would talk about it later.

"You say you and your sister used to look exactly alike?" said Mr. Rupert.

"Up until the point where I got married, had kids, and blew up like a blimp," said Lenora.

"That's a shame," he said.

The warm, fuzzy feelings Lenora felt previously instantly evaporated. Her face turned red. He thought she was huge too.

"Well, I'm trying to get back to close to that size, but it's not easy, and it doesn't happen overnight," explained Lenora.

Mr. Rupert smiled. "No, it's a shame she can't look more like you. She's way too boney. A man likes something he can hold on to. You said she was single, right? Maybe if she gained some weight she could get a husband. Don't lose too much weight, Lenora. It's not necessary. You're lovelier than you think. By the way, I love that dress you're wearing. The brown brings out the color of your eyes. Is it new?"

Lenora smiled. That dress was one of a few pieces she bought a few weeks earlier to reward herself for the weight loss. This was her first time wearing it. Herman didn't say anything about it that morning when she left, but that was because he didn't see it. He was asleep.

"Why, yes, it is. Thank you for the compliment. I'm glad you like it." Mr. Rupert sure did know the right thing to say.

"I meant what I said about you being an asset to our school. I will be looking for an instant improvement, Lenora. Don't let me down. The administration is watching you."

"I won't, Mr. Rupert. I promise," she said.

Mr. Rupert was staring at her again, but this time she didn't mind. Actually, she was staring back at him.

Chapter 45

Turn on the Lights

"Good night, Boss Lady," said Sheba. "Are you sure you don't want me to stay and wait on you?"

She and Tee both had a long day at the office, but it appeared her employer wanted to make it even longer. Sheba and the two temporary workers were still getting a steady stream of calls from people who said they had information on Becca or her brother. Tee left the phone calls to Sheba while she focused on their clients. Sheba closed the phone bank and told everyone else to go home. The answering machine could do the job until tomorrow.

"No, I want to go over a couple of marketing proposals before I go. I try not to bring my work home if I can help it. Let me finish now so I can leave and focus on my man."

"Sounds like a plan to me. I'll lock the door behind me."

"Thanks, Sheba. Be careful and good night," said Tee.

It had been a busy 10 hours, but Tee was dedicated to making MiTee Management a success. Blak was headed to Houston soon, and she wanted to make sure he got plenty of exposure while he was there. Promoting him was turning out to be a full-time job. He already had a reputation in the industry, and people really wanted to know what would make a platinum-selling rapper turn his back on a multimillion-dollar contract and start performing gospel hip hop. Others wanted to know if his music would have the same appeal it did before. Many people were skeptical that he could enjoy the same type of fame and command the same number of dollars in the gospel world. Tee was doing all she could to make sure Blak stayed on top. She knew that he might not be able to sell out arenas anymore, but he could maintain his current standard of living if he diversified his offerings and solidified his brand. Endorsements and products were the direction she was trying to push him. She was in negotiations with a jeweler to launch a signature watch line called Blak Ice. It would feature watches covered in diamonds that only those with deep pockets could afford, and it would have a less expensive selection with other kinds of stones. She was sure she could get him six figures out of the deal.

After making a couple of phone calls, Tee packed up her things to leave. She was so busy lately that she hadn't taken the time to visit the condo upstairs and see for herself how it was progressing. Michael came home after his inspection Friday and gave it rave reviews. He said it was almost finished and hoped to be able to move in within a couple of weeks. Tee was glad to hear that the elevator was now working.

Since becoming pregnant, she had nothing but contempt for stairs, and she avoided them whenever possible. She decided to take a quick look at the condo before going home. She left her purse and briefcase on the desk and boarded the elevator. It was very nice as far as elevators go. The interior was made of wood grain, brass, and mirrors. She looked at herself in the mirrors that ran from top to bottom and were on every wall but the doors.

She thought her face was fat and her nose was spreading across it. She was not particularly enjoying all the changes her body was experiencing but having a little more hips and booty was a bonus. She smoothed her dress along the curves of her hips. She hoped they wouldn't get much bigger. She looked down and noticed several small brown spiders on the floor. Tee hated bugs. She made a mental note to call an exterminator in the morning. She pressed the button for up. The condo was only one level up so she wouldn't have far to travel. As she ascended, Tee looked in the mirror again and this time she focused on her growing baby bump. She rubbed her stomach and said, "Hello, little one. You nice and comfy in there?"

Suddenly the elevator jerked. Tee grabbed the brass bars attached to each side to steady herself. The elevator jerked again, and then stopped. She pushed the button to open the doors, but nothing happened. She pushed it again, still nothing.

She pushed the button that should have been connected to some type of emergency assistance, but unbeknownst to her, it hadn't been enabled yet. She let out a deep breath and told herself not the panic, everything would be okay. Tee hated tight spaces. The pep talk to herself was working—until the lights went out. Tee gasped for air. This couldn't be happening. She was trapped in the elevator inside her own condo. She couldn't call for help because she left her cell phone in her purse which was sitting on the desk. It was pitch-black in there. She couldn't even see her own hand in front of her face.

She frantically pushed every button she could find, but nothing happened. She beat on the door and yelled until the sides of her fists hurt and her throat felt sore. She wiped her sweaty face in distraught frustration. No one could hear her, and no one knew she was in there. It could be hours before anyone realized she was missing. She had no idea what time Michael would be home. He left the office early to go work out and play basketball with their church league team. Physical activity was his therapy. He worked out, played basketball, or ran around the neighborhood at least five days a week. Tee planned to leave work and surprise him by going to watch his game. She slid her body to the floor of the elevator and sat there in an effort to calm herself.

"Please, God, let this elevator start," she prayed.

The elevator was hot. It was June in Memphis, Tennessee, and for the last few days, the temperatures topped 100 degrees. Evidently, the elevator wasn't equipped with air yet either because she couldn't feel anything coming through the small vent in the ceiling. Fear and lack of air were causing her to sweat profusely. Her hair and clothing clung to her body like rice on sushi. She was hungry, and she had to use the bathroom. Tee knew someone would come looking for her eventually, but how long would that eventually take, and would they even think to look in the elevator? It was about 6:30 p.m. Michael probably wouldn't start to worry until about 9 or 10 p.m. Tee suddenly screamed and jumped up from the floor. The spiders were crawling on her arms and legs.

Chapter 46

Girl, Please!

"Is there something you need to tell me?" asked Lenice.

"No, is there something *you* need to tell me?" asked Lenora.

"Why were you having lunch with your attractive boss when you should be at school teaching children how to use watercolors?"

"Why were you at lunch with Milky Moses when you should have been at work helping single mothers get enough money to care for their kids?" shot back Lenora.

Lenice hated when she answered her question with a question. After her evening yoga class she came by Lenora's house and found her in the studio working. After lunch, with Mr. Rupert he told her to take the rest of the day off. She picked the kids up from school, gave them a snack, and then took them to Mrs. Rosemond's house. The elderly woman enjoyed the company. Her own grandchildren lived six hours away in Atlanta, so doting on Lenora's children came natural to her. She told Lenora to leave them there as long as she needed to in order to get her work done. Lenora was grateful for the quiet time. Her show was this weekend, and she wanted it to be perfect. She had a few more pieces completed.

"I'll go first, but you have to answer my question if I answer yours," said Lenice.

"Deal."

"He's one of the men I met online. I signed up for the site called Richdates.com. Every man on there is guaranteed to make $300,000 or more."

"When did you become a gold digger, Twin?"

"I'm not. I signed up for multiple sites. That just happened to be one of them. I thought it would be nice to meet a man with culture and the ability to enjoy the finer things in life. Don't you think I get tired of men asking, 'What cho name is? You gotta mayne?' and offering to take me to dinner at Chili's? Your turn."

"My boss wanted to talk to me about my performance at work. It seems faculty, children, and parents have been complaining about my attitude. I don't mean to be mean, but this thing with Herman is making me crazy. I hate that he works at a strip club. I see him less and less each week, and I'm scared he's messing with those nasty women."

"First, just because a woman strips doesn't automatically make her nasty. Some of them are very professional. They strip, put their clothes back on, and go home to their families. Second, your husband lost his job, and instead of sitting around here looking at you, he went and found work. No, it's not in the most savory of places, but he's working. Has he given you any reason to think he's cheating?"

"No, but he hasn't given me any reason to think he's not cheating. Whose side are you on anyway?" Lenora put down her paintbrush and placed her hands on her hips.

"Yours. I'm always on yours. In this economy, I know plenty of men who have lost their jobs and after looking for a few months and not finding anything they become a permanent fixture on the couch, like the pillows and cushions, making their families miserable. They think they're too good to work a lower-paying job or get out and cut some grass or rake some leaves to bring in some extra money. Their whole family is suffering because of their ego. Herman didn't do that. You said yourself he was a good bartender in college."

"He was, but why does he have to work there? I know the pay is good, but why couldn't he have gone to a bar or restaurant that doesn't serve women swinging on poles. I can't compete with those girls, Lenice. They're gorgeous. I can't even compete with you."

"You and I aren't in a competition. Don't you ever let me hear you say that again. If you want your husband not to cheat on you, I suggest you stop nagging, whining, and complaining about his job. It isn't helping. I'll put some feelers out and see if anybody is hiring, but if I were you, I'd start making my husband feel happy to come home to his house before he starts going home after work to somebody else's. Working at a strip club doesn't mean he'll cheat on you, but it does mean he has options readily available. Don't give him an excuse to utilize those options."

"Shut up! Just shut up!" screamed Lenora. "Doesn't anybody care how *I* feel? I'm angry that my husband actually thought it was okay to get a job at a whorehouse and hide it from me for months. He didn't think enough about me or my feelings to consult me or to even tell me he was fired. That truly shows there is a breakdown of trust and communication in this marriage. This is supposed to be one of the happiest times in my life, and I'm miserable. My husband and I reconciled, I look better than I have in years, I have a job I love, and my first art show is coming up. I'm supposed to be singing and clicking my heels right now. Instead, I'm stressed, depressed, and listening to your fat mouth!"

Lenice struggled to remain calm as she responded to her sister's rant. She could be such a brat. "You need to donate yourself to science at the medical college because you have got to be the only person who has lost brain cells while losing fat cells. You are only thinking of yourself. I am not a fan of your husband, and you know it, but if I can see the good in what he's trying to do, why can't you? Do you have any idea what Herman being out of work is doing to him? He's a man. Yes, he was wrong for not telling you, but that's in the past. Address it and move on. He's doing what he can to keep this beautiful ship you call a life from sinking, and all you can do is complain. I'll support you when you're right, but I'll be the first to tell you when you are wrong. You could have creditors threatening to take everything you own, but you don't. Your children could be hungry, but instead their bellies are full.

"Did you forget that I work for a welfare agency? I know what real poverty looks like. I see mothers who can't afford to feed their children, and they live with family members who don't want them there. Stop beating Herman over the head when he's trying. You go ahead and have your art show and sell your paintings. Hide out here in your garage instead of talking to your husband and keep going out to lunch with men who are clearly attracted to you. I'm sure that will solve the problem! I suggest you get that attitude in check, or Herman won't be the only one fired. You can be such an idiot sometimes. By the way, that painting looks great. Add some more pink to the flowers to make them pop!"

Lenice stormed out of the studio and slammed the door behind her. She didn't understand how some women couldn't see how good they had it. Herman wasn't perfect. He had his flaws, but he was a good provider, a good father, and a decent husband most of the time.

She got in her car and did what she did almost every evening: go home to kiss Webster, fix them both some dinner, get on the Internet, and chat with strangers for a few hours, and then go to bed.

Lenora picked up her paintbrush and resumed painting. She needed to make this show great. She didn't care what anyone said. She could not support Herman at this time. He was disrespecting her by working at a strip club without her consent. His behavior was going to bring damnation to their house. She had to make sure that no matter what happened, she and her babies would be okay. Her sister was right about one thing, though. The painting would look better with more pink.

Chapter 47

Baby, Come Home

It was 9:30 p.m., and Tee still hadn't made it home. Michael called her cell phone several times, but each time it rang until the voice mail picked up. He left multiple messages and sent several texts, but they all went unanswered. He called Sheba to see if she heard from his wife, and she informed him that last time she saw her was at the office.

Michael decided to drive downtown to the office. It was unlike Tee to work this late or not check in to let him know she was safe. He expected her to be at home, curled up in the living room watching TV or in the kitchen fixing something to eat when he got home from his game. When he arrived at the office, he saw Tee's Denali sitting behind the building, but the building was completely dark. They always left a few lights on to make passersby think someone was there. He went inside and attempted to turn on the lights. When they didn't come on he went to the circuit breaker and moved the lever up. The lights came on, but it was eerily quiet inside the building. He made his way to Tee's office and saw her purse and laptop bag sitting on the desk.

He knew she wouldn't leave without them unless something was wrong. He began calling her name loudly, but there was no answer. Michael decided to check upstairs. He went to the elevator and pushed the button. He waited a few minutes for the elevator doors to open, but they did not. He pushed the button again and noticed that it didn't even light up. He called Tee's name loudly again. This time he heard a faint voice answer with his name. He pressed an ear against the elevator doors in an effort to hear more clearly.

"Michael! Michael, baby, I'm stuck in the elevator!" screamed Tee.

"Are you okay?"

"No! There are spiders in here, and they're biting me. I can't see a thing. It's really hot in here. I think the power went out. Please get me out, Michael."

"Hold on, Tee. I'm calling for help."

Michael called everyone he could—the fire department, the police department, and the contractor in charge of renovations. Within 15 minutes, their building looked like a crime scene with several emergency vehicles and flashing lights outside. The contractor tried to get the elevator to start, but several wires were cut. This was no accident. The elevator was stuck between two floors so there was no way to open the doors. Rescue workers were able to pry open the doors on the second level and gain access to the elevator shaft. The opening at the top of the elevator was too small for a person to crawl through so they used an ax to widen it. Once the hole was large enough, one of the workers reached inside and pulled Tee through the top of the elevator. He then helped Tee stand on the top of the elevator and hoisted her up to two rescue workers standing above them in the second-level elevator opening.

Michael saw his wife and hardly recognized her. While in the hot elevator, sweat poured from Tee's body as if it were coming from a faucet rather than the small pores in her skin. Her hair was damp and matted to her head and her eye makeup was running down her face. She tried not to release her bladder while in the confined space, but eventually she could no longer hold it and had no choice. As a result, her clothing was soiled with sweat and urine. She was also covered from head to toe in small red spider bites, and her body was swelling from their torturous toxin. Her lips, tongue, and eyes were swollen, distorting her face. The skin around her eyes was so puffy it hard to tell if they were open or closed.

Michael picked her up. Tee draped her arms around his neck and sobbed softly. The paramedics tried to take her from him, but he refused to let anyone touch her. He needed to hold her, to comfort her, and let her know he was there. How did this happen?

Tee's body felt like an oven. A firefighter said she was lucky she didn't faint from the heat inside the elevator, which he estimated to be at least 130 degrees. Michael carried her to a waiting ambulance, and they were immediately transported to the hospital. The paramedics attended to her during the drive. Michael held her hand, and with his other hand, he called her family and asked them to meet him at the hospital. Tee was admitted to the hospital for heat exhaustion and a severe allergic reaction.

The next day, Tee looked and felt much better. The hospital gave her some medicine to counter the effects of the spider bites. The swelling was gone, but she was still covered in small red bumps. The itching was so bad Tee wanted to scrape off her skin. She tried her best not to scratch to prevent any scarring, and she hoped that the bumps would go away without leaving a trace that they ever existed. She prayed that this ordeal wouldn't have a negative effect on her baby. The doctors said it shouldn't, and they gave her a low dosage of medication to make sure. To everyone's surprise, Tee's spirits were up, and she was quite talkative. She even cracked jokes about being a grown woman who peed on herself. Throughout the day, she received visits from Sandy and Patrick, Momma Pearl, Sheba, Lenora, Lenice, Tiffany, and Teresa. Michael never left her side the entire time.

To everyone she appeared to be fine, but Momma Pearl knew better. Her daughter was afraid of something, and when they were alone she would ask what it was. Soon, Tee grew tired and asked Michael to halt visitation so she could rest. Before she went to sleep, she asked him to go to the cafeteria and get her some ice cream. She was craving something cold. After enduring such intense heat, it only seemed natural to want something the same temperature as ice.

Michael didn't want to leave her alone. He knew at some point he had to tell her that someone deliberately cut the wires on the elevator but now wasn't a good time. He didn't want to upset her during her recovery. Tee was under the impression that it was some type of electrical malfunction and would be fixed by the time they moved in. However, she was in no hurry to use the elevator again. Tee assured him she was fine and asked him again to please get her ice cream. Michael reluctantly left the room. While he was gone, Tee began to drift off to sleep but was startled by the loud ringing of the phone in her hospital room. She reached over and grabbed the receiver from the cradle.

"This turned out better than I anticipated," said the voice. "I only intended to scare you. Who knew you were allergic to spiders?"

"Who is this?" demanded Tee.

"Your worst nightmare," said the voice.

"You did this?"

"Of course, I did. I bet you aren't feeling so big and bad now. Did you really think that getting on TV would flush me out? It's going to take more than that. How's the baby?"

"Don't you worry about my baby! We're both fine."

"For now," the voice scoffed.

"What do you want? Why are you doing this to me?"

"Tee, darling, it's really not about you. You are simply a means to an end. This is about Michael. I want his demise."

Tee was afraid. There seemed to be no lengths this person wouldn't go to get to Michael. "And you're willing to hurt me and an innocent child to get it?" she asked.

"And anyone else who I think I could use to hurt him."

"What would it take to get you to leave us alone?"

"I'll never leave you alone as long as Michael is alive and well. I have a job to do."

"What would it take to get you to leave me and our child alone?"

"Hmm. I never thought about that," said the voice. "I know. Leave Michael and get a divorce."

"What?"

"You heard me. Walk away from the man and his millions, and I'll stop my assault on you. Simple, right?" said the voice and hung up.

Michael walked in Tee's hospital room smiling and carrying six small containers. "You didn't tell me what kind you wanted so I got a little bit of everything. There's vanilla, chocolate, angel food, fudge, caramel mocha, and rainbow sherbet."

"Michael, *she* did this to me!" Tee's voice was high-pitched and animated as if she were someone other than herself. She waved her hands around in broad movements, shaking the bed. "I'm in this hospital bed and covered in bites because of her. This is the third time Becca has tried to harm me, and this time she's after my baby. I don't know how much more of this I can take. What did I do to deserve this? NOTHING but love a man who has a crazy woman who will stop at nothing to hurt him. Get out! I'm in this mess because of you! Get out!"

"Baby, this isn't my fault," said Michael. He tried to put his arms around Tee, but she only screamed louder.

"Don't you touch me! This is all your fault. Get out!"

"Tee, you don't mean that. Didn't we say we were going to face our problems together?"

"Don't you dare throw my words in my face. Look at my face! I look like somebody is playing connect the dots on my head because of you! I sat in a hot, dark elevator with spiders for over four hours because of you. I was starving, thirsty, and pissy-scared all because that crazy wench hates you. I don't know if you're worth all this anymore, Michael. Leave now!"

"What are you saying?" Michael felt a hard lump forming in his throat and tears threatened to sting his eyes.

"I'm saying that maybe I need to be more concerned about me and my baby than I am about you. I keep putting you first and look what it gets me."

Michael had never seen Tee like this. Lately, she seemed a little emotional, but he thought it was a result of her pregnancy. He knew she endured a lot to be with him, but he never imagined once that she would consider leaving him. Michael suddenly didn't feel well. It was if the walls were closing in around him. Tee was generally the nauseous one but this time, it was him. He needed some fresh air, and he needed it right then.

"I'm going to leave, but I'll be back tomorrow. Hopefully, you'll see that we're stronger together than apart after you get a good night's sleep." He moved closer to kiss Tee good-bye, but she put her hand up to stop him.

"Whatever! Leave!" she shouted.

Michael left and with each step he prayed to God to change her heart. He didn't know what he would do if she left him.

Tee cried herself to sleep. Not because her skin was itching so bad she wished she could peel it from her body but because she knew what she had to do if she wanted to keep herself and her unborn child safe. It broke her heart to even think about waking up each morning without Michael, but it seemed that living without the man of her dreams was the only way she could get Becca to leave her alone. No one should have to live their life in fear. No one should have to live without love either, but she was afraid she might have to learn the true meaning of the words *til death do us part*.

Chapter 48

Tattletale

Mac pressed the button to make a call on his cell phone, dialed the number and then pressed another button to end the call before anyone could answer. This was his third time doing so. He was trying to convince himself to call Tee's office and tell whoever answered the phone what he knew about Casper. Perhaps his tip would lead to her capture. If she was apprehended it would work in his favor, but he also feared that her activities could somehow be traced back to him. That would make him an accomplice to whatever she was doing. Mac wasn't sure what she was doing with the money, but he had a strong feeling that Casper was somehow tied to all the problems Michael and Tee were having.

Mac was desperately trying to find a way to stop giving her money without ruining his career. He shared his thoughts with Amy, and she told him that whatever he decided she would stand by him. She and Patrice were willing to do whatever was needed to clear his name if those pictures were released to the media. He clicked the mouse on his computer and looked at Tee and Michael's *Today Show* interview again. He had already viewed it once that day. She looked tired. He felt sorry for her.

Mac knew that she didn't deserve what was happening to her, but he didn't see how he could help her without implicating himself in some way. For now, he would wait and see how things played out on their own. He hoped they would work in everyone's favor. Mac wasn't a religious man, but since Casper came into his life, he was doing a lot more praying. He needed a God he couldn't see to help him get rid of a woman he couldn't see. He put down his cell phone and said a quick prayer for peace. Mac's soul was tormented by what he was helping to do to a woman he used to imagine himself spending the rest of his life with.

Chapter 49

Torture

The next morning, Michael tried to visit Tee at the hospital, but she had been moved to a private suite on a different floor and gave strict instructions that under no circumstances was he allowed access to her room. Michael tried everything he could to get hospital personnel to tell him where she was, that included an attempt to bribe security with $1,000. The guard was not amused and escorted him from the building with instructions not to come back unless his wife requested to see him. Michael felt defeated. As he crossed the parking lot to his car, he decided to text Tee in hopes that she would answer.

Michael: Tee, I love you.

Tee: It hurts me to say this, but stay away from me. I'm leaving you.

Michael: NO! Please don't do that. What can I do to stop this?

Tee: Find whoever is stalking you and put an end to this. Until you do, don't come home.

Michael: I'll end this and then I'm coming home.

Tee: Please be safe. I hope you can understand why I have to do this. She said she would leave me alone if I left you. I have to think of the safety of our child.

Michael: I can get you 24-hour security. You don't have to do this.

Tee: She tried to kill me three times. I can't take any chances. It's not about me. It's about our child.

Michael: I'm getting you security whether you want it or not. I'll find her, but what am I supposed to do in the meantime? I need you. I love you.

Tee: Do what you always do when life doesn't go your way. Go home to your parents. I love you too.

How could Tee say that she loved him when she was breaking his heart? Michael put his phone in his pocket and rammed his fist through the window of the closest car to him. The glass broke, and the car's alarm sounded loudly announcing his deed to anyone that was nearby. His fist hurt, but it paled in comparison to the pain in his chest. He felt as if some evil person had his hand around his heart and was squeezing with all his might. Hot tears burned his face. His wife was leaving him. Someone was going to pay.

Michael reached into his wallet, took out three one hundred dollar bills to pay for the damage to the car, placed them under the windshield wiper, and walked away.

Chapter 50

The Fragrance of You

Lenice signed the electronic device the deliveryman handed her. She instructed him to set the vase containing two dozen red roses on the table in her office. They looked beautiful next to the two dozen white roses she received the day before. She read the card and blushed. *These roses don't compare to the fragrance of you. I can't wait to see you again. Brighton*

Last night, he took her to the symphony. She felt like Cinderella going to the ball. He sent a car to get her, and when she got inside she found gifts for her and Webster. When she arrived at the venue, Brighton was waiting for her at the door and escorted her to their seats in the first row.

Lenice was completely mesmerized by the atmosphere. She loved live music, and she had never been that close to the stage before! She could see the crisp precise movements of the musicians and hear the rustle of the pages as they turned them to play the next song. She could even see the sweat streaming from the conductor's brow after leading a particularly rousing selection. Her closeness amplified the sound and she almost felt as if she were part of the show rather than a spectator.

Brighton seemed to be getting serious very quickly, but Lenice didn't feel the need to run like she had with her other dates. Could this be the start of something meaningful?

Chapter 51

This House Is Not a Home

Renovations to the condo weren't complete, but Michael moved in anyway. He told the contractor he needed to have everything completed in a week instead of two weeks. For two days he didn't leave the condo. Hammering, whizzing saws, and more were going on outside his bedroom door, but Michael was oblivious to it. On day three he went no further than the office parking lot.

Most of his day was spent looking out of his window at the passing cars and pedestrians. He was never one to lick his wounds, but he had never been in love with a woman like this before. His first night away from home, he had another nightmare. Once he realized that he was in that condo alone instead of in their house with his wife, he wept.

Dr. Foster was devoting all of her time to helping him. Calls were still coming in to the office from people who claimed to have some information about Becca and her brother, but so far, none of the information they received provided anything useful. News that he and Tee were separated had already become public knowledge. Several tabloids were running "Tell-All" stories with details that were totally fabricated.

One publication said he and Tee broke up because she found out the stalker wasn't really a stalker but Michael's mistress. He planned to sue them when he was feeling better. Another said he was suicidal. He didn't want to kill himself. He wanted to kill the individual who was responsible for the demise of his marriage. He texted Tee every day to check on her and the baby. Each day she responded with, "We're fine. Please don't hate me."

Michael was scheduled to participate in a golf tournament soon. He planned to go in hopes that it would help him take his mind off his troubles. Tee hadn't been back to the office since her elevator entrapment, but he knew she would have to return eventually. She enjoyed her work too much not to. He was working on something that was sure to put a smile on her face when she did. It was Lenora's idea, and she was downstairs working on it. He hoped Tee would like it. He laid down to try and get some sleep, but it was hard. He kept having nightmares that someone was trying to harm Tee and their baby.

Chapter 52

Guess Who Came for Dinner?

Lenora went back to the truck to get her wall-mounting kit. She hung one of the paintings in the area of the office where she and Tee previously discussed it would go. She decided to go ahead and put two of the paintings up and save the other two for her art show. She didn't need all four. After they were hung, she had to devise a plan to get Tee to the office to see them. Tee didn't know it, but one of the paintings was a portrait of her and Michael standing in front of the MiTee Management logo. She hoped her friend would be pleasantly surprised when she came back to the office.

Michael was nice enough to let Lenora borrow his truck to transport them. Her station wagon was too small to do so. Michael hardly drove his tricked out F-150 truck because it attracted so much attention. It was pearl white with all the extras: 24-inch rims, chrome trim with a large chrome grill, multiple televisions, customized brown and white leather interior, and a booming sound system. She felt like a rock star driving it because everyone turned toward her to see who was coming. Good thing the windows were tinted. She could see them, but they couldn't see her.

She easily transported her framed paintings in the truck's large covered bed. Herman helped her load them, and Michael helped her unload them before he went back upstairs. He told Lenora that if anyone other than Tee came looking for him, he wasn't home. He offered to help her hang the paintings, but Lenora assured him that she could handle that part by herself. He didn't look well. She urged him to rest.

While she worked, Lenora moved her body to the sounds of one of her favorite stations, V101. She loved the variety of old-school and new-school music they played and all with no rap. She stopped listening to hip hop when she had children. She despised a lot of the newer artists. Many of them laced their music with negativity about premarital sex, drugs, violence, and doing anything to get money. She hated the songs that were demeaning to women the most.

It seemed like almost every other song was about some woman shaking or clapping her booty and she was being referred to as a whore or worse. She was trying to raise Christian young people, and she didn't want her children's heads filled with filth. Lenora knew they would be introduced to that type of music at some point, but by then, she hoped she would have ingrained in them a love for more positive entertainment.

She was surprised when she heard the doorbell for the private entrance ring. Tee gave her friends and family a preview over a month ago and showed them which entrance was strictly for the office and which entrance they needed to use when they came to visit her and Michael. Lenora walked to the door and looked through the peephole. "What is she doing here?" she said aloud to herself. She opened the door to find a startled and embarrassed Tiffany Tate.

"H-h-h-hello, Lenora. Sugah, what are you doing here?"

"I was about to ask you the same thing." Lenora looked Tiffany up and down. She was wearing one of her signature form-fitting, low-cut dresses and carrying two bags of food. Tee and Michael hadn't been separated a week yet, and the vultures were already circling. She was supposed to be Tee's friend.

"Um, I came to check on Michael. Is he here?"

"No, he isn't. You should have called before dropping by unannounced. Have you been by to check on Tee? She was released from the hospital. I talk to her almost every day, and I don't remember her once saying you came to visit her."

"Well, I haven't been to visit her yet, but we've talked. I will go visit her soon. I was in the neighborhood and saw Michael's truck. I thought he might be hungry, so I picked up some food."

"He's not here, and I'm driving his truck. He left this morning to attend some celebrity golf tournament for charity," she lied.

"You?"

"Yes, he let me borrow it so I could bring the paintings I did for Tee to the office. He wanted to surprise the only woman he wants with them when she returns to work."

"Oh, I see," said Tiffany. She tried to ignore Lenora's attempts at rubbing Michael's love for Tee in her face. As if she didn't know that.

Lenora smiled. "Why don't you come in? There's no need to let good food go to waste, and hanging paintings has helped me work up an appetite. We can eat together and catch up. I haven't seen you in a while."

Tiffany was hesitant at first, but then accepted the invitation. She was hungry herself and didn't feel like waiting until she got home to devour her meal. As they walked down the corridor that led to the break room of the office she said, "I know what this looks like, but it's not what you think. Michael and I have become very close. He's a great friend and enormous asset to my company. I know this separation has been hard on him, and I wanted to see if he was okay. Tee has family here, so she has a great support system; but Michael, on the other hand, has no one."

"Uh-huh. That's nice of you. We should all have a friend like you. Would you excuse me for a minute?" said Lenora.

Lenora left the room and texted Michael that Tiffany was in the building so he probably didn't want to come downstairs. He responded, "Thank you. I won't." Lenora never really liked Tiffany, but she wasn't as vocal about it as her sister was at one time. As a married woman, she always thought that Tiffany's willingness to play the role of a mistress was pathetic and disgraceful. She never cared for her diva attitude, either. It became obvious to her years ago that Tiffany was jealous of Tee. She always wondered why Tee couldn't see it, but Lenora didn't think she was all bad. She was able to see Tiffany's good qualities as well. She was smart and funny, and when the girls went out on group outings she generally enjoyed her company, but she always had the nagging feeling that something wasn't right about her. So, she kept a little distance between them. The ladies entered the break room. Tiffany set her bags of food on the table, took out the individual containers, and put them on the table.

"You went to Capriccio's. I love that place. I gave up pasta during my diet, but I guess it won't hurt if I cheat today," she said. The scent made her mouth water.

"Dig in, Sugah. I love Italian food. I've got fettuccini with grilled chicken and shrimp, tortellini, bread with olive oil and spices, and I even had them throw in some calamari."

Lenora retrieved some plates from the cabinets, and they both piled them high with food. Conversation was pleasant between them. They talked about their jobs and kids. Lenora enjoyed the pleasantries, but she knew that she couldn't let Tiffany think what she was doing was okay.

"I know why you're here, Tiffany, and you are dead wrong. I know you have a crush on Michael, but he is Tee's husband, and if nothing else, your friendship with Tee should keep you from making moves on him. She has been nothing but nice to you."

"No, it's not like that. I truly wanted to check on him as a friend. He won't answer my phone calls. I got concerned."

Lenora wasn't buying her innocent act at all. "Michael is busy trying to figure out how to save his marriage. Normally, when someone doesn't answer your calls that means they don't want to talk. I know you're jealous of Tee, but you have no right to be."

"I'm not jealous. I love Tee. I think she deserves everything she has."

"That may be true, but let me give you my definition of jealousy. It is when you're so busy counting someone else's blessings that you forget to count your own. God is raining blessings down all over you, and instead of being at home with your son who has claimed the victory over depression, spending time with your boyfriend who is an awesome man of God, or working on your business, which has allowed you to upgrade your standard of living, you are here trying to spend time with Tee's husband. That's sad."

"You act is if they are still together," said Tiffany. "If Tee was so wonderful she would be here with him."

"They're separated not divorced. And the only reason he left is to keep Tee safe from whoever is stalking them. Don't act like you didn't know that. He's still very much in love with her, and you know that as well. I have no doubt you consider Michael a friend, but you aren't the shoulder he needs to cry on because it's obvious you are attracted to him, and you would gladly give him more than a shoulder. You need to go home and pray that God delivers you from the pathetic spirit of mistressness you have over you. You seem to have no problem playing second fiddle to another woman. Besides, you have a man. What would William say if he saw you here dressed like this for someone else?"

"Mistressness? That's not even a word. There is nothing wrong with my outfit, and leave William out of this. He doesn't even know if he wants a relationship with me," said Tiffany. "You don't understand. Michael brings something out of me no one else has. He believed in me. He encouraged me and—"

"And Tee didn't? She gave you money, but more importantly, she trusted you with her husband. She knows Michael has connections that she doesn't, and that's why she agreed to let him work hands-on with you. She wants you to be successful. She wants to show you that the life you have been waiting for a man to give you, you can give to yourself. And *this* is how you repay her? Don't make her regret her decision.

"You have allowed yourself to develop feelings for her husband. The Bible says shun the very appearance of evil, and you got SKANK written all over you right now. Go home, Tiffany. And you better be glad I'm Lenora and not Lenice because she would have shut the door in your face rather than let you in. But there is one thing me and my sister have in common. We are both fiercely loyal to our friends. You can trust that I will be telling Tee about this little visit of yours, and the next time you have the urge to drop in and check on Michael, DON'T. Thanks for dinner. It was delicious."

Lenora had a way of telling people off that made it seem like she wasn't. She never raised her voice, and it possessed the same calmness one would have when soothing a wounded spirit. It's hard to get angry with someone when their mean words ooze sweetness.

"Now come here, girl, and let me pray for you." Before Tiffany could object, Lenora grabbed her hands and bowed her head in prayer. Tiffany let her hold her hands, but she didn't bow her head and her eyes remained open. Lenora called on Jesus to touch Tiffany's heart and deliver her from her carnal desires. She also prayed for Tee and Michael to reconcile their marriage. Afterward, she pulled Tiffany toward her and gave her a hug. Tiffany didn't return the embrace and held her body as rigid as a board. She was in disbelief. Did Lenora really go off on her, and then pray for her?

"You are better than this, Tiffany. Stop letting the devil use you and stop being an untrue friend to Tee. I've been there when people have spoken badly about you and called you out of your name, and Tee defended you. She loves you like a sister. Don't do this to her. You're saved now. You're a changed creature. Act like it." Lenora then exited the room and went back to finish hanging up the last painting.

Without uttering another word, Tiffany gathered her things and ran down the corridor. Lenora was right. What was wrong with her? She was being a horrible friend.

Chapter 53

Good Times

Tee and Sandy sat quietly watching reruns of the sitcom *Martin,* while eating rocky road ice cream with oatmeal cookies. Tee's dog, Chesnutt, sat between them chewing quietly on a rawhide bone. Lately, Tee's cravings were becoming stranger. She put mustard in her oatmeal that morning. She added a side of pickles and onions to her ice cream. Sandy found it difficult to watch her down the concoction. She turned her head in disgust each time Tee took a bite.

Sandy's life was hectic but good. Business was booming, her marriage was healing, and all three of their children were healthy and happy. She and Patrick both learned the value of forgiveness and were working on forgetting each other's indiscretions, which was easier than they initially thought it would be. Who had time to point fingers and place blame with two businesses, three children, one of which was a newborn, and a cat? Their former lovers, Armondo and Sheniqua, were a thing of the past. Neither of them had tried to make contact in months. Sandy and Patrick were quite grateful for that.

Yes, Sandy was busy, but there was no way she was going to let her sister continue to sit at home wallowing in what could best be described as coerced regret. The doctor cleared Tee to resume her normal duties after she was released from the hospital, but she refused to go back to the office. She worked at home on the days she felt like working. Her excuse was that she didn't want to be seen in public with red splotches on her face, but Sandy knew better. She didn't want to go to the office and run the risk of bumping into Michael. Sandy had never seen a woman more miserable after putting her husband out. The way she behaved one would think that Michael was run over by a car rather than living in their downtown condo. Their mother moved in to keep an eye on her, but Momma Pearl was getting on Tee's nerves. Tee convinced her to go home for the night since Sandy was coming over.

"Tee, you know I love you, right?" said Sandy.

"Yeah, sure," said Tee absentmindedly.

"I think you're making a big mistake."

"Fine. If you want to watch *Good Times* instead of *Martin,* I'll put it back," said Tee.

"That's not what I meant, and you know it."

"Sandy, when you refused to tell Patrick that you slept with Armondo and the baby you were carrying could have possibly been his, even though we both knew telling Patrick was the right thing to do, did I badger you about it?" asked Tee.

"No," said Sandy.

"I need you to return the favor. I appreciate the company, and I truly appreciate the break from Momma, but I can do without the lecture. I know what I'm doing, and if I'm wrong, let me come to that conclusion myself. Okay?"

"Okay."

"Thanks."

"Don't thank me for being quiet when I want to scream at you until you go get your husband back."

Tee handed her a cookie. "Put this in your mouth. It will help stifle the screams."

They both laughed.

"You're right. I would rather watch *Good Times*. Please change the channel," said Sandy.

Chapter 54

Proverbs 31 Woman

Lord, what's wrong with me? prayed Tiffany. *I want to do better. Help me to do better.* She wanted to be a better woman. She was tired of bringing sabotage into her own life. She remembered that Tee recommended she read Proverbs 31. Tiffany pulled out the Bible Tee gave her shortly after she dedicated her life to Christ. It was a beautiful red leather-bound Bible, and on the cover was her name engraved in gold letters. Inside Tee wrote, *Welcome to the Kingdom. Everything you need to become a strong woman of God is within these pages. Follow directions.* Tiffany opened the Bible and turned the crisp pages to the section she sought and began to read.

"A wife of noble character who can find? She is worth far more than rubies. Her husband has full confidence in her and lacks nothing of value. She brings him good, not harm, all the days of her life. She selects wool and flax and works with eager hands. She is like the merchant ships, bringing her food from afar. She gets up while it is still night; she provides food for her family and portions for her female servants. She considers a field and buys it; out of her earnings she plants a vineyard. She sets about her work vigorously; her arms are strong for her tasks. She sees that her trading is profitable, and her lamp does not go out at night. In her hand, she holds the distaff and grasps the spindle with her fingers. She opens her arms to the poor and extends her hands to the needy. When it snows, she has no fear for her household; for all of them are clothed in scarlet. She makes coverings for her bed; she is clothed in fine linen and purple. Her husband is respected at the city gate, where he takes his seat among the elders of the land. She makes linen garments and sells them, and supplies the merchants with sashes. She is clothed with strength and dignity; she can laugh at the days to come. She speaks with wisdom, and faithful instruction is on her tongue. She watches over the affairs of her household and does not eat the bread of idleness. Her children arise and call her blessed; her husband also, and he praises her: Many women do noble things, but you surpass them all. Charm is deceptive, and beauty is fleeting; but a woman who fears the Lord is to be praised. Honor her for all that her hands have done, and let her works bring her praise at the city gate."

Tiffany wanted to be considered noble, honored, and blessed. She wanted to be seen as precious. She wanted to be respected. She didn't quite understand everything she read, though. God didn't really expect her to make her own clothes and comforters for her beds, did He? Was it necessary for her to rise before the crack of dawn every morning? She normally asked Tee about such things, but she didn't think it was a good time to call her with her problems. She wasn't sure if Lenora was serious about telling her that she came to see Michael. Instead, she called Lenice. She was quite familiar with the passage.

"Honey, my grandmother used to read this to me and Lenora all the time. We called her Nana, and Nana wanted to make sure we knew what kinds of skills we needed to not only be good women but good wives. Let me get my Bible and we can go through it together."

She returned quickly. "It's really quite simple. The man is supposed to be the head of the household, but he shouldn't be expected to do it all. It's his woman's job to not only help him run the house, but she has to know how to handle business in his absence too. It says 'she brings him good, not harm.' If a woman understands that marriage is a partnership, she won't do anything to sabotage her husband or make things hard for him because she realizes that she is only harming herself and their household as well. She'll make sure the home is pleasant. After a hard day's work, he has a place of rest and replenishment. When he gets home, she's not nagging and fussing and saying negative things to him that make him wish that he was still at work. 'She sees that her trading is profitable and her lamp doesn't go out at night' is about planning for the future. When she shops, she isn't spending money frivolously or spending bill money on wants instead of their needs. She is actually at home trying to figure out ways to save money and make money.

"She makes sure she's stocked up on the things they need at home so they don't run out. Now, let's bring it into this century. Your man is in the shower and he runs out of soap. He yells for his wife, which is you, to bring him some more so he can finish washing his stanky body, and you respond that you are completely out. You've got to run to the store and get some. Or maybe you're really creative and you hand him some dishwashing liquid or some shampoo so he can finish his shower. Can you imagine your husband with shampoo, with built in conditioners for extra body and shine, on his balls because you forgot to buy more soap when you were at the store? What does his hair down their need extra body and shine for? Or maybe it's light bulbs, and you are literally sitting in the dark because you ran out of bulbs, or even worse, the utility company cut off your lights because you forgot to pay the bill like your husband asked you to. You see where I'm going? Plan ahead and be prepared not only in your household but all aspects of your life. The woman in the scripture is making sure that she has the tools necessary to take care of her own needs, her man, and her children, as well as those who are less fortunate."

"What about the verse that says, 'She makes coverings for her bed; she is clothed in fine linen and purple?'" asked Tiffany.

"That means sister girl has got skills. She is capable of making things for her home, and she makes sure she looks good. Now, God is not telling you that you need to become a seamstress. I recognize we're new millennium women and very few of us ever took sewing or even home economics. What the scripture is saying is that you need to make sure you are capable of keeping your household and yourself looking good and well covered. Your children shouldn't be wearing summer jackets in the winter. They will get sick. No man wants to come home to a filthy house. The house needs to be tidy, somewhere he can lay his head without wondering if roaches are in his bed.

"When I was making home visits for my job, I would go to some houses that were so dirty you didn't want to sit down, use the bathroom, or even ask for a drink of water because you doubted the cup they gave you would be clean. There was one woman we had to threaten with removing her children from her home before she would clean her house! It was so filthy that bugs and rodents were lying around as if they belonged there, like they paid the rent or something. I think she thought they were pets. She had the nerve to wonder why her children were always sick. It was because of all the bacteria and infection everywhere. That should NEVER be any woman's house, especially one with a family.

"It upsets me when I hear women saying they don't cook or clean regularly, but they expect the man to pay all the bills, not cheat, and treat her like a queen. If you're not domestic, at least have the good sense to pay someone to do the cooking and cleaning for you. These male chauvinists have got it all wrong. Nowhere in that passage does it say that we need to be barefoot and pregnant, but it does say we need to make a pleasant, clean environment for our families and be business savvy. It says we need to be of good moral character. It says we need to look out for the less fortunate, and it says we need to know how to put in a hard day's work to help take care of our families. In short, a Proverbs woman is a woman who knows how to handle her business in every aspect of her life: marriage, family, business, and home. My Nana used to say if you want to keep your man you better know how to cater to him and make him feel like a man, and if he's a good man, he'll return the favor without you ever having to ask.

"I know I jumped around, but did anything I say help you?" asked Lenice.

"Yes," said Tiffany. "You explained that rather well."

"Good. Tiffany, I know this isn't why you called me, and it's probably the last thing you want to hear, but my sister told me you tried to visit Michael without an invitation."

"It wasn't how it looked at all. My intentions were purely innocent. As I tried to tell her, Michael has been a good friend to me," defended Tiffany.

"That may be true, but hasn't Tee been an even better friend? You wouldn't even know Michael if it wasn't for her. She's hurting behind this separation too. You didn't go to her house with dinner. Are you sure your intentions were pure? From what I was told, you had on your 'freak'um' dress and full 'get a man' makeup. When I go see men I'm not interested in, I have on jeans, a T-shirt, and lip gloss.

"Do me a favor and turn to the book of Proverbs with me. Go to chapter 18. I'm going to read the first and the last verse. 'An unfriendly man pursues selfish ends, and defies all sound judgment.' That's verse one. Now, let's skip to verse 23. 'A man of many companions may come to ruin but there is a friend who sticks closer than a brother.'"

"I like that last one," said Tiffany. "I keep my circle of friends small because you can't trust everybody."

"That's so true. I don't have very many friends myself. Actually, if I had to count them I could use one hand: my sister, Tee, and you. Everyone else is pretty much an acquaintance. But you need to pay attention to the first verse too. I don't think you're exercising sound judgment in this situation. Did I ever tell you how I met Tee?"

"No."

"As teenagers, we were in a summer enrichment program for high school graduates. The purpose was to make sure we had adequate study skills to survive in college. It was designed for low-to-middle income students. They wanted to make sure that when we went to college we were successful. Me and Lenora instantly bonded with Tee. That entire summer we were like the Three Musketeers. Sandy was in culinary school and working as a cook in a hotel and would let Tee have her car when she was at school and work. We explored the whole city in her '85 Topaz, burning up Sandy's gas and going places our parents would never take us," Lenice laughed.

"We all cried when the summer ended and Lenora and I left for college. Over the years we stayed in touch and visited each other as much as possible. I've had three life-altering moments during my adult life, and Tee was there to help me through all of them. The death of my Nana, the death of my mother, and my breakup with Scott. When my mother died, I almost lost my mind, and that's probably when I started to lose my faith. I tried to shut out the entire world. Lenora had Herman to help her deal with our mother's passing, but I was single. Tee wouldn't let me shut her out. She practically moved in my house and made me breakfast, lunch, and dinner. She made me get out of the house when I didn't want to go out. I would wake up in the middle of the night and cry like a child who lost her blankey, and Tee would sit there with me and hold my hand. I even woke up a couple of nights to find her deep in prayer for me and my sister. She was praying that the spirit of depression that had come over me would leave. One time I woke up with holy oil all over my forehead, and I knew nobody put it there but her.

"Yeah, I know Tee can get on your nerves sometimes. She's a little old-fashioned and a Miss Goody Two-shoes, but you'll never find a truer friend. She's the friend I'd lay down my life for. I don't appreciate what you're doing. She's still very much in love with her husband, and the last thing she needs to hear is that someone she considers a friend is trying to date him. I consider you a friend too, Tiffany, but if I ever had to choose, I'll take Tee's side without batting an eyelash. Is Michael worth losing two friends? Money can buy you a lot of things, but a true friend isn't one of them."

Tiffany sat on the phone in silence. She didn't appreciate Lenice's last comments. She really wished people would stop judging her. Lenice kept talking even though she didn't get a response.

"You know why I didn't like you. It wasn't only because you were dating a married man, but because you can be very selfish. You act without considering how your actions might hurt others. If you did, you would have never dated Quincy.

When he started offering to give you money and take you out, you should have told him to go home to his wife.

"Did you ever stop to think about how your actions would affect William? He really does care about you, but maybe his exit is for the best. You seem to be proving whoever told him to leave you alone right. You aren't ready to be a first lady. All you see is the prestige and the money that could come your way if he should get his own church one day. Did you ever think that you also have to share your husband with an entire congregation of folks? All the nights he's going to be with them instead of you? Not to mention all the women who would be willing to do anything to be with him even if it's for one night?

"I saw it all the time with my Papa. Nana was one strong woman. Women old and young threw themselves shamelessly at my Papa. Never once did I hear Nana raise her voice or see her stop being a lady in order to put them in their place. I remember one Sunday this lady asked me for Papa's pager number. Now, proper church protocol is to call the church secretary and set up an appointment if you wanted to speak to the pastor, especially if you're a woman. I knew good and well she wasn't supposed to be calling his pager. I gave that trick the number to a funeral home instead. I knew it by heart from working in the church office and helping those who lost loved ones make arrangements with the church. When that woman saw me at Wednesday night Bible Study she was hotter than fish grease and asked me why I did that. I told her because that was where she would end up if she didn't leave my Papa alone!

"When word got back to my grandmother, she wore my behind out for being disrespectful to an adult. She even made me go to that woman and apologize. I asked her why was I in trouble when it was obvious that hoochie was after her husband. She told me if she tried to put every woman who was after Papa in their place, she would have no time to focus on the important things like her relationship with God, the ministry she helped build with her husband, and her family. Instead of fighting those women, she prayed for them and let God handle it. The best defense she had against those women was being a good wife, a Proverbs 31 wife.

"I realized that my grandmother wasn't as blind as I thought. All that time I thought she didn't see what those women were doing, but those women didn't see what my Nana was doing. She was nice to the staff at the church so they would help her fend off those women. Many times the church secretary ran defense and offense for her. My grandfather's armor bearers did the same thing. She was always cooking Papa's favorite foods and making sure she kept the house how he liked it. And from what I know, my Papa was faithful. He knew that three woman couldn't amount to his wife. She stood by his side until the day he died.

"You think those women in that church are cold toward you now, wait and see how they act if you and William get back together and he puts a ring on your finger. You better pray about that thing, Tiffany, but first you need to get yourself together."

"Why does everyone always think the worst of me?" asked Tiffany.

"Because you don't make it a habit to show people the best of you. I know you have a good heart, Tiffany. I know you're talented and you're smart, but most people never get below your surface to see it because they're too busy looking at that tight dress you're wearing with your titties hanging all out. You got 'danger' written all over you, girl. Stop dressing like you're going to the club all the time. Well, therapy with Dr. Lenice is over for now. I got myself another date tonight, and I need to get ready. This one's a surgeon."

"When are you going to stop seeing all these different men?"

"When I get bored with seeing all these different men. Bye!"

Tiffany looked around her home. There were piles of dirty clothes that needed to be washed. On her desk was a list of contacts she had yet to cold-call in hopes they would be interested in a complimentary massage. She also needed to finish putting together her business plan for her bath-house. But first, she needed to help the number-one man in her life with his homework. Quincy 2 was in a summer program to help strengthen his math and English skills.

"Tiffany," she said to herself, "you've got work to do. Let's get busy."

Chapter 55

Peek-a-Boo Baby

"Thanks for coming to my doctor's appointment with me," said Tee.

"You don't have to thank me," said Lenice.

Tee and Lenice sat patiently in the waiting room of her OBGYN's office waiting for the nurse to call her to the back. This would be her first visit without Michael. She purposely didn't remind him so he wouldn't come. She knew it was her fault he wasn't there for her checkup, but that didn't make the reality any less harder to bear. Her husband should be there to see how his baby was doing.

"You don't understand. My mother is driving me crazy," said Tee. "She moved in after I was released from the hospital because she said she didn't want me pregnant and at home by myself. Her constant doting on me is nerve-wracking. She won't even let me get my own glass of water. The only reason she went home last night was because Sandy was there."

"I don't mind being here. Since it seems I won't experience the miracle of birth for myself, I have to live vicariously through my sister and my friends."

"Stop putting negativity into the atmosphere. I never knew you wanted children. I never heard you mention them once," said Tee.

"I didn't think I did, but now that I'm getting older, it seems I'm feeling more maternal. All of a sudden, Webster doesn't seem to be enough."

"You're not that old. You can still have children."

"It doesn't matter now anyway. I don't have a husband, and there's no way I'm becoming anybody's baby momma." Lenice rolled her neck and eyes for emphasis.

"You don't know what God has in store for you. How was your date last night?"

"It was okay. He took me to Ruth's Chris Steak House and ordered almost everything on the menu. I almost wet myself when the bill came and it was $400. I knew he was a doctor before the date, but throughout the course of the evening, I found out he was an anesthesiologist so he could afford it, but it seemed so excessive. He didn't eat most of what he ordered. He said he wanted to taste it and when it was time to go he didn't want to-go boxes to take it with him. He said he didn't eat leftovers."

"Wow. Well, how was the conversation?" asked Tee.

"It was all about him. His education, his job, his hobbies, his condo by the river, his Mercedes. I think he may have asked me one question about myself the entire night. Then after dinner, he had the nerve to invite me over to his place.

"You should have seen his face when I turned him down. It was obvious that he's used to women falling at his feet.

"He even asked me a second time to see if I really meant it. He then informed that most women can't wait to jump his bones and asked me if I was on my cycle. I told him most men were smart enough to tell that I'm not the kind of girl you have sex with on the first date. Then that fool asked me if I have a three date, five date or 30-day rule. He wasn't used to waiting, but he might be willing to give it a try since I was fine."

Tee laughed, "No, he didn't! What did you do?"

"I told him I had a no-arrogant-butthole rule and left. I left him sitting at the table alone and asked the bartender to call me a cab. The bartender was a sister who was all too happy to give me the goods on him. Apparently, he brings his dates there all the time and flashes his cash in front of them. She said most of the time they don't even get to dessert before he's convinced them to go home with him. She rarely sees any of them twice."

"Lenice, I'm sorry that happened to you, but can I ask you something? Has James ever asked you for sex?"

"Never. He's celibate."

"Does he ask you about yourself?"

Lenice smiled. "James always wants to know how I'm doing and what I'm doing. Sometimes I have to make him talk about himself. He's a great conversationalist, and he's smart. Did you know he loves tennis? I don't meet too many black men who keep up with tennis."

"Sounds like you two have a good time when you're together."

"We have a great time!" Lenice thought about all the laughs she and James had and smiled. Brighton listened to her too. She hadn't told Tee about him, yet. The only reason Lenora knew was because she saw them together.

Tee sat there and let what she said sink in for a few minutes before she continued. "Then, why are you wasting your time with all these other men if you're so good together?"

"I'll answer your question if you answer mine. Why are you letting some killer you can't even see run you away from your husband? Get some extra security and go home to your fine husband, and every time you get scared or start worrying, screw him to take your mind off things."

"I wish sex was the cure for all our problems. We would never have any. Look at me, Lenice. I look like I have a small beach ball in my belly, and I'm getting bigger every day. I'm always sleepy, tired, and hungry. If I were attacked, I'm not sure I'd be able to fight off my attacker, and I never have been much of a runner. I have to think of my safety for my baby's sake, and what kind of life are we going to have surrounded by security 24/7? That's not the life I want for me or my family. I love Michael, but I won't live in a prison, and I won't live in fear."

"What makes you think that this person is going to keep her word and leave you and the baby alone because you're not with Michael? I wouldn't trust some manipulative stranger," said Lenice.

"I don't, but I have to try. I love Michael, but it's not about me or him anymore. It's about our child. Your turn," said Tee.

Lenice was about to answer her question when a nurse in green scrubs called them to the back.

"I want my answer when this is over."

Lenice smiled but didn't utter a word.

Chapter 56

Disappointment & Love

Lenora wanted to drop the phone and scream. The owner of the art gallery called to tell her that her showing was being postponed so they could host a private party this weekend. She couldn't turn down that type of money for a free event with an unknown artist. The owner offered to let her hang her paintings in the gallery before the party in hopes that some of the partygoers might want to purchase them as if that was a fair trade. The next available weekend the gallery could host her showing was in three months.

Lenora tried to stop the tears from spilling from her eyes, but she couldn't. She was devastated. She went to her studio to try to paint her anxiety away, but she couldn't focus. The kids were with their grandparents. They agreed to come get them so she could focus on finishing her artwork, but there was no rush now. She doubted her babies could make her feel better anyway. There was only one person who could make her feel better when she felt like this, and his name was Herman.

Unfortunately, Herman was at work. She wanted to feel her husband's arms around her. She wanted him to kiss her face and tell her it was their loss.

She needed to call everyone and let them know her show was cancelled, but she didn't want to talk to anyone right now. Instead, she got on Facebook and updated her event invite she posted announcing the showing. In all caps she typed "CANCELLED. I will let you know when it's been rescheduled." Then she went to her bedroom to lay down and waited for sleep to overcome her. An hour later, she awoke to Herman standing over her.

"Baby, are you okay? I saw the art exhibit was cancelled. I tried to call you to find out why. You didn't answer the phone. I got worried and came home early." Lenora immediately wrapped her arms around her husband's neck.

"Whatever it is, it's probably not as bad as you think." He rocked his wife back and forth until she felt like talking. Lenora explained in as few words as possible what happened.

"Baby, that's not the only art gallery in Memphis. There's no way we're going to wait three months to showcase your paintings. Not after all the work you put in. Tomorrow, I'm going to go downtown and walk from gallery to gallery personally until I find one that has an opening. We'll rent one out if we have to."

"Herman, we can't afford that," whimpered Lenora.

"Don't you worry about that. I'm the man of this house. I'm supposed to be the primary breadwinner. I'll take care of it."

Lenora winced at hearing the mean words she said to him come out of his mouth. "No, baby we're a team. It's OUR job to provide for this family. I'm sorry I've been so insensitive. I know you're doing the best you can. I don't like you working there, but I'm sure it's only temporary. I can deal with it until you find another job. I miss having you around, but the kids and I will survive."

Herman was touched. He missed his family too. "Thank you, but I put in my notice yesterday. I found a job as a bartender at a bar and grill. The pay won't be as good, but I'll be home more, and I won't be working around naked women. I could never continue to do something I know you hate. You mean the world to me. It's not fair that you have a husband, but you have to handle the day-to-day duties by yourself. I see how stressed you are."

Lenora smiled. She gave Herman a kiss. He squeezed her tightly as he kissed her back.

"Why don't you go to your studio and paint? It will make you feel better. I'll cook us dinner," said Herman. "I can pick up the children from my parents after we have a quiet adults only dinner."

"If you don't mind, I'd like to paint right here in our bedroom," said Lenora.

"Okay." Herman got up to go to the studio and get her supplies.

"Where are you going?" she asked.

"Don't you need your supplies to paint? I'll go get them."

Lenora laughed and gave him a mischievous look. "You don't understand, sexy. I have everything I need right here. You are my canvas. Come here so I can show you how talented I really am."

Herman felt a surge of lust for his wife. He loved when Lenora got naughty. It was such a change from her usual good-girl persona. At that moment, she looked incredibly sexy and seductive to him. "Yes, ma'am," he said and kissed her slow and deep.

Chapter 57

Video Chat

Tee couldn't believe Michael arranged to be at her doctor's visit using video chat. When she questioned Dr. Walker about how she could do that without her consent, her doctor reminded her that she signed paperwork allowing her to share any medical information with Michael. When he called and told her he wanted to know if he could view her visit via the Internet, she agreed and made accommodations for him to do so. She didn't know they were separated.

Tee had to admit that it was good seeing his face. He looked so handsome as he watched the ultrasound of the baby. He smiled the entire time. Tee wanted to touch, kiss, and hold him so badly. She prayed that Michael would keep his promise and find her attacker soon. They were both so excited about the baby. When Dr. Walker pointed out what she thought was the beginnings of a penis, Michael said he was gonna be blessed just like his daddy. Tee blushed and told him to stop talking dirty in front of her doctor. After her appointment, Tee returned home and found a note inside her mailbox among the store circulars. It read:

You're not keeping your entire end of the bargain. Start divorce proceedings now.

Attached to the note was a picture of her and Lenice leaving the doctor's office with a bull's-eye drawn on her stomach. Tee cried as she dialed the number to her attorney's office.

Chapter 58

Wake-Up Call

The next morning, Tiffany was awakened by a loud banging on her door. She wasn't expecting visitors at 7 a.m. She was surprised to find that Quincy's daughter, Priscilla, was the cause of the noise. She didn't remember telling her to come tutor Quincy 2 that morning. She opened the door with a smile.

"Well, good morning, Sugah."

"Is he here?" asked Priscilla without any type of proper greeting.

"Is who here?"

"My daddy."

"No, why would he be here?"

"He's cheating on my momma again, and I figured he might be here with you," she said with much attitude.

Tiffany snarled at her. Even a teenager won't let her forget her past. "Wait a minute, young lady. You show some respect. I may be your father's former mistress, but I am also your elder. Watch your tone."

"I'm sorry, Ms. Tiffany, but I can't let him do this to my mother again. She was so happy, but now he's back to his old ways, and he's hardly at home and barely paying any of us any attention like he did when he was with you." The teenager began to cry. "Last night, he didn't come home. She called him several times, and he didn't answer. My mother sat up all night waiting on him."

"Come in, child. Let's talk, but first you go to the bathroom and wash your face. It's going to be all right." Tiffany gave her a hug as she passed her.

While Priscilla was in the bathroom she called Quincy and told him she had an emergency, but she didn't tell him what it was. He said he would be right over. He arrived 20 minutes later. He was quite surprised to see his daughter and son in the kitchen eating a bowl of cereal and French toast. Tiffany fixed him a bowl of cereal and told him to have a seat. Priscilla adored her father, and she wanted to see the best in him at all times. She seemed to really enjoy those few moments of just having him at the breakfast table with her. Tiffany was sure that his wrinkled shirt and pants and the lipstick on the collar of his shirt didn't go unnoticed. When they finished eating, she told Quincy 2 to go to his room and get ready for his swimming lessons.

"Quincy, I asked you over here because your daughter is very upset. I didn't want to send her home driving and crying. She needs to talk to you."

"Okay, Priscilla. What's so important that you felt you needed to come over here to Tiffany rather than talking to your mother or me?"

"Daddy, I'm tired of you cheating on my mother! I came over here to see if you were cheating with Ms. Tiffany, again. I was happy to see you weren't here, but it's obvious you were somewhere," said the 16-year-old.

"Young lady, you are out of order. It is not your job to check up on me. *I* am the parent. I spent the night at the office. The firm is working on a proposal to land us our first multimillion-dollar engineering project. We've all been putting in late hours."

Tiffany shook her head. This man would even lie to his own daughter. She wondered what she ever saw in him.

"Daddy, don't lie to me! You've got lipstick on your shirt, and you smell like a woman's perfume!" screamed Priscilla.

"It's not what you think. That was from a female colleague who wears way too much makeup and perfume. She gave me a hug, and it got on my shirt."

"Daddy, I'm not a stupid little kid. If that was true it would be on your shoulder or maybe on the outside of your collar, but it's on the inside. Can you tell the truth? I need you to stop cheating. It's breaking my mother's heart. She does everything she can to please you. We all do in hopes that you will spend more time at home with us. When you and Ms. Tiffany broke up you did that. You were the daddy I always wanted. Now, you're hardly at home anymore and you're always busy. Daddy, whoever this woman is, please leave her alone! Puhleeeeeease!"

Priscilla threw her arms around her father's neck and began crying uncontrollably on his shoulder. Tiffany's heart went out to her. She was happy that this time she wasn't a part of his child's pain.

Quincy rubbed his daughter's back and whispered words of comfort in her ear. Tiffany couldn't hear everything he said, but she heard the words "I'm sorry" repeatedly. When Priscilla calmed herself, Quincy walked her to the front door. "Go get in your car and trail me home. We'll finish this discussion at home with your mother.

"Tiffany, I'm sorry we brought this to your house. I promise you that it will never happen again," said Quincy.

"It's okay. I like your daughter, and I appreciate the way she has taken to our son. She's good for him."

"I agree," said Quincy. "She is always raving about her little brother. The littlest one isn't there yet because she doesn't like not being the baby anymore, but she's coming around. My oldest, Quincetta, likes him too, although she tries to hide it." Tiffany winced at the mere mention of Quincetta's name. She hadn't seen her since she and her friends ambushed her at the spa months ago. Although, she did write her a letter apologizing.

"Quincy, are you cheating on your wife?" asked Tiffany.

"Tiffany, that isn't any of your concern," said Quincy.

"You've already answered my question. Why? I understood us. We were actually in love, but why now?"

"It's my nature, Tiffany. I've never been a one-woman type of guy. My wife knew that when she married me. The only reason I married her was because she was pregnant and she pressured me into it. I think she thought having children would change me. Boy, was she wrong. It actually made it worse. Parenting and trying to be a good provider is a lot of pressure. My female friends help me relax and unwind. You and I were different, though. I ended up falling in love with you, and if things were different I would have married you. I never wanted us to end. I still love you, Butterfly, and I guess part of me is looking to fill the void you left behind. I didn't mean to stay out all night and upset my family. I guess I'm slipping. My wife has always wanted something I couldn't give her—all of me. I'm not that type of guy. I've got to figure out a way to keep this thing balanced. I've got to learn how to keep my wife, my children, and lady friends happy."

Tiffany couldn't believe Quincy actually let those words come out of his mouth. How could she have fallen for such a jerk? She shook her head.

"Don't go teaching my son your womanizing ways. That's not the type of man I'm trying to raise!"

"Believe it or not, Tiffany, I want him to be a better man than me. I promise not to try to groom him into a player, but if he's anything like his old man, it's in his blood." Quincy chuckled.

"If he's anything like his momma, he'll by loyal to those he loves. I never once desired another man while I was with you."

"I know, and I appreciate that," said Quincy. He walked to the door. He needed to get home and try to smooth things over with his child and his wife.

Tiffany issued a silent prayer for Quincy and his family. Some people never learn. She decided it was time for a vacation. She would leave to give herself time to get over Michael. It might even be good to make William miss her a little. Sierra and Siendy were still avoiding her calls. It was time to check on Sierra and Siendy in person. She had a feeling they were taking jobs without giving her, her cut. Yep. L.A. would be perfect. Nobody there knew her as the former mistress of a city official. She also wouldn't have to worry about anyone coming to her house looking for their father.

Chapter 59

What's Love Got to Do with It?

This was Brighton and Lenice's fifth date. He rented a section of the Memphis Botanic Gardens for a private dinner for two. Lenice was getting used to being pampered. Brighton was full of surprises; she never knew what was next—roses, a day at the spa, a limo to take her shopping. He even arranged for Webster to have a spa day. It was obvious that he really liked her.

She was still seeing other men, but her rendezvous with Brighton was lasting longer than any of the other men she went out with, except James. Most of them were gone after the second date. She enjoyed Brighton's company, but she thought of him as more of a friend. Lenice planned on telling him today that the feelings weren't mutual. She hoped that he wouldn't have a problem being friends because she needed a big favor from him. She also planned to ask him to give Herman a job. She was glad that Lenora and Herman were doing better. Their money woes seemed to be bringing them closer together, but Lenice hated seeing her sister struggle. Just yesterday, Lenora asked her if she was allowed to ask for public assistance since she was related to the woman who ran the department that granted it. Lenice had no problem getting her sister assistance, but it broke her heart to know that their situation had brought them to the point where they needed to ask. Lenice went out the same day and bought them $300 worth of groceries. She would have given them money, but she knew Lenora would never take it.

Lenice tried to enjoy her dinner with Brighton. It really was a lovely gesture. They were surrounded by exotic plants and flowers. The air was fragrant, and the night sky was littered with stars that surrounded a bright crescent moon. The candles on their table cast a soft glow on each of them. The summer heat produced a mild mugginess, but it wasn't unbearable at night like it was during the day. Brighton also arranged to have a large fan blow cool air on them from a distance. The Cornish hen dinner they ate with roasted baby potatoes and sautéed spinach was delicious. She wondered what was for dessert. A violinist appeared and began to play as the waiters brought out an assortment of cheesecakes.

Brighton stood up and cleared his throat. He was nervous. The soft manufactured wind caused a few wisps of his thinning gray hair to reposition themselves in his face. He took his hand and smoothed them over to the side. He cleared his throat again.

"Lenice, it's been five years since my wife died, and I'm tired of being alone. I don't have to have love. I've already had that, but I do need companionship. My time with you has been indescribably enjoyable. You're smart, witty, and beautiful, and I spoil you because I believe you deserve it. I have a proposition for you. How would you like to be spoiled every day for the rest of your life? You wouldn't have to work, and I have enough money to give you anything you need or want, for that matter. We can travel the world and enjoy ourselves to the fullest. Life would be one big vacation. I think you're gorgeous and having someone like you next to me would look good, but most of all, you make an old man feel young again. There's no reason for one of the richest men in Memphis to not have a beautiful woman on his arm."

Lenice was in disbelief. Things like this only happened in fairy tales. Poor little black girls from the hood don't get selected by high-class, insanely rich white men. This had to be a dream. Did a millionaire really ask her to marry him? Was this some new kind of affirmative action program nobody bothered to tell her about? You can marry a rich white man and elevate your entire standard of living.

"You want me to be your trophy wife?" she said. Her words were slightly above a whisper.

"No, I want you to be my partner. I don't want someone who merely possesses good looks. I want someone who has brains and beauty that I can also teach to run my company. I don't have any children, and I'm not getting any younger. I want my company to go to someone who is deserving of it. I think you would do a fine job of running it. You're also young enough to give me one or more sons or daughters I could groom in case something happened to me."

"What are you talking about? You're one of the healthiest men I've ever seen. Are you sick? You don't look sick. Why would I want a husband who's going to die on me?"

Brighton laughed. "I'm healthy, but as an older gentleman, I have to be honest with myself. I have more years behind me than in front of me. I can't live forever, and I want a beautiful woman and family to share all that I've accomplished with."

Brighton reached into his suit coat and pulled out a ring box. He opened it and set it on the table in front of Lenice. He then got down on one knee. Lenice stared at the sparkler. It made Tee's ring, Godzilla, look like a mere pebble. The massive diamond ring resembled an antique, but Brighton had it custom-made for her so it wasn't old by any means. He took it out of the box and slid it on her left hand.

Lenice gasped. "This looks kind of like the ring my Papa gave my Nana. How did you . ." Her words trailed off.

"I saw the portrait of them you have in your living room. I took a picture of it with my phone and sent it to my jeweler. I embellished the details a bit and added larger diamonds. I hope you don't mind. You will be the wife of a rich man. You deserve to have a ring that rivals all others. Lenice, will you marry me?"

Tears spilled from her eyes. How could she possibly spoil this magic moment by saying no? Opportunities like this didn't happen every day, but she had to play her cards right and make this beneficial for everyone.

"I'll marry you, but on one condition. I need a huge favor from you. You have to hire my brother-in-law and give him a beginning salary of at least $80,000 and an excellent benefits package. He is an IT project manager, and I know he could be an asset to your company. He's unemployed, and he and my sister are barely holding on by a thread. They recently received their third foreclosure warning. I would loan them money, but they won't take it from me. I've never seen two more stubborn people. Actually, they have three children that we could probably groom up in the company along with our own. It would truly be a family business."

Brighton placed his hand on his chin as if he were thinking about her request. A smile spread across his face, and he chuckled. His eyes sparkled like the ring he put on her finger. "I knew you were a shrewd businesswoman. Lenice, you don't have to bargain with our marriage. Get me his résumé. I'll have someone in my office set up an interview."

"I don't want you to interview him. You have to hire him," said Lenice sternly.

"I will, but won't he be suspicious if a job he didn't apply for appears from nowhere? If he's as proud as you say he is, he won't appreciate you treating him like he isn't capable of securing his own employment. If he's as good as you say he is, he'll want to think it was his talent that got him the job offer not his sister-in-law's beautiful face and incredible body."

Brighton sidled next to her, placed his hands on her face and gently kissed her on the lips. His lips felt thin and dry. She made a mental note to introduce him to Carmex. Brighton rarely touched her, and she liked it that way. Lenice fought hard not to stiffen during the kiss. When it was over she said. "You have a point. You can't tell him I had anything to do with this. I don't even want to announce our engagement until he has been hired and starts work."

"That's fine by me. I prefer to keep this quiet for a little while anyway. By the time we announce this, I want us to be close to walking down the aisle. I'm sure I will have several friends, business associates, and family members who will try to talk me out of marrying you," said Brighton.

Lenice gave him an inquisitive look. "Why?"

"I have to be honest. My family isn't racist, but we generally don't intermarry. You're African American. My parents are deceased. I don't have any siblings, and I've never been close to my remaining family. They're all hoping I'll stay single and leave them a large piece of my wealth in my will, but, my dear, it shall all go to you. What do I care? I can't do a thing with it if I'm dead. Besides, most of them have been mooching off me for years. As far as I'm concerned, they've already gotten their inheritance."

"Oh, thank you, Brighton. You are such a kind man." Lenice gave him a hug and a sweet kiss on the cheek.

"Is that a yes?" His bright green eyes danced as he asked the question.

"Yes, Brighton, I'll marry you," she cooed.

Brighton picked up a glass of champagne, handed it to Lenice and picked up a glass for himself. "I propose a toast. To Mr. and Mrs. Brighton Stone. May we both live long and prosper."

Lenice clinked her glass with his and gulped down her champagne hard and fast. She thought to herself, *So what I'm not all that attracted to him? I don't love him, and he smells like ointment. He is capable of taking good care of me and my family. I can set us up for life.*

Chapter 60

Welcome to California

Tiffany got off the plane and headed to baggage claim. In most cities she traveled to, her Louis Vuitton luggage was easy to spot, but she was in L.A., the land of Hollywood's rich and famous. She saw at least three pieces of luggage that were similar to hers roll around the carousal before she recognized her own brown and black pieces coming toward her. She was happy that she was smart enough to tie a red ribbon around the handles so she could identify them quickly. Her driver helped her retrieve her luggage and carried them to the car. She and Quincy came here a couple of times on one of their many lovers' getaways, but this time was different. She was single and ready to mingle!

As she sat in the back of the black limousine waiting for her driver to finish loading her luggage in the trunk, Tiffany almost thought she saw a glimpse of Michael getting into a white SUV two cars in front of hers. She had to be hallucinating. As soon as she got to the hotel, she was going to change clothes and go to the pool and lounge. Some rest and drinks with little umbrellas in them would help her get her mind off men, whether it be Michael, William, or that stupid, cheating baby daddy of hers.

Tiffany watched the scenery as her driver traveled down unfamiliar territory. She looked at the tall palm trees that lined the streets and the people dressed in trendy warm-weather attire. She loved L.A. The West Coast had an entirely different vibe than the South, and what she loved most was no flies and no mosquitoes. She was sure they had them somewhere, but she never experienced them on her visits. She could sit out on the patio of any restaurant and eat her food in peace. She fit right in here. When she was out she didn't see anyone out in public in pajamas, house shoes, and head scarves. You needed to look good at all times in LA. You never knew what star you might bump into.

If the cost of living weren't so high she would consider moving to California, but it didn't matter how much money she made; she would feel like she was being robbed every time she paid a bill.

Tiffany's driver pulled up to her hotel. She was staying at the Ritz-Carlton in Beverly Hills. She had a surprise for Sierra and Siendy. Before she left Memphis, she got William to pretend to be a customer and book a massage directly with them. Sierra gladly gave him their rates and scheduled the appointment. She was in direct violation of their employment agreement.

All bookings were supposed to go through MiTee Management. MiTee negotiated the fees, and they accepted the payment. The girls were paid once a week through direct deposit. Tiffany also paid for their apartment and their transportation. She couldn't wait to see their faces when they showed up at her suite to give their boss a massage. They were stealing money from Tiffany, and she wasn't going to stand for it.

Tiffany's driver pulled up in front of the hotel and unloaded her bags. She gave him a tip and walked to the front desk to check in. Her eyes weren't playing tricks on her. Standing in front of her in all of his magnificence was Michael Stokes. She couldn't contain her joy and ran over to him.

"Hello, Michael! Fancy meeting you here," she said. Tiffany's vacation was going to be better than she thought.

Chapter 61

Bottoms-Up

Lenice needed a drink. She pulled into the parking lot of the first place she saw that served liquor. The blaring neon sign above the door read The Peacock. She had never been there before, but she didn't care. Her day was absolutely horrible, and she needed to unwind quickly. She was sure that something alcoholic would do the trick. It wasn't always easy being the boss. Budget cuts made it necessary for her to eliminate some jobs in her department.

Today, she had to tell three people that their services were no longer needed. One poor man started crying right in her office. He pleaded with her not to let him go because his wife was pregnant and they needed the money. Her heart went out to him but her hands were tied. All she could do was hand him some tissues, say she was sorry, and tell him that if he needed a reference she would be happy to give him a glowing review.

The reduction was going to make the department understaffed, which meant she was going to have to start going to homes to evaluate cases herself. She wasn't looking forward to spending her days in apartments questioning single mothers about their income, children, and the whereabouts of their babies' daddies. Yet, she did enjoy being able to help them provide for their families. Some of them needed someone to believe in them and encourage them to better themselves for the sake of their children. Although, her job wasn't the only thing on her mind. She was still very uneasy about accepting Brighton's proposal.

It's seemed so right, but yet so wrong. That only added to her desire for a drink.

She walked in The Peacock and looked around. It was only 3 p.m. and there weren't very many people there. She sat at the bar and asked for a Crown Royal and Coke with light ice and easy on the Coke. Before she received her drink, Sheba walked up to her.

"Hey, Lenice, how are you?" she said.

Today, Sheba was wearing a pair of purple leggings and a T-shirt that barely covered her stomach. Despite the fact that she was skinny, with very small breasts and no hips and virtually no booty, Sheba insisted on wearing form-fitting clothing.

"Hello, Sheba. I'm fine, and yourself?"

"I'm great. I'm happy to be out of the office. I took off today to go see my gynecologist. You know how it goes: breast exam, Pap smear, pee in a cup. We gotta take care of ourselves. It's a shame what happened with Tee and Michael. She still won't come back to the office. I go by the house every day to help her handle business. Michael, on the other hand, isn't that great. Although he lives above the office, I barely see him and when I do he looks a mess. He wore the same clothes three days in a row."

Lenice wasn't sure how much Sheba knew about what was going on between Michael and Tee so she really didn't want to talk about that. "Keep both of them in your prayers. I could use a Pap myself. I haven't had anybody in that area in so long I might enjoy it," joked Lenice.

"Girl, you crazy! There's no enjoying somebody holding your legs wide open with cold clamps, and then taking out a piece of you for testing. I never thought I would see you in here. It's a cool spot, though. Have fun. I was on my way out. You should try the wings. They're great."

After Sheba left, the woman sitting next to Lenice said, "Honey, who is she fooling? That's a man if I ever saw one."

Lenice looked over and saw a seven foot tall drag queen sitting next to her. She was wearing a platinum blond wig, a tank top, and short shorts. Her long legs were shaved and perfectly toned. She also wore hot-pink lipstick with fingernails and toenails painted the same color.

"Excuse me?" said Lenice.

"That queen you were talking to. She hasn't been to no-body's gynecologist to have her reproductive organs checked. The only eggs she has come in a carton. Pap smear? More like turn your head and cough. I been a queen long enough to recognize one. Bartender, bring me what she's having and give me the tab for both."

Lenice wondered if she was trying to come on to her. She was wasting her time. "That's very nice of you but unnecessary," said Lenice. "I can buy my own drink, and the young lady you're speaking of, I'm pretty sure that's a woman. She works for my friend. I'm sure she would have told me if she suspected she was a man."

"Don't worry, doll. I'm not trying to hit on you. You're not my type. At least, not anymore. I like men who look like women. Not women who look like women, but I can tell when someone has had a rough day, and 'the man rode me hard today' is written all over you. If you say that's a broad I won't argue with you. I'll leave you so you can enjoy your drink in peace, Rough House. By the way, nice shoes. I have that same pair in pink. I love Jessica Simpson."

Lenice looked down at her black platform heels. "Thanks," she said.

The drag queen picked up her drink and began to walk away. Her shorts were so small they didn't fully cover her behind and the bottom of her tan cheeks hung out from the bottom. They were riding up uncomfortably. She reached back to pull the material out of her behind in full few of everyone. *Gross*, thought Lenice. *I'm glad I didn't shake her hand.*

She was suddenly overtaken by an emotion she couldn't recognize, but she didn't like it. *Did she call me Rough House?* Her ex-boyfriend used to call her that. He gave her the nickname because she loved to wrestle with him. She never won, but she always came back for another round.

"Scott, is that you?" Lenice called out.

She turned around. "You don't really want to know. Enjoy the drink. The next one's on me, too. You're probably going to need it. You look good, Rough House. Don't you let them work you too hard. By the way, I noticed the ring. Congrats! He must be loaded. I'm glad you found someone who deserves you," she said and winked.

Lenice brought her glass to her mouth and swallowed its entire contents in one gulp. She pushed her stool back from the bar with such force that it teetered with her still on it. She quickly regained her balance and ran toward the door. She almost knocked over a lesbian couple on their way out. Her feet couldn't seem to carry her to her car fast enough. Her chest grew tight, and she couldn't get any air into her lungs.

Lenice had very bad asthma as a child, but it improved as she got older. It was rare for her to have an attack, but occasionally it did happen. Especially, if she was upset. She reached her car, opened the door, and dove in headfirst, almost bumping her head on the passenger-side door. Her chest heaved up and down as she struggled to breathe.

She searched frantically in her glove compartment for the inhaler she kept there for emergencies. Once she found it, she put it up to her mouth and pumped the medicine. She sat still as it began to take effect. A few seconds later, her breathing returned to normal. Her entire body was now shaking. She had to get away from there. Lenice cranked up her car and drove away, never to return to The Peacock, again. She didn't want to believe that the man she used to love was now living as a woman. And it didn't help that he looked better than she did.

Chapter 62

Smile for the Camera

"Hi, Tiffany. What are you doing here?" Michael asked.

"I decided that I needed a little vacation. It's so good to see you." She gave Michael a tight hug.

Michael was in town on business. While in L.A., he had a full schedule with a celebrity golf tournament, a book signing, and a speaking engagement at a private yacht club. He hoped his busy schedule would help keep his mind off Tee, but it would be hard. During their gynecologist video chat, he wanted to jump through the screen and plant kisses all over her. She was the sexiest pregnant woman he'd ever seen. He really didn't feel like being bothered with Tiffany or any other woman that wasn't his wife.

Suddenly, a man with a camera appeared out of nowhere.

"Hey, I'm Bruce with Celebrity Profile. Welcome to California, Mr. Stokes. Is this your new girlfriend? I understand that you and your wife are separated, and she's pregnant. Is this woman the reason that you two broke up?"

Michael turned back toward the counter without saying a word to the man. He demanded that the woman at the front desk issue him a key immediately so that he could escape the paparazzi. The woman apologized and called for security.

The man was not deterred by Michael's silence or the security guards that were quickly approaching him. "Ma'am, what's your name, and how long have you been Mr. Stokes' mistress?"

Tiffany decided to follow Michael's lead and say nothing, but she tried to pose for the camera without making it obvious that she was doing so. If she was going to be on television, she needed to look good. Security came and stood in front of the man and his camera and ordered him to leave. Michael snatched his key from the woman at the front desk and left Tiffany and the cameraman as fast as he could without saying another word.

Chapter 63

Viral

By 7 p.m. that evening, the video of Michael and Tiffany hugging was all over the Internet and the TV. The captions read "Michael Stokes' Mistress Revealed" and "Reason for Split Now Known." About 7:30, Tiffany received a text from Lenice that read, I warned you. Tiffany tried to call Tee several times to explain that it wasn't what it looked like. It was a coincidence that she and Michael ended up at the same hotel. Even when she was trying to do right she was accused of doing wrong. How was she supposed to get William back with lies linking her to another man floating around?

Her identity wasn't known yet, but she knew that it was only a matter of time before the media connected a name with her face. Michael wasn't answering his phone, either. Who knew that a hug could cause such a frenzy?

She hoped the twins didn't see the news and realize that she was in town. They were scheduled to arrive at her hotel at 8:00. At 7:45, there was a knock at her door. Tiffany looked out of the peephole. It was Siendy without Sierra and without security. She was wearing a French maid costume instead of her standard company-issued uniform. The bottom of the skirt barely stopped below her behind. Tiffany had a mandatory dress code and that outfit was not one of their company issued outfits. They were to wear scrubs and similar nurse attire at all times unless otherwise authorized. She opened the door and snatched Siendy into the room. The poor girl looked at her as if she were a ghost.

"T-T-T-Tiffany?" she stuttered.

"Yes, I'm here in the flesh."

"What are you doing here?"

"I'll ask the questions. What are *you* doing here? My office did not book this job, and you are under contract to work exclusively for Tiffany's Magic Touch. And why are you dressed like a costumed call girl? Are you tricking?"

"No. Me and Sierra decided to start wearing costumes to spice things up a bit. The clients really like it," said Siendy.

Tiffany was livid! "I run a professional massage service. There is no spice in what we do. Do you know what could happen to me if people thought I was pimping girls out? And where is your security? You are never supposed to do a private job without security. Do you have any idea what could happen to you two? Two pretty young thangs showing up dressed like this could give a man the wrong idea about why you're there. Suppose the client is the kind of man who can't take no for an answer. Where is your sister?"

"We didn't want to be late for this job so I left her at the last one and came by myself. She is supposed to wrap up and follow," said Siendy.

"You did *what?* If my memory is correct, you two were scheduled to do a fraternity party tonight. You mean to tell me that you left your sister with a bunch of horny college kids? Please tell me that security is there with her," said Tiffany.

"We stopped using security weeks ago. It's so expensive here, and nothing ever happened when they were with us, so it started to feel like it was a waste of money. Don't worry, though. The guys at the frat house were really sweet. I wouldn't have left if I thought she was in danger. Besides, we each carry a gun and mace."

"Of course nothing happened when security was there. Their job is to prevent bad things from happening and protect you if it does. I'm the boss, young lady, and cancelling security was not your call. I require security so that me and your parents can have some peace of mind. I promised them I would take care of you two. You carry a gun, huh? Show it to me. There is no way you have a gun on you in this skimpy outfit!"

Siendy stood there feeling stupid. They were busted, and there was nothing she could do about it. "We're going to get your sister, and then the two of you are in big trouble!" screamed Tiffany.

Tiffany made Siendy drive as fast as she could to the frat party, which was being held at a private residence in Malibu. Their eyes widened as they approached the house and saw flashing blue lights and an ambulance. Siendy bolted out the car door and headed toward the house, where she was halted by one of the officers.

"Excuse me, ma'am. You can't go in there. This is a crime scene," he said.

"My sister was in there. What kind of crime?"

"I'm not at liberty to say, ma'am. What a minute. You look exactly like the woman that was raped."

"RAAAPED!" Siendy screamed. She tried to run toward the house again. The officer caught her around the waist and tried to subdue her. "Where's my sister? You've got to let me see my sister!"

"Calm down, ma'am. Tell me who you are, and I'll see what I can do."

Siendy continued to struggle.

Tiffany approached the officer. "Excuse me, sir. My name is Tiffany Tate, owner of Tiffany's Magic Touch Mobile Massage. This young woman and her sister work for me, and they were scheduled to give massages during a fraternity event being held at this house. Both of these women are my responsibility. Please tell me what happened. If one of them is hurt I need to get to her."

"You're the reason these girls were here?"

"Yes, sir. They work for me."

The officer let go of Siendy, retrieved his handcuffs from his belt, and said, "Ms. Tate, you are under arrest." Before Tiffany could react, her arms were being forced behind her back and handcuffed. Another officer came and did the same thing to Siendy.

"You are under arrest for the unlawful crime of prostitution. We were tipped off that you moved your operation to this area, and we knew it was only a matter of time before we ran into you. Although we never expected that it was because one of your girls would be raped and beaten half to death."

Tiffany couldn't believe what was happening. "Prostitution? This is a big mistake. Officer, you must have me confused with someone else. I run a reputable massage business."

"It's no mistake. You have the right to remain silent. Anything you say can and will be used against you in a court of law."

Dazed, Tiffany half-listened as the officer recited the Miranda rights to her. This couldn't be happening. She was a law-abiding business owner. She felt a throbbing pain around her wrists because the handcuffs were too tight. She looked over at Siendy, who was frantic and begged relentlessly to be allowed to see her twin. She kicked and screamed as the officer tried to detain her.

His fellow officers realized that he was having a hard time and two more came to help. Within 10 seconds, Siendy was face down on the ground. She continued to scream for her sister.

Once the handcuffs were securely on both of them, the officers informed Tiffany and Siendy that Sierra had already been transported to the hospital, but that was not where they were going. They were going to jail. Tiffany prayed silently to God for help. What had these money-hungry little girls gotten her into? She needed to get to a phone. She had to call Michael. He was close by, and he could bail her out quickly.

Tiffany wanted to wring Siendy and Sierra's little necks. She took them under her wing, paid them a generous salary, and relocated them to the City of Angels. She knew that with their looks the locals would love them. It seems that they loved them a little too much. How did she let her dream turn into a nightmare?

Chapter 64

You're Hired

"Lenice! Lenice! I have wonderful news. Herman got a new job, and he's making almost $30,000 more than he was making before. He's going to be a manager. Can you believe it? And there's more. Someone at the Marshall Art Gallery called and asked if I would submit two of my paintings for an upcoming art exhibit featuring Memphis artists. I'm the only new artist in the bunch. It's going to be hard to pick just two. I already have like 12 paintings completed. Not only that but all of the artists will be featured in newspapers and magazines. My God is so good. Also, a gallery downtown called and said they want me to have an art show there. They're not even going to charge me for the space. You have to help me promote it, and I have got to get Tee out of this funk so she can help too."

Lenice sat quietly and listened. Lenora was talking a mile a minute. She let her sister have her moment of bliss, but she was too upset to share it with her. She was at home recuperating from her Scott sighting and her asthma attack. Lenora had no idea that Lenice and Brighton orchestrated all of her good fortune. Brighton told the CEO of his company to hire Herman and let him write his own job description. He also made a phone call to the Marshall Art Gallery and convinced them to include Lenora's art in the upcoming exhibit. He was chair of their board of directors and gave a generous donation each year. There were definitely benefits to being engaged to a millionaire.

Lenice had been engaged for an entire 48 hours and had yet to tell a soul. Partly because she wanted to see if Brighton fulfilled his end of the agreement and partly because she was still trying to convince herself that marrying so that she and her entire family could live happily ever after was, indeed, the right thing to do. Earlier in the day, she prayed for peace in her situation. She read her Bible looking for words of wisdom but none seemed to reveal themselves. She asked for the Lord to give her a sign that she was doing the right thing. The signs she was getting weren't what she was looking for.

The knot in her stomach seemed to twist tighter every time she thought of anything that had to do with a wedding. She popped another Rolaids in her mouth and continued to listen to Lenora talk about her "good fortune."

Chapter 65

Evil Knows No Bounds

Michael checked out of his hotel as soon as the paparazzi left. He was silly to think he could run from his problems. Now, the world would think he was having an affair. He was going home to handle this today! The television news program on the private jet he charted informed him of Tiffany's arrest. It was the lead story on every major news outlet. He couldn't believe the headlines that were swirling across the screen. She was being labeled a pimp, a madam, and Michael Stokes' alleged mistress-turned-girlfriend. They also said that one of her employees was raped. He knew it had to be one of the twins.

He couldn't watch. This was terrible. He knew Tiffany wasn't running a prostitution ring. Who was funneling them all that wrong information? Michael turned off the TV. The flight attendant approached him with the plane's phone and told him he had a call. Who could be calling him on the plane? He didn't even know the number.

"Hello," he said.

"You just don't get it, do you?" said the voice.

"Becca?"

"Maybe, maybe not. I want you lonely and miserable. Do I have to systematically exterminate every woman in your life in order for you to get the picture?"

"What are you talking about?"

"Did you think you could hide a girlfriend from me, Michael? Well, kiss her good-bye. She'll be Big Bertha's girlfriend in cellblock B before this is all over."

Michael felt like he was going to be sick. "*You* did this? Tiffany is *not* my girlfriend. Leave her alone," said Michael.

"I don't believe you. Cameras don't lie, but just in case you are telling the truth, oops, my bad. There's nothing I can do about it now. The damage is already done."

"You arranged for one of the twins to be raped and Tiffany to be blamed for it?"

"Of course not. Siendy and Sierra were sluts. They did this to themselves. I simply arranged for the police to believe that Tiffany was a part of it. It's amazing what an anonymous tip can do. I gotta go now. Buckle up. You never know what could go wrong during these long flights."

Michael sat there holding the phone in his hand long after the caller hung up. First, Tee, and now Tiffany. Becca really wanted him to suffer. Tiffany was in this trouble because of him. If he had never bumped into her in the lobby of the hotel none of this would have happened. Momma Pearl was right. He *was* poison. He called Dr. Foster and told her what happened. She suggested they bring in reinforcements. This case was becoming too big for them to handle alone.

Michael cut the TV back on and the media was still running pictures of him and Tiffany hugging. He wondered if Tee was watching.

Chapter 66

Looks Can Be Deceiving

Tee snatched a lamp off the table and hurled it across the room. It hit the wall and broke into several pieces. The bulb within it shattered to little slivers. She watched the TV as pictures of Tiffany and Michael hugging were shown over and over again, alongside the news of the "Memphis Madame's" arrest. She assumed her estranged husband was in Akron with his family. That's where he usually went when he was upset. Instead, he was in California with that harlot! She couldn't wait to sink her claws into Michael.

This was terrible for Tee's personal life and business. Was Tiffany trying to ruin her? Since her company was being managed by MiTee Management, it was possible that she and Michael could be implicated somehow. Tee wondered if she should fly out to L.A. to do damage control. No. She was finished helping Tiffany. The best thing to do was to distance herself from Tiffany, her company, and her horrible husband.

Tee had been at home feeling sorry for herself and considered taking Lenice's advice and getting back with her husband. She felt bad that he was alone and unhappy in their condo, but he wasn't. The entire time he was cheating with someone she thought was her friend. Just wait until he got back to Memphis. He was going to get a welcome home present he wouldn't soon forget.

Chapter 67

Heartbreak

Lenice logged on her computer. Even though she was engaged she still enjoyed visiting the various dating web sites. She visited James' page on singlecelibates.com. He hadn't spoken to her since their last date. During the date, she told him that she still wasn't ready for a relationship with him. He gave up on her after that. He wasn't going to continue to pursue a woman who didn't want him. He wasn't a millionaire, but he actually did pretty well as an accountant. In addition to his job, he did taxes on the side, and he had a couple of small companies whose books he maintained. His various activities gave him a nice annual salary.

Lenice had to admit that she missed James, but she couldn't give him what he wanted. She wasn't ready to give any man all of her. Her sighting of Scott in full drag made her more cognizant of that than ever. It was a good thing Brighton wasn't asking for love, only companionship.

Lenice typed his name in the search box and was surprised to see his latest post. "I'm getting off the site. I have found the one." Below the post was a picture of him and an attractive Asian woman laughing. Her heart sank. "Good for him," she whispered to herself. She really didn't mean that, but his relationship was even more reason for her to move on with Brighton. He was a nice man. They would have a good future together. She no longer saw a need to wait to marry Brighton. The sooner the better. She was getting pretty good at lying to herself.

Chapter 68

Actions & Consequences

Tiffany was arraigned the next morning. Her bail was set at $50,000. She tried to call Michael several times for help, but he wasn't answering his phone or returning her phone calls. She called her parents who promised to get her out as soon as possible. They informed her that her arrest and the rape of her employee were all over the news.

Two hours later, Tiffany was released. She assumed her parents hired a bail bondsman because when she talked to them that morning they were still in Memphis. There was no way they could have gotten to her in two hours. She was surprised to find William standing in the police station lobby waiting for her. He hugged her and said, "I came as soon as I saw the news. I knew you weren't guilty. There's no way my Tiffany is a pimp."

Tiffany smiled and hugged him again. She loved the way he said "*my Tiffany.*" "You bailed me out?"

"Of course, I did. I would never leave you when you're in need. I realized something these last few days without you. I don't want to be without you. Yes, there are some things about you I don't care for, but there are lots of things about you I love. I came to take you home, Tiffany. We're going to fight this together. If you want to?"

Tiffany let out a sigh of relief. She wasn't alone, and for that she was thankful. William was a good man. He was handsome and successful, but most of all, he loved the Lord. He was the man for her, and she needed to start showing him how much she appreciated him before he found someone who would.

"I would love that," said Tiffany. "I want to go home so I can see my son, but first, can we stop by the hospital to check on Sierra?"

"Of course. Michael has arranged for a private flight to take us home. It won't leave until we're ready."

"Michael? Why didn't he come and bail me out himself? I know he's here," said Tiffany. "I've been calling him, but he won't answer."

"He said he had an emergency and left before he learned of your arrest. He was in Memphis when he called me to explain the picture of you two and arranged for me to come get you. C'mon, let's get to the hospital so we can get you home."

Tiffany didn't appreciate being placed on the back burner when she was in need. She also didn't appreciate being labeled a madam, a mistress, and a pimp. This wasn't the first time she was called a mistress, but this time it wasn't true. The more she tried to clean up her image the worse it got.

While in jail, a police officer was kind enough to fill her in on the twins' activities. Turns out they were offering their clients far more than massages if they were willing to triple their fee. Sierra offered to have sex with one of the men at the frat house, and he accepted. During intercourse, several of his frat brothers came in the room and attempted to join in. She refused. The men were drunk. They got angry and began to punch and kick her before taking what they wanted. The police said as many as four men had their way with her before another young man in the house realized what was happening, intervened, and called the police.

The twins' parents were contacted, but they couldn't catch a flight until that morning. They were scheduled to arrive in about an hour. Tiffany didn't know what to expect when she walked into Sierra's hospital room, but nothing could have prepared her for what she saw. The beautiful young lady's entire face was bruised and swollen. She had several shattered ribs and a collapsed lung, making it necessary for her breathing to be aided by a machine. The hospital gave her a sedative to help her rest and pain killers to numb her aching body. Sierra was oblivious to what was going on around her.

Tiffany and William said a prayer over her and decided to wait until her parents arrived. Leaving her alone seemed like the wrong thing to do. While they waited, Tiffany called the courthouse and arranged to have Siendy's bail paid. She knew the twins' parents were people of meager means and paying that money would probably prove hard for them. Because of those two ladies she was in big trouble, but Tiffany wasn't heartless. Helping them was the Christian thing to do. The twins were going to need each other to get through this.

Chapter 69

Let No Man Put Asunder

Michael pulled the divorce papers out of his back pocket, tore them up into several pieces, and tossed them on the floor of the home he and Tee used to share. He was quite surprised to return to the condo and find a sheriff's deputy there waiting to serve him. After handing him the papers, the deputy had the nerve to ask for an autograph and a picture.

"I will not lose my wife to such foolishness! Baby, I know you're scared. I'm scared too, but I am not about to let this lunatic make me lose the best woman I have ever known." He fell to his knees and placed his head on her stomach and listened to his baby's heartbeat. Tee tried to hold her body rigid and not succumb to images of the erotic emotionally charged night they had the last time he did that.

"Michael, you don't understand. I *have* to do this," she said.

"I need you, Tee. Don't do this. I'm miserable without you. We both stood in front of a church full of people and God said we would stay together until death do us part. I'm still alive, and so are you, and as long as I've got breath in this body, I'm going to fight for you. Don't leave me. Please don't leave me. I promised you I would find Becca, and I will. I just need more time."

Tee finally gave in to what she was feeling and burst into tears. Tears were becoming a familiar sight. She cried several times since she made the phone call to her lawyer and told her to draw up the divorce papers. She didn't think she had any more tears left, but evidently she was wrong.

"Becca said she would leave me and my child alone if we left you. I don't want to live without you either, but I'm tired. There's only so much one woman can take. How long can I allow myself to be punished simply for loving you? Now that I'm pregnant, it isn't just about me anymore. Of course I'm scared. And how can you expect me to believe that I'm the only woman for you when you've been taking trips with Tiffany?"

"I didn't take a trip with Tiffany. We happened to be in the same place at the same time. This is all a trick of the enemy to ruin me. I would never cheat on you, Tee. No other woman compares to you. You are the very definition of a good woman. It doesn't get any better than you. I'm not stupid enough to mess us up. You have to believe me."

"A trick of the enemy? The problem with this entire situation is no one knows *who* the enemy is. Is it really Becca? Or is it some sick imposter? We don't know. I love you, Michael, but this has become too much. Why is this woman doing this to us?"

Michael raised her shirt and began kissing her tenderly on her stomach. "I am so sorry, baby. It's my job as your husband to protect you, and I'm sorry that I haven't been doing a better job of that, but I promise to start doing so today. Pack your bags," he ordered.

"Where am I going?"

"It's better if you don't know, but you'll be safer away from here."

"No. Stop! Take your hands off me!" Tee pulled Michael's hands from her body and stepped back. "I'm not running because we'll have to keep running. This isn't easy for me, but it's what I have to do. You have to respect that.

My decision has been made. I love you, Michael. I truly do, but this is the only way."

"I can't live without you, Tee!" Michael protested. "Please don't do this."

Tee looked at Michael. He looked like he hadn't slept a wink in days. His clothes were wrinkled, his shoes were dirty, and he hadn't shaved his head. He had a small fuzzy layer of hair sprouting up. Michael never let his hair grow. It pained her to see him this way, but she believed in her heart that her decision was the best for everyone. Tears spilled from her eyes as she saw the man she loved at a low point that she helped to cause. He was pleading with her to not give up on him.

A small voice she didn't even recognize escaped her throat and said, "I can't be with you anymore, Michael. This is the only way I'll ever be free of her. I can't live like this. I'll have my attorney send over the divorce papers again. This time, I implore you to have your attorney look them over so we can get together and hash out the details of the divorce. I know you didn't make me sign a prenup, but don't worry, I have no intention of taking you to the cleaners. I just want my life back."

Michael bent his head, and the emotion that was sorrow was quickly replaced by rage. "You want your life back! I *made* you my life! I moved here to be with you! I helped start a business we could both run together! I've been helping out your friends. I could have been happy in Akron with my family helping raise Michelle, but instead, I'm here. You want your life back? What about me? You're being selfish!"

With each sentence, Tee's body flinched as she felt the intensity of his words. Michael couldn't believe what was happening. His life was unraveling before him, and he was powerless to stop it. He took his fist and rammed it into the wall creating a hole. Tee screamed. He was destroying the house she bought with her hard-earned money.

"Get out! How dare you! This is my house! Get out!"

"This is *our* house!" yelled Michael. "We're married. We're one, and you're throwing it all away. The time I really need you to stand and fight with me, you cower and run. I love you, woman. With everything inside me I love you!"

They both stood there with tears in their eyes. Each of their chests heaved up and down as they breathed heavily. They were both frustrated with the situation and tired of being unable to love one another in the manner they were accustomed too.

Tee wanted Michael at home as badly as he wanted to come home. Michael gazed longingly as his wife. Even with running mascara and agony in her face Tee was still beautiful to Michael. He wanted to kiss her, touch her, make love to her, and make her believe that he could protect her. He knew that no matter what he did at that moment she wouldn't believe him. She was a mother who feared for her life and the life of her unborn child. Her love for her child seemed to overrule her love for him. It pained him to admit that to himself, but it was the harsh truth. Michael broke his gaze away from her and looked down at his hand. He had several cuts on his knuckles. Some were from the car window he punched earlier and some were from the wall.

"I'm sorry, Tee. If a divorce is what you really want, I'll give it to you," he said sounding defeated. He then rushed past her and out of the house.

Tee fell to her knees and cried out to God. "I did everything right, Lord. Why? We did everything right. I don't deserve this. Michael doesn't deserve this. Why are you letting this happen to us? Help me! Get this woman out of our lives. You promised not to leave nor forsake me. Why do I feel so all alone?"

Tee heard the front door open. She thought Michael was back. She didn't really want him to leave. She really wanted him to hold her and make her believe everything was going to be all right. She turned around anticipating his handsome face but was greeted with faces she didn't recognize. Two men dressed in all-black were standing in her living room. She stood up and rubbed her stomach. She had to be brave for her baby.

"I think you have the wrong house. Leave!" she yelled trying to sound menacing.

"No, ma'am, we have the right house," said one of the men. His voice contained a lot of bass and a ting of a West Virginia drawl. "We're here to show you what happens when you don't follow orders."

"What? I filed for divorce like she said. I'm doing everything she said." Tee's voiced cracked with panic. She looked around for something to defend herself with but saw nothing within her reach. "Get out of my house!"

The men lunged toward her. Tee fought them with her fists, but she was no match for their brute strength. She grappled with one of them briefly, scratching and clawing with all her might, but he quickly managed to grab both her arms. She kicked and screamed as loud and as hard as she could.

"Michael! Michael! Help! I need you!" Why did she send him away? If he were there the men probably never would have entered her home, or at least he would have been there to kick their butts.

But Michael was nowhere around. The other man placed a black cloth bag over her head, and then grabbed her legs. She continued to try to struggle, but her efforts were in vain. One of the men placed a damp cloth over her nose and mouth. She breathed in its contents through the bag. She was being chloroformed. In a few seconds her body went limp. They transported her to her truck and placed her in the backseat. One of the men got behind the wheel and slowly backed out of the garage into the driveway and into the street. The other walked out of the house to the car they came in and drove away too.

Chapter 70

Lovesick

Lenice was popping Rolaids like candy. Her stomach hurt at all times of the day and night, and she wished it would stop. Her decision to marry Brighton was a financial decision and a good one. He upheld his end of the bargain, and it was time for her to uphold hers. She decided to have a private ceremony at the courthouse so no one could talk her out of it.

By the time everyone heard about it, it would be old news in the society section of the local papers. She would have to tell her sister, though. There was no way she could get married without Lenora. She was debating whether she would tell her everything on the phone or if she would trick her into coming to the courthouse and tell her everything once she arrived. She thought about inviting Tee, but if she came Lenice was sure that Tee and Lenora would double-team her and talk her out of getting married.

Inviting Tiffany was out of the question. She had no desire to speak or see that home wrecker. As far as she was concerned, "The Memphis Madame" was getting exactly what she deserved. Lenice was getting married tomorrow no matter what, and Lenora would be her only invited guest.

It wasn't how she envisioned her wedding, but that was the way it would have to be. She could handle her sister.

Chapter 71

Kidnapped?

"Sleeping beauty has awakened," said Teresa. She hugged her friend and helped her sit up comfortably in her seat.

Tee felt groggy, and her mouth felt like cotton. Thoughts of her encounter with the two men in her home came flooding back to her. "Where am I?" she asked.

Teresa handed her a bottle of water. "All I can tell you is on a plane. I agreed to come along to take care of you and one of the stipulations of my doing so was that I wouldn't ask any questions about my or your whereabouts."

"You helped to have me kidnapped? Why? You're a cop. Shouldn't you be helping to keep the streets of Memphis safe or be at home with your husband and your son? Is this about money? Tell Michael how much you want, and I'm sure he'll pay it so I can go home. Teresa, I thought you were my friend."

Teresa laughed. "Girl, you must have bumped your head. I'm hurt you would even think such a thing. Michael is the one doing this, not me."

"Michael? Why?"

"He believes that getting you out of Memphis is the only way to keep you safe. He asked you to come nicely, and when you refused, he had no choice but to have you abducted. Calm yourself. You're safe. No one here is going to hurt you.

"I didn't tell you this, Tee, but I started drinking again. I made some serious mistakes on the job, and my captain told me not to come back until I've kicked the habit. I'm doing much better, but I'm not ready to go back yet. Taking care of you is a perfect distraction from the liquor and the shambles I'm making of my career. My son is grown and doesn't need his mother like he used to. As for Zach, he told me to go. He knows how much I love you. If anything ever happened to you and I didn't do everything within my power to prevent it, I wouldn't forgive myself. All I know is we're on a plane headed somewhere to keep you safe. When we get there we will have very little access to a phone, computer, or any other form of communication."

"That seems a little extreme," said Tee.

"Extreme times call for extreme measures. Did you really think Michael was going to allow anyone to rip his family apart? I've never seen a man love a woman with such intensity as Michael loves you. I actually think this was pretty smart. If he doesn't have to worry about you he can work on finding whoever is doing this. Whoever is stalking you is watching your every move, and it's highly likely that they have your house and your phones bugged. If we cut off their ability to monitor your every move, we cut off their ability to intimidate you."

Tee took a long drink of the water. Her head was spinning, and she couldn't believe what she was hearing. She was too weak to get angry. Her muscles felt sore. She assumed it was from the struggle in her home.

"Where's Michael?"

"Now, that I do know. He is still in Memphis working to flush whoever is bothering you two out. He's hoping he can get her to face him once she realizes that her ability to hurt him through you is gone."

Tee looked out the window. She saw blue skies filled with fluffy white clouds. Below them were large masses of land that she didn't recognize and large bodies of water. "Will I get to even talk to my husband?"

"Yes. And we're not alone. Michael got a group of mercenaries for hire to help him find whoever is terrorizing you two. They kind of remind me of the A-Team. I met them a few years ago when I was working on a kidnapping case. The kid's parents didn't like the way the police were handling the situation so they called in these guys. Their son was home by dinnertime. I don't know how they did it, but we were grateful for their assistance."

Tee looked around the cabin of the plane and saw three men and a woman dressed in all-black. She recognized two of them as the men who kidnapped her. They were each wearing a gun and a bulletproof vest. Everything seemed so surreal. She was grateful that Teresa was there. She probably would have freaked out if she wasn't.

"Michael made a video for you. It's on this phone. The phone has no service so you can't make a call, but you can take pictures, watch videos, and play games. Here."

Teresa handed Tee a smart phone. The video was paused on the smiling face of her husband. She recognized the background. Michael was in the living room of their home, and he was wearing the same clothes he had on when she last saw him. He must have recorded the video after she was kidnapped. She was going to give him a big piece of her mind when she saw him, but for now, she wanted to sit in the chair and wait for the grogginess to completely wear off. She touched the play button. Michael's voice came through loud and strong.

"Hey, Beautiful. I'm sorry I had to do this, but I knew if I told you what I was planning you would try to argue with me and there was no time for that. I had to get you somewhere safe. Don't worry about me or your family. I'll be fine, and I have 24-hour surveillance on my family and yours. I don't take Becca's threats lightly. Especially after she locked you in that elevator. I'm not bringing you home until this is over. So, I need you to sit tight. You're going someplace exotic with a beach and a staff that's going to pamper you and Teresa until you can't take it anymore. Don't worry about our clients. Sheba is handling them. You may have to postpone the I'm A Good Woman Empowerment Conference, though. I love you. If anything happens to me I need you to know that. Well, I'm gonna go now. I got a killer to catch and with the help of those guys on the plane, I'm sure I will."

"Wait until I see him," Tee said.

"Don't be too hard on him. He only wants to spare you more pain while he ends this. He's a good man, Tee. He's a good, good man," said Teresa.

Tee nodded her head in agreement. This is was what she and Michael had come to. He had to send her away to protect her. Teresa came and sat beside her. Tee placed her head on her friend's shoulder and closed her eyes. She said a prayer that God would protect her husband and their families and bring this horrible ordeal to an end soon.

She suddenly opened her eyes and yelled, "You guys better be good. I want my husband back with me as soon as possible. You find that woman and get her out of our lives for good. This makes no sense. Here I am in the middle of nowhere, hungry, pregnant, and horny, and I can't do a thing about it."

The woman with the team spoke. "We can't do anything about you being pregnant or wanting a little loving, but we can feed you." She opened a small refrigerator, pulled out a sandwich and a soda, and handed them to Tee. "Here you go, ma'am. My name is Jade." She pointed to her teammates. "That's Maverick, Cult, and Bass. I promise you that my team and I will do everything we can to have you and your husband back on the same continent as soon as possible. I'm a huge football fan, and I have always admired your husband. It's an honor and a privilege to help one of the best players that ever lived."

Tee looked at each of them. She recognized Maverick and Bass from her home. Maverick was an older gentleman with silver steaks of hair on each side of his head. Bass was short and stocky with a huge scar on the side of his face that ran from his temple to his chin. He also looked mean, as if he could beat the crap out of anyone. Cult, on the hand, was extremely attractive. He had friendly eyes and a lean, muscular build. He looked almost as good as Michael. He winked at Tee and Teresa.

"Why do they call you Cult?" asked Tee.

Jade answered. "Because he is capable of getting almost any woman to do anything he wants. It's almost as if they are part of a cult once they get with him. Or *think* they've gotten with him."

"No one asked you, Jade," he interjected. My mother named me Mercutio." His accent was thick and sexy, but Tee couldn't quite place it.

"Mercutio?" she asked. That was an odd name for a black man.

"William Shakespeare was one of her favorite authors. She loved *Romeo and Juliet*," he explained.

"Where are you from?" asked Teresa.

"Barbados. The home of Rihanna."

"Who?" said Teresa.

"You know, the lovely woman who sings me and my umberella-ella-ella-ella-eh-eh-eh." Everyone laughed at his attempt to sing.

"I know who she is. I was just messing with you. Keep your day job, Cult. Your singing is horrible," said Teresa.

"Are all of you going to babysit me when we get to where I'm not supposed to know I'm going?" asked Tee.

"No, that's Teresa's job," said Maverick. "We've got to get back to your husband and help him catch a killer, like he said."

Chapter 72

I Object

Lenice and Lenora stared at each other in silence. They were in the office of the judge Brighton found to marry them. The judge was about to begin the ceremony. He told Brighton and Lenice to stand, and he took his position in front of them.

Lenora's head was swimming with reasons she concocted to help her justify why her sister was getting married in a fly-by-night ceremony to some old man she barely knew. She tried to talk her out of it when she first arrived, but Lenice wouldn't listen. Lenice was determined to marry Brighton today, but she had to give it one last try.

"Excuse me," Lenora said. "I know this probably isn't the right time, but I have to go to the bathroom. Lenice, will you accompany me?"

Chapter 73

Surprise!

Michael received word that Tee was okay and was en route to the house he rented for her on a private island in the Caribbean. He hated that he needed to resort to having his wife kidnapped, but after she refused to come with him peacefully, she left him no choice. He was in his condo waiting for his own personal A-Team to return to him so they could get busy working on their plan of action.

He heard the doorbell ring. He wasn't expecting any visitors. He knew Sheba was downstairs working, but he left strict orders not to be disturbed. He went downstairs and looked through the peephole.

"Junior, you open this door right now!" yelled his father.

Michael opened the door. "Dad, Maxwell, what are you doing here?"

"Don't you ever put a tail on me again as long as you live. What gives you the right to have somebody watching me and my family without me knowing? Did you forget I'm ex-military? I spotted that turkey after the first day. I snuck up behind him with my Glock and gave him 30 seconds to tell me why he was outside my house. He sang like a canary. I tried to take your mother's advice and wait for you to contact me, but I couldn't. I know when my children are in trouble. First your wife is throwing up on famous TV people, then both of you are on TV asking the world to help you find a stalker, then your wife leaves you, and now you're all over TV with some big booty woman wearing a lot of makeup they say is running a prostitution ring. Tell me something, how do you retire and end up on TV as much as you were when you were still playing ball? You should have your own reality show. Your momma, Tomeka, and Michelle say hello. Michelle threw a fit when I told her we were coming to see you, but she couldn't go. Be sure to give her a call."

"Excuse our father's horrible sense of humor," said Maxwell. "I know my brother, and you wouldn't be caught dead with a thick chick like that Tiffany. I mean, that's a big ole ghetto booty. It would take you a week to rub it all. Everyone knows you're married. At least for now, and you're so whipped you would never cheat on Tee. So, I came to take Ms. Ghetto Booty off your hands."

Max and his father laughed. "Seriously, it's obvious you don't have it all figured out so me and Maxwell came down here to help," said his father.

Max wasn't finished giving his brother a hard time. "We got to get your wife back first, though. When's the last time you shaved or took a shower? You look like hell. Is this what a broken heart looks like?"

"Shut up, Maxwell!" said Michael, Sr. "Look, son, I know things between the three of us haven't been the best, but I'm your father. I know something's wrong, and Maxwell and I came to see what we could do to help. I need to know who has my boy so spooked that he's got to have armed security watching his family. Neither me nor your momma will sleep well until we know what's going on."

"Yeah, Mike. We got our differences, but if anybody is messing with you, they got to deal with all of us. I may be little, but I don't play when it comes to my blood," said Maxwell.

Michael laughed and gave them both a hug. "Man, I'm glad to see you, but I need you to go check into a hotel because I think this place may be bugged. Call me when you're all checked in, and I'll come over and explain everything."

"Okay, son. We can do that. But I gotta know before I leave. You're not really tappin' that big booty girl I saw on TV, are you?"

Michael shook his head. "Tappin' that? Who have you been talking to? No, Pop. Tiffany is a friend and a former client. All I did was give her a hug, and the paparazzi happen to catch that on camera."

Michael, Sr. laughed. "I knew that was too much woman for you to handle. That back shole was fat."

Chapter 74

Fired

"MiTee Management, how may I help you?" said Sheba.

"Hello, Sheba, I need to speak with Tee or Michael," said Tiffany.

"Sorry, Ms. Tate, but neither is available. They have both taken a leave of absence."

"Then who is running the business?"

"I am," Sheba said proudly.

"Quit playing. This is no way to run a business. Why wasn't I informed of the change? I tried to call Michael and Tee on their cell phones, but they are both going straight to voice mail with instructions to call the office."

"I would have called you, but you were incarcerated at the time the decision was made, and I was unable to reach you. How did you like being in the slammer?" Sheba snickered.

"Oh, you find that funny? Tell Michael and Tee somebody better call me because I have a business to run. What does their leave of absence have to do with me?"

"Ms. Tiffany, I am sorry to inform you that you are no longer a client of MiTee Management. MiTee Management cannot be involved with a business that has been pinpointed by authorities for shady business practices. Please understand that we in no way believe that you are running a prostitution ring, but we are a new company, and we cannot be placed under such scrutiny. It's bad for business. I put your final check in the mail yesterday. You should receive it shortly."

"You're the secretary! You have no right to talk to me like this. Put Michael or Tee on the phone now!" screamed Tiffany.

"Correction, I have been promoted to the position of account executive and acting assistant manager. I am the only one you can speak to at this time, but I assure you that everything I told you came directly from the owners of this company," said Sheba without an ounce of compassion in her voice.

"I want a list of all clients that have been booked on my behalf since I signed my contract!" yelled Tiffany.

"Sorry, no can do. Those clients were secured by MiTee Management, and we no longer represent you or Tiffany's Magic Touch. All information regarding past clients is property of this company. Therefore, any future appointments we booked for you have been canceled. However, when canceling the appointments we did give you the courtesy of providing each client with your cell phone number in the event that they would like to schedule an appointment with you personally. However, in light of your current negative news coverage, I doubt they will."

Tiffany wanted to reach through the phone and rip out her trachea. How dare the help talk to her like that! "Why would they do this to me? I thought they were my friends!" screamed Tiffany.

"I'm sure it's just business, Ms. Tate. Now, good-bye. I need to work on campaigns for the people we still represent." Sheba hung up the phone.

Tiffany couldn't believe it. She lost her best friend and manager over a man she wasn't sleeping with. She didn't need them. She could run her business without them. All she needed to do was call up her regular clients and offer them a discount for continuing to do business with her. To hell with MiTee Management and its owners. She was mightier than both of them combined. Tiffany picked up the phone to begin making calls. Before she could dial a number, she heard her front doorbell ring. She hung up the phone and went to see who it was. Standing on her porch was a woman and a deputy sheriff.

"Are you Ms. Tiffany Tate?" said the woman.

"Yes, I am. How can I help you, and this officer?"

I'm Ms. Gwendolyn McKinney with the Department of Human Services and this is Officer Todd Mabon. The deputy handed her a document. "By court order we have been instructed to come get your son Quincy Tate and place him in the temporary custody of his father, Quincy Matthews, until the court of law convenes to determine if you will retain your parental rights." He handed her the official legal document.

"You can't be serious! I haven't done anything. Don't take my child. He's all I have. If Quincy thinks he can take my child he's got another think coming. I'm calling my lawyer!" screamed Tiffany.

"I'm sorry but your recent arrest and pending charges have put your ability to adequately care for your son into question. However, there are steps you can take to petition the court to give him back. You will definitely have your day in court," said Ms. McKinney. "I'd be happy to tell you more about it."

"Ms. Tate, please go in the house and pack some things for your son and get him ready to leave. I am really sorry to do this, but he has to come with us," said the Deputy Mabon.

Tiffany shut the door and turned her face to the wall. Her world was crumbling around her. What could she have possibly done to deserve this?

Chapter 75

Wedding Bells Are Ringing

"Lenice, you know what you're doing isn't right. What's going on with you? I'm worried about you. You can tell me. I'm your sister," said Lenora.

Lenice looked in the bathroom mirror. "Nothing is going on with me. I decided to have an impromptu wedding, that's all. Brighton and I have been engaged for a few days now, but I didn't tell anyone because I didn't want you or anyone else to talk me out of it. I knew you wouldn't understand. I don't see a reason to delay if two people want to be together. I'm so glad you came."

"A few days? Who hides that they are getting married from their friends and family? I know you. You want a traditional wedding not some wham-bam-you-may-kiss-the-bride junk like this. You look beautiful, but don't you think everyone who loves you deserves to share in this moment?"

Lenora stared at her sister's reflection in the mirror. "This isn't you, and I know what this is about. I've kept my mouth shut for far too long hoping you would work this out on your own, but I see you won't. This is because Scott left you for another man, isn't it? At first you were scared of rejection so you shut everybody out. Well, it seems you got over that, but then you went on this dating frenzy to prove to yourself that you are still hot. I mean, you have to be because all these men want you, right? You've been out with more men in these past few months than most women go out with during their entire lives. I didn't bother you about it because you weren't sleeping with them, so I didn't see much harm in it. I see I was wrong, though. I should have killed that nonsense months ago because you think what you're doing now is an upgrade. Not only do you want to be the woman every woman envies and that can have any man she wants, but you want to have the man most men envy. The rich man who can buy anything he wants and can have any woman he wants. You're going to show Scott and the rest of the world that you can pull a multimillionaire! Does that sound about right?"

"I don't have anything to prove to anybody. I want to marry this man," lied Lenice.

"That's crap, and you know it, Twin. You're letting a good man slip through your fingers. No, James isn't a millionaire or the finest man you've ever seen, but he cares for you deeply and he'll treat you the way you deserve. Stop this. It's not too late for us both to walk out of here right now. Look me in my face and tell me you love Brighton and you can't wait to spend your life with him."

Lenice continued to stare in the mirror and began to toy with her hair. Lenora grabbed her by the shoulders and turned her sister's body toward her. "I'm over here."

"I see you. Let me go. Lenora, you don't understand what it's like to have a man leave you for another man. It's devastating. Do you know how hurt and embarrassed I was? I heard people whispering. 'Poor Lenice,' they said. They pitied me like I had some life-threatening illness. I had ugly, grossly overweight, unemployed chicks with five kids by five different men thinking they had it better than me because at least none of their boyfriends left them for somebody with no breasts and a penis."

Lenora understood, but Lenice was handling her pain the wrong way. "You never could lie to me. Forget what those fools think. They don't know you. Who are they to pity you? You had it going on before Scott, and you have it going on now. Scott damaged your self-esteem, and he broke your heart. Don't let him destroy your spirit. Keep fighting for love. It's out there. I know exactly where it is."

"He's got a girlfriend," said Lenice.

"That Chinese chick? I saw her when he brought her to evening service last week. That will never last. You know James doesn't like Chinese food. She's a rebound. I'll bet you my paycheck if you say the word, James will break up with her for you. That man wants you, but you keep pushing him away. Let's go. We've got a wedding to call off." Lenora grabbed her sister by the hand and pulled her toward the door.

Lenice snatched her hand away. "I won't ruin James' life. I'm a mess. He deserves better. Besides, I have to marry Brighton. I gave him my word."

"Don't you think James sees your flaws? He loves you in spite of them. That is what real unconditional love does. It takes you as you are and commits to stand by you as you make improvements. James is more than capable of loving you while you heal. You deserve that.

"Tell Brighton you made a mistake. It happens all the time." She turned on a faucet and water came rushing out. Lenora cupped her hands and splashed some of it on Lenice. "Oops, see, I made one. Now you've got water all on the front of your pretty dress. You can't get married like that. Let's go find you some dry clothes to put on."

"Stop it, Lenora! This is Vera Wang!" She walked over to the paper towel dispenser and pulled out some towels to blot her dress with. "I can't walk out on Brighton. I know what that feels like. I can't do that to him. Did you see how happy he is? That man wants me. Out of all the women in the world, he wants me."

"And? You don't owe him your loyalty. You and Scott had a history. You barely know this man. Is it the ring? Then give it back. You want to be some man's trophy? Really, Lenice? Really?"

"I saw him."

"Saw who?"

"I saw Scott. He's the most beautiful woman I've ever seen. After I realized it was him, I ran to my car and had an asthma attack. All I could think of is I made love to him. He was probably thinking of another man every time. Why wasn't I enough, Lenice? What did our lawn man have that I didn't?"

"It wasn't you. Scott liked men all along, and he was trying to hide it by dating you. The best way for him to mask his homosexuality was by dating a beautiful woman. No one was going to question his masculinity when he was dating the baddest chick on the block. That wasn't your fault. You didn't do anything wrong, but you're doing something wrong now. Don't you see you're doing the same thing to Brighton? You're pretending to want him when you really don't. You can't force love, Twin. Don't do this," Lenora pleaded.

"You don't understand. We have a deal. Brighton is not jaded. He knows I don't love him, but he wants a lovely woman to share his wealth with. Why can't it be me? I tried true love. It failed me. This way I win. We all win. Do you know how much good I can do for this city, this country, or maybe even the world with his money and connections? I can help our family. I can even make my dreams come true and create a job skills center so women who are on the system can get off. I thought about this. It's a good thing. I need you to support me."

"No! I will not support a marriage where there is no love. I have a very bad feeling about this, Lenice. Something in my spirit is telling me that if you do this there are going to be some disastrous consequences. If you go out there and marry that man, I'm leaving," said Lenora.

Lenice laughed. "No, you won't. I'm your sister, your best friend. You're not going to miss my wedding. You're my matron of honor. And I don't appreciate you trying to jinx my wedding with that gloom and doom forecast you just gave. It won't work. I'm getting married."

Lenora looked at her in defiance. "I won't be there. I won't stand there and watch you make this mistake. My presence will say it's okay, and it's not. Heed my words, Twin. God is not pleased."

They were both confident enough in their bond to one another to call each other's bluff.

"Now, you listen, Lenora. I need you, and you will NOT turn your back on me. Let's go!" said Lenice.

"You won't get married without me. I'm doing this for your own good," said Lenora.

Lenice and Lenora walked out of the restroom. Lenice headed back toward the judge's chambers where Brighton was waiting for her. She heard Lenora's feet behind her and smiled. She turned around to let her know how much she appreciated her support, but her smile quickly faded. Lenora was headed in the opposite direction toward the elevators.

She called out her name. Lenora turned around and blew her a kiss.

"I love you, but I can't support this," she said. She then turned back around and continued to walk away from her sister.

Lenice stood in the middle of the hallway in a long, white, strapless wedding gown. It was beautifully crafted with dark pink embroidery around the edges. She watched Lenora until she disappeared from view. Her stomach was still hurting, and it was only compounded by the pain of knowing she had to do this without her only immediate family member. Lenice wanted to cry, but she didn't. She wasn't going to ruin this day for Brighton. He was so happy. Her sister didn't understand that she was doing this for her too. "You're doing the right thing," she said to herself. She looked down at the wet spot on her dress. She was about to marry the richest man in Memphis with what looked like a pee spot on the front of her dress. Oh well . . .

Lenice wore a smile during the entire ceremony, but she wasn't focused on Brighton or the judge. She thought about Scott and how he left her for a man. Now that he was living as a woman, Lenice felt like her womanhood was under attack. She had to prove to herself that she was still desirable and could get any man she wanted. Who could deny that she was all woman with one of Memphis's most eligible bachelors on her arm?

No one would call her "poor Lenice" or laugh at her after this. She was going to be filthy rich and have the last laugh.

Chapter 76

A Mother's Love

"Michael, where is my daughter? Yesterday, I went to take Chesnutt to the vet and when I got back to the house she was gone. The house looked like it was ransacked in two places. The living room was a mess and someone went through Tee's drawers. Her toiletries are gone and so is one of her suitcases," said Momma Pearl.

Michael stepped outside his condo and led Momma Pearl to the farthest corner of the parking lot. He lowered his voice until it was barely above a whisper. "Calm down, Momma Pearl. Tee is fine. I sent her on a little vacation. She left in a hurry. That's why the house looks like that. I'll come over and clean it up later," he said nonchalantly.

"Why are you whispering? I can clean up the mess, but it's unlike my baby to leave without telling me, and she left her cell phone. Your phone isn't working either. I called it multiple times with no answer. That's why I came over here."

"Momma Pearl, I'll be honest with you. I think our home and our phones are bugged, and that's why she left it and why neither one of us is answering our phones."

"When will she be home?"

"As soon as I figure out who's stalking us."

"Maybe you should talk to M—" Just as she was about to say his name, Momma Pearl remembered that she promised Mac she would never tell what he knew.

"Talk to who?" asked Michael.

"No one."

"Momma Pearl, if you know something please tell me. The faster I can resolve this, the faster I can bring Tee home."

"You're really not going to tell me where my daughter is?"

"No. She's safer that way. Now, tell me what you know."

"Son, you must promise not to hurt him. He loves Tee as much as you do, and sometimes when we love someone we do crazy things, but he's come to his senses now."

"Who?" demanded Michael.

"Don't raise your voice at me, young man. It's disrespectful, but the who is MacKenzie. A woman contacted him and told him that she would help him get Tee back if he gave her money. He said he initially agreed, but he stopped because whoever she was kept asking for more and more money and because he realized how happy Tee is with you."

"I'll kill him! The door is open. Make yourself at home, Momma Pearl. I suddenly have an urge to talk to a lawyer," said Michael.

Mac's office was three blocks away from the office of MiTee Management. Michael took off running as if his life depended on it and got there in no time at all. He leapt up the three flights of stairs leading to Mac's suite and burst through the door.

Patrice was at the desk opening the mail. "Where is he?" barked Michael.

"Hey, Mr. Stokes. It's me, Patrice. Tee's mentee. I met you a few months ago when Tee had me over for dinner. How are you, and where's who?"

Michael wasn't in the mood for conversation, but he had a soft spot in his heart for all the girls Tee mentored.

Tee gave him the history of each of them. Most of them were being raised by single mothers or other family members with little or no contact with their fathers. He wondered why she was working for a scumbag like Mac.

"I guess you're wondering why I'm here," said Patrice. "This is my new job. I come here three days a week after cheerleading practice and help Mr. Patton. He's teaching me so much. I think I want to be a lawyer when I grown up."

"That's nice. Is Mr. Patton here?"

"Yes, he is, but he's with a very important client. I can tell him—"

Michael didn't wait for her to finish. He turned the handle to the door, entered, and closed the door behind him.

Mac was leaning against the desk kissing Amy and had no idea someone else was in the room. She stopped by during her break to bring him a burger, fries, and some kisses for dessert. Mac had both hands on her behind, and they were kissing as if they hadn't been together in months. Michael snatched Mac from her embrace and slammed him against the wall.

"You want my wife so bad you would hire someone to get rid of me?" He slapped Mac across the cheek. He screamed like a girl.

"No, I mean yes, but I stopped," Mac stammered. "This wonderful young lady with the horrified face over there, that's my girlfriend, Amy. Say hi, baby."

Amy waved hesitantly.

"Baby, would you please excuse us. Michael and I have some business to discuss," said Mac.

"Do you want me to call the police?" she asked.

"No, that won't be necessary. I'm sure we can resolve this as men, right, Michael?"

"Yeah, sure," said Michael through clenched teeth.

Amy walked out of the room. Michael threw Mac into one of two chairs on the opposite side of his desk.

"Talk before I punch you in the face."

Mac straightened his tie and cleared his throat. "I owe you a huge apology. I was wrong. Once you married Tee I should have moved on. I tried, but I couldn't. You know what an extraordinary woman she is. About four months ago a woman contacted me and told me she would help me get Tee back if I gave her some money. I didn't ask any questions. I merely gave it to her, but she kept coming back asking for more. I told her I couldn't help her anymore, and that's when she set me up. She has pictures of me in a compromising position with an underage girl. I didn't do anything with her, I swear. She found a girl who looks like a grown woman to ask me out on a date, and she took some pictures when I was passed out drunk. That woman is threatening to release the pictures if I don't keep giving her money."

"You're still giving this lunatic money?" Michael growled.

"I haven't lately but she is threatening to release those pictures if I don't give her something soon. Do you know what pictures like that would do to my reputation, my career, my practice? Everything I've built would be gone in an instant. Not to mention I could lose that wonderful specimen of womanhood you scared the crap out of."

"What does she look like?"

"I don't know. I've never seen her."

He grabbed Mac by the lapels of his shirt and held him in the air. His feet dangled beneath him. "Don't lie to me! I ought to kill you. Then, your practice would no longer be a concern."

"I swear to you. I'm telling the truth. I've never seen her. We only communicate by phone and an occasional e-mail."

Momma Pearl came running in with Michael's father and brother. They returned to the condo after Michael took too long to come to their hotel. Momma Pearl was there when they arrived, and she brought them to Mac's office. She was afraid Michael was going to hurt him.

"Son, don't do this!" she screamed.

"Junior, let him go! Beating him up won't resolve this issue," said Michael, Sr.

Michael dropped Mac back in the chair. "It's cool, Pop. I tell you what, fool. I won't beat you to a pulp if you help me catch this person."

"Gladly. She's bleeding me dry. She asked me for $10,000 last night."

"Where's the drop-off?"

"I've been transferring the money into an account. I tried to have the account traced, but it seems to be registered to a company that I can't find any record of anywhere."

"Tell her the next drop must be in person because you are tired of giving your money to someone you've never seen. If she doesn't agree, you better come up with something creative to make her agree. Someone will contact you later with the place and time for the exchange. Do this and I'll let you live. Mess this up and I'll make sure the next picture taken of you will be one of you lying in your casket. Understand? And stay away from my wife!"

"I haven't been near your wife, except for that one time I came by the house, but nothing happened, I swear."

"You've been to my house?" Michael slapped him again only harder.

Mac screamed like a girl a second time. "Don't hit me again, please! I bruise easily. I won't go near her again. I promise!"

"You better be glad I'm saved, punk!" He stomped out of Mac's office. Michael, Sr. and Maxwell followed.

Momma Pearl was close behind but stopped for a minute and directed her attention to Mac. "I'm so sorry, MacKenzie. I had to tell him. Tee is my baby. Put some ice on that so it doesn't swell. Some makeup will help cover the bruising."

As they walked out of the building, Michael caught a glimpse of Maverick and Bass. Maverick gave him a nod. That meant that they heard everything, and they would handle it. Michael suspected the two of them were going to pay MacKenzie a visit soon and tell him exactly how the drop was going to go down.

Chapter 77

Mrs. Tolliver

"Tiffany, what in the world is going on? Larry and I are in London. I looked at my tablet to get the local news, and I almost spit out my dentures when I saw the headlines with your name in it. 'Memphis Madame'? My word, child, what have you gotten yourself into?" asked Mrs. Tolliver.

Tiffany hadn't seen her client and confidante since her husband's retirement party. After 30 years of service, he retired from juvenile court and took his wife on a second honeymoon. They were expected to be gone for at least three months.

"Mrs. Tolliver, everything that could go wrong is going wrong," wailed Tiffany. "My employees started selling more than massages, and I am being implicated in their prostitution. Quincy is using this opportunity to try to take my son from me. It seems his wife now loves the idea of having a son, but not one that comes along with a former mistress. They want to take him from me and raise him themselves. This scandal was exactly what they needed to try to label me an unfit mother. Of course my business is suffering. My management company dropped me, and several of my regular clients either don't want to do business with me or they want to know why I didn't extend sex services to them. I showed up for a massage yesterday, and the man greeted me at the door naked. He said he was willing to pay extra for 'full service'.

"The only thing that seems to be going right is my relationship. My lawyer says I should see if he'll marry me because a spouse who can provide a more stable home for my son would look good in court. I can't ask a man to marry me in order to keep my son!"

"Slow down, Tiffany, take a deep breath," said Mrs. Tolliver. "These are growing pains, or better yet, the storms that come before the sunshine. When Satan attacks you like this it's usually because God has a major blessing coming your way. Don't get discouraged. Hold on to your faith and keep fighting. Larry and I are willing to do anything we can to help you, but you have to be completely honest with me. Did you have any knowledge that your girls were selling sex?"

"No, ma'am. I run a clean business."

"I believe you. Next question, are you sleeping with Tina Stokes's husband?"

"No, ma'am. She and Michael are my friends and business partners, or at least they used to be. The media blew that hug completely out of proportion. Besides, they're separated."

"So, you *wanted* to," said the old woman knowingly.

"I didn't say that."

"Tiffany, I've raised three children. I know when I'm not being told the whole truth. If you want my help I need to know exactly what I'm getting into."

"Mrs. Tolliver, I never slept with Michael. I admit I am attracted to him. I mean, look at him. He's handsome, successful, charming, and rich. He's everything I ever wanted in a man, but he's taken, and he's head over heels in love with his wife. If I were to try to date him, I wouldn't stand a chance."

"Tiffany, you're doing what's called coveting. You're badly wanting something that belongs to someone else and is rightfully theirs. That's a sin. What about this boyfriend you have?"

"I told you about William before you left. He's the nice young man I bought my car from. He's also an associate pastor at his church. I can't complain about him. He was my shoulder to lean on when I finally decided to get rid of Quincy, and he's been defending me throughout this whole prostitution thing. Like I said, he's nice. I like him a lot, but there seems to be something missing. He's not like . . ." Tiffany's voice trailed off.

"Like Michael?" finished Mrs. Tolliver. "You seem to have a knack for sabotaging yourself by wanting men you can't have. I'm proud that you haven't crossed over into inappropriate territory with Michael, but it sounds like if given the opportunity you would. It also sounds to me that this William fellow has great potential."

"Oh yes. He's smart. He's funny. He's got an amazing body, not that I've seen it because we're not sleeping together, and he's an anointed preacher. Every time he gets in the pulpit somebody gets the Holy Ghost and gets saved."

"Do you like him?"

"Yes, Mrs. Tolliver, I do. I really do."

"I suggest you check yourself before you wreck yourself, as my granddaughter says. Stop focusing on superficial things like money and look at that boy's heart. I told you my story. My husband didn't have two nickels to rub together, but look at him now. Even if my parents weren't rich we would still live a pretty good life.

"Whether you realize it or not, Tiffany Tate, you're not so great yourself. You're a work in progress just like William. Get off your high horse before the good Lord sees fit to knock you even lower than you are now. You are about to lose your reputation, your business, and your son, but he's still right there with you. Where's Michael? Don't tell me. He's with his WIFE and that's exactly where he's supposed to be."

Tiffany sat in silence. She had great respect for Mrs. Tolliver and her wisdom. Her words were eating at her very core.

"I'm done. You don't have to say a word because you know I'm right. Sometimes God has to break you down so He can build you up correctly. Now, you be good to this William and work on loving him and only him. I have a feeling he's part of your blessing. Don't mess it up. I'm about to make some phone calls to see if I can't get you some help. Keep your head up, child. You didn't do anything wrong, so there's no need for you to bow your head in shame."

"Mrs. Tolliver, what do you do when you start to feel like God is turning His back on you?" asked Tiffany.

"That's when you worship Him even more. It's easy to praise God when everything is going well. It's easy to have a testimony when all your skies are sunny. It's when things are going wrong and thunderstorms are drenching you from head to toe that you show God how much you truly love Him. You worship Him for who He is, what He has done, and what He is going to do. Can you do that?"

"Yeah. Sure," Tiffany said halfheartedly. "I've come this far. There's no reason for me to turn back now."

"That's the spirit. Let's pray before I go."

Mrs. Tolliver prayed a fervent prayer for God to intercede in Tiffany's situation and turn what the devil meant for bad into good. When she finished, Tiffany felt a peace that she didn't have before. She knew everything was going to be all right. She had to muster the strength to ride out her storm.

She was grateful for Mrs. Tolliver's friendship. She hadn't heard from Lenice since that story about her being Michael's girlfriend aired. It was clear who her allegiance belonged to.

William was supposed to come visit her after he got off work. She was going to order something to eat but decided to cook instead. He loved greens. She needed to go to the grocery store to get a few fresh bunches so she could make her man smile.

Chapter 78

Island Girl

The private island that housed the villa Michael rented for Tee could only be described as paradise. Lush green vegetation and flowers bursting with bold, vibrant colors greeted them as they entered the place she and Teresa would now call home. Every room was spacious and decorated in contemporary home furnishings. The closets and bathrooms were the size of a master suite. Tee was particularly fond of the outside Jacuzzi located on the deck, which held a magnificent view of the white sand beach. The master bedroom's king-size bed held the softest mattress she had ever felt in her life. It seemed to cradle every part of her body. The next morning, it was a chore to drag herself from beneath its smooth-as-silk sheets. There was no need to hurry. It wasn't as if she had something to do or some-place to be. When she did rise she was greeted by bright sunlight streaming through French windows and doors that seemed to be everywhere, allowing the occupants to view the natural beauty that surrounded them.

The house was equipped with a full staff whose only job seemed to be to fulfill whatever needs she and Teresa had. She didn't have to lift a finger if she didn't want to. She almost had to beg the housekeeper, Ms. Marita, to let her put her own house shoes on. Tee enjoyed not having to cook. The two women were treated to delicious meals and decadent treats from one of two private chefs. One was available during the day and the other at night if they should wake and want something specially prepared. Tee tried not to overindulge so that she didn't become the size of a whale. In that type of environment it was easy to sit around and do nothing but eat all day. Other amenities available to them included full-body massages, manicures, and pedicures. The house also contained a private movie theatre, bowling alley, basketball, and tennis court. They were bathed in beauty, comfort, and luxury everywhere they turned.

Tee imagined this was how the insanely rich lived. Then she realized that she and her husband were insanely rich. Sometimes it was still hard for her to believe that a year ago she was a hardworking member of the middle class, and now she had access to over $100 million. Tee was grateful for Teresa's company; she would have been quite lonely without her. It was like a never-ending slumber party. Their first night they stayed up playing every card game they knew. Tee was particularly fond of spades. Each day they had conversations about various topics: love, motherhood, politics, work, etc.

Tee knelt and thanked God for His goodness. If it were not for the wonderful man He placed in her life she would have no idea that such places existed. She prayed for God to keep Michael safe as he fought for her safety and that of their unborn child. The next morning she and Teresa took a stroll along the beach for exercise. The beautiful blue waters that kissed a clear blue sky reminded her of the time she and Michael vacationed in Jamaica. She missed him terribly. She longed to see his smiling face, bald head, and chocolate skin. Teresa was good company, but she wasn't her man. There was no denying that Tee was enjoying her own private paradise, but it wouldn't be perfect until she was with the man she loved.

Tee rubbed her stomach often to remind her that she carried a part of Michael with her wherever she went. She loved to feel the movements of her little one. There was an OBGYN on the island who was alerted to her arrival, and she was scheduled to visit with him sometime that week. Today she lounged around the house doing nothing in particular. She was bored and yearned for some sense of normalcy. Lunch with her friends would be nice. She desperately wanted to call Sheba and check on the business, but she didn't have a phone.

The doorbell rang. No one ever came to visit them so Tee was excited when Ms. Marita announced there was a package for her. She moved as fast as she could to see what it was. Lying in her arms and kissing Ms. Marita's face was her cocker spaniel Chesnutt. As soon as Chesnutt saw Tee, he struggled to be released from Ms. Marita's arms. Then he launched his furry body from her arms onto the floor and ran to his mistress. Tee knelt down and accepted all of his kisses. She usually shied away from the ones he tried to plant on her lips, but at this moment, she didn't care. Chesnutt licked her and danced his little body around with glee. When he had his fill of lavishing Tee with love, she read the note around his neck. It read. *"I thought you might like a small piece of home. Love, M."*

Tee picked Chesnutt up in her arms and nuzzled her face in his soft fur. It was cut low and filled with the fruity scent he always had when he returned from the groomer. Tee certainly welcomed this familiar face, but it wasn't the one she hoped for. Teresa walked softly down the steps behind her.

"That was so sweet of Michael. We can take Chesnutt shopping with us. Put on your shoes. We've stayed around this place long enough. Today we will go into town and mingle with the locals. I understand there's a crafts square with some beautiful handmade pieces."

Tee liked the thought of getting out of the house. Maybe while she was there she could figure out where she was. She had no way to contact the outside world. She was not a prisoner, but there was no phone, no television, no computer, and no Internet access. It was explained to her that such seclusion was to prevent anyone from being able to locate her. A technology-savvy person could track her down by something as simple as her logging into her email account. She felt so weird not being able to see what was happening in the world around her. Tee would be happy when she could go home and get back to life as usual.

Chapter 79

Liar, Liar, Pants on Fire

Michael took his family to Mae Lillie's to eat, and they were all stuffed. He felt a little better after getting some food in his stomach. Momma Pearl ate so much that she excused herself to go to the bathroom to take off her girdle. Periodically, Sandy would sit at the table with them and chat for a little while.

No one at the table was aware that Michael was wearing a wire at the suggestion of the Maverick. Jade, Bass, and Maverick arrived shortly after his family. They were the reason he didn't go to his father's hotel as planned. They told him their plan, outfitted him in a wire, and gave him a secure cell phone to prohibit any more listening to his phone calls. Maverick decided it would be best if his team, which he referred to as Resolve, went into stealth mode on his case. Michael typically didn't employ security except during events and other functions where there was guaranteed to be large numbers of people. He didn't want anything to appear out of the ordinary. Now that Tee was away and his loved ones were under watchful eyes he could be a little craftier with his plan to pluck out the human thorn in his side.

He was more convinced than ever that it was Becca behind these shenanigans, but he hadn't figured out how she survived the shooting. She was cunning enough to get Mac to help her. He wondered who else was on her team.

"Michael, have you talked to Tee?" asked Sandy.

"Yes, she's fine. She's out of town enjoying a maternity spa retreat. It was my gift to her. I know she's stressed. I wanted to do something nice for her before the divorce."

"I tried to call her, but her phone keeps going straight to voice mail."

"The retreat doesn't allow cell phones."

"Well, do you have a number where I can reach her?"

"No, the spa only allows one point of contact when you're there, and since I'm paying for it, I'm her only one. Besides, you can't call her. She has to call you. Is there a message? I can give it to her the next time we speak."

Sandy did not appreciate being told she could not talk to her baby sister. "Did you send her to a spa or a prison? Just tell her I said hello and call me soon."

"It's pretty exclusive, and all guests get top-notch pampering. They want them to focus on themselves and not worry about anything. They make it mandatory that you leave the outside world outside when you're there. All communication devices are confiscated when you arrive. Sorry, Sandy, but I will give you her message."

Michael hoped what he said was enough to pacify Sandy for now. He also hoped Maverick and his team of merry gunmen could live up to their name. He needed them to resolve his issue quickly.

"Son, can you send your mother? I could use a break from her," said Michael, Sr. "Did I tell you that she's thinking about retiring? I can only imagine all the things she would nag me and Tomeka about if she was home all day. She said something about school being too violent and maybe Michelle should be homeschooled. I avoided the subject and told her we would have to talk about it later."

"Where is this place?" asked Sandy.

"I can't tell you," said Michael.

Sandy got up and left the table. She had nothing left to say. Michael was lying, and she knew it.

On the way home, Michael received a call from Dr. Foster. Maverick told him not to answer his old phone, but he recognized the number and did it anyway.

"Hey, Michael, I know I've been out of touch, but I promised myself I wouldn't call you again until I had something to report. I can't talk long. I'm in trouble, and I have to make this quick. I've located Sean, and he should be contacting you soon. I think you should know that he's mentally ill as well. He suffers from multiple personality disorder, and one of his personalities has already contacted you. She goes by the name of—oh, God, no!" she screamed. "I gotta go."

"Dr. Foster!" yelled Michael. "Dr. Foster, what's wrong? Tell me who she is." The phone went silent.

"Dr. Foster! Dr. Foster! Dr. Foster!" No one answered.

Chapter 80

Church Gossip

Tiffany didn't want to go to church, but William told her that hiding wouldn't solve anything. Since she was innocent there was no reason for her to hide as if she were guilty. Since arriving back in Memphis, Tiffany tried to stay out of sight as much as possible. She was the hot topic on all the local news stations. Several news reporters showed up at her house unannounced, asking for interviews. Her lawyer advised her not to do any interviews for fear that someone may try to use something she said against her. She followed her directions and didn't open the door.

Tonight the church was having revival, and William urged her to come. Tiffany arrived at church early. Normally, she was fashionably late, but today was not the day to be late. If she was already seated when church began, she wouldn't have to stomach all of the eyes that would be staring at her as she walked down the aisle. She didn't sit in her usual seat in the middle, either. Today, she sat in the front to allow the bulk of the congregation to sit behind her so she wouldn't see them, and they would have to look at the back of her head. Tiffany went to the ladies' room before she went to her seat. This would prevent her from having to get up to go in the middle of the service. She wanted to allow the congregation as little access to her as possible. While she was in the stall, two of the church's most notorious gossips, Sister Sonya and Sister Nadine, came in to freshen up their makeup.

"Nadine, did you see Tiffany Tate come in?" said Sister Sonya.

"Yes, I did. The nerve of that tramp traipsing up in the Lord's house like nothing is wrong. I hope she came to repent of her sinful ways."

"She said she didn't do it," said Sister Sonya.

"Child, please. Do you look at the way she dresses? It's got 'I got five minutes for $5' written all over it. I feel sorry for Pastor William. I wonder how he feels knowing he was sleeping with a slut."

"Nadine, what are you saying? You know everybody knows Pastor William isn't having sex."

Sister Nadine looked at her like she was an idiot. "Did you see how he got more pep in his step and more stride in his glide when they started dating? That man is getting him some. She's Jezebel and Delilah all wrapped up in one. I'm so glad my husband and all the other deacons talked him into leaving her alone. I'm trying to hook him up with Sister Gloria. Now, *that's* a good woman. Her divorce is final now, and she and those six kids need a man like William in their life. She said he's been giving her the eye. With me playing Cupid, it's only a matter of time."

Tiffany had heard enough. She flushed the toilet and walked out of the stall. Once the two women noticed it was her they stopped talking. Neither one of them would look her in the eyes.

"Don't stop talking now, ladies," said Tiffany. "You seemed to have plenty to say a few seconds ago. Since you're so interested in my life why don't you let me enlighten you?" She straightened the skirt on the Donna Karen suit she wore. It stopped below her knees and not an inch of her cleavage was showing from her Versace top. The conservative look was actually starting to grow on her.

"First, I am innocent. I had no knowledge that prostitution was being implemented in my California office. I am a woman of God. I do not stand for such disgraceful behavior. Second, you give that meddling husband of yours and the rest of the deacons a message for me, and I'm going to say it loudly so you can hear me. PASTOR WILLIAM AND I ARE STILL TOGETHER. WE ARE GOING TO BE TOGETHER DESPITE WHAT YOU EVIL SO-CALLED SAINTS TRY TO DO! Now, run tell that. If my William's got more pep in his step it's because *I* make him happy. I'm capable of doing that quite well with my clothes on. If you took the time to talk to me instead of talking about me you would know that I have a wonderful personality. I am blessed to have him in me and my son's life. Not that it's any of your business, but he and I are having a saved and celibate relationship. So, whatever dreams you had of him getting with Gloria, pack them away in that cheap dollar-store compact of yours. That foundation you're using is so thick that it reminds me of the kind they use on corpses. But I realize you two are getting on up in age. Perhaps you're practicing for the inevitable."

She looked at Sister Nadine. "How dare you come up in this bathroom and pass judgment on me. You don't know me. You don't know a thing about me, but you better be glad I know Jesus. Instead of slapping that nappy wig off your head I'm going to tell you who I really am and I know it because my Heavenly Father says so. I am the head and not the tail. I am the salt of the earth, and I'm also the light. So, I have no time to waste on you and the rest of the gossips in the church. I have to be about my Father's business. I suggest you get you some business and get out of mine!"

The bathroom door opened, and William stepped in. "Tiffany, I can hear you yelling down the hallway. Are you okay?"

"I'm fine, baby. These two gossiping heifers unknowingly took the time to enlighten me on what they think of me and my relationship with you. It seems they think you would be a much better match for Sister Gloria."

William shook his head. Sister Nadine tried to defend herself. The last thing she wanted to do was offend the clergy. "Well, Pastor, it's not like that," she protested, "Sister Sonya and I—"

William put up a hand to silence her. "Sisters, I would appreciate it if you would not make comments about my personal life. Sister Gloria is a fine woman, but I'm already spoken for."

"Pastor, we didn't mean any harm," Sister Sonya defended. "You know I think the world of you. Will you still be joining me and Deacon Webster for dinner after church Sunday?"

"No, I'll be dining with *my* girlfriend after church, but thank you for the invitation." He gave Tiffany a peck on the cheek. "You look lovely tonight. Let me escort you to your seat."

"Please do. Excuse me, ladies. I'm going to go watch *my* man lead praise and worship now."

Tiffany and William walked out of the restroom and were met by a crowd of congregants standing outside the door listening. William readied himself to push past them but instead stopped and said, "Excuse me, everyone. I want to make an announcement. Tiffany Tate and I are an official couple. I'm sure you've heard about the pending allegations against her. I'll have you know that this beautiful woman is innocent, and anyone who has any comments about her or our relationship needs to keep them to themselves. Now, if you call yourself a Christian, what you'll do is get on your knees tonight and pray that the truth will come out and justice will be served. Ask God to be her judge and lawyer in the courtroom and that everything will work out in favor of this wonderful woman who loves the Lord."

William gave her a sweet peck on the lips, and then took her by the hand and led her to the front pew that was generally reserved for the mothers of the church and the pastor's wives. Tiffany sat next to the first lady of the church and beamed with pride. Even when you're at your lowest, God is still in control. Tiffany's custody hearing was the next day. She was certain God was going to give her son back.

Chapter 81

Tonight Is the Night

Lenice wasn't looking forward to making love to a man she didn't love, but had to do it. She hoped that it wouldn't be a horrible experience. Immediately after the ceremony, Brighton and Lenice went out to lunch. Afterward, they went to his lawyer's office to sign some documents. He was a man of his word, and if she stayed with him she would reap all the benefits of his hard work.

Brighton hoped that would cheer her up. He saw how disappointed she was that her sister didn't support her decision to marry him. He felt like the luckiest man in the world. He always found African American women exotic, but as a youth he knew his parents would cut him off he ever dated or married one. Now, he was a grown man with his own money and he could do as he pleased. The delicious chocolate kiss in front of him belonged to him and him alone.

Lenice wasn't quite sure how much Brighton was worth or what he owned, but when she saw his extensive list of assets on the papers his lawyer had them sign, she almost had another asthma attack. He had property in five states and on four continents. His bank accounts contained more zeros than she had ever seen in her life. The paperwork contained a clause that she had to be married to him for the duration of his life to receive everything. If she opted to leave for any reason, she was only entitled to $100,000 for each year that they were married.

Lenice expected to have to perform her wifely duties that evening, but Brighton had other plans. Later, they went to the country club for a rousing game of tennis. Lenice hadn't picked up a tennis racket in years. She was quite rusty but enjoyed playing just the same. She had forgotten how invigorating it could be. Afterward, she and Brighton wrapped themselves in towels and entered the club's sauna and shared a conversation while sweat poured from their bodies underneath the stifling heat. Lenice enjoyed the sauna, but the hairstyle she got the day before specifically for the wedding was ruined.

Afterward, they went to dinner, and it was there Brighton revealed his surprise. He was taking her to Italy for their honeymoon. They would board a plane that night and wake up in Venice. He wanted to make love to his wife for the first time there. He planned to give her an evening she would never forget.

Chapter 82

All Bets Are Off

Michael and his family sat around a table puffing on cigars and playing poker. He was enjoying this time with them. They helped him keep his mind off his problems. He entrusted his situation to Resolve, but he found it hard to wait for instructions on what he was supposed to do next. He told Maverick about Dr. Foster's phone call, and he said he would look into it. Michael was very worried about her. He tried to call her back several times, but she never answered.

Another woman was also giving him grief, and she was named Sheba. He left the condo to escape her. Each day she grilled him for information about where Tee was and when she would be home. Each day she had a new question or problem she swore only Tee could answer. She finally shut up when Michael told her if this was an example of what type of manager she was going to be then she would always be their assistant. She was there from the very beginnings of the company and was fully aware of how things were done. If she had any questions she could ask during their daily conference calls. He made himself available to her once in the morning and once in the evening.

Other than that, he was not to be disturbed. He could tell Sheba was very upset about being separated from her beloved Boss Lady, but she would have to deal with it for now.

"Michael, get your head in the game," said Maxwell. "You're starting to play like Pop."

Michael looked at his hand. He didn't see one card he liked.

"Son, I've been meaning to ask you something," said Michael, Sr. "Are we being watched here and why?"

"Pop, this is the only time I'm going to address this because the less you know the more natural you'll behave. I am never completely alone, and neither is everyone I love, and that's the way it's going to be until the people who are watching me catch whoever has been stalking me and Tee."

"I'm sure you're doing what's best for you, son, but it's making me nervous. Is there anything I can do?"

"Yep, act natural and stop dealing these crappy hands." Michael threw his cards on the table. "I'm out."

His phone rang; it was Sheba. Didn't he tell her not to contact him? *It better be an emergency,* he thought.

"I'm sorry to bother you, Michael, but I thought you would like to know there's a man here to see you who claims to be Becca's brother."

"What?"

"Yeah. He claims to be your crazy ex-girlfriend's brother. He said Dr. Foster paid him a visit and asked him to get in touch with you. Rather than call, he decided to come introduce himself."

Michael couldn't believe it. Sean had finally surfaced. They definitely needed to talk. "Tell him to sit tight."

"Game over, guys," said Michael. "Becca's brother is at my office. Anybody want to meet him?" His father and brother were eager to meet him too. Perhaps he had clues to help Micahel end all this drama.

Chapter 83

Lord, Lord, Lord

Tiffany's custody hearing was the last one of the day. Her lawyer, Maria Willis, asked her to arrive at the courthouse early to go over some new information she received. Tiffany hated talking to lawyers, but under the circumstances she had no choice. She and her lawyer were in constant communication concerning her case.

"Ms. Tate, I have good news for you. The Malibu police have completed their investigation and all charges against you have been dropped. Siendy and Sierra were extremely cooperative, and both gave statements that you knew nothing about their prostitution activities. They also supplied a list of their clients. Some of them have already been picked up for questioning, and each one said they have no idea who you are or had no conversation with you regarding sex with the twins. Lucky for you and your company most of their solicitation was among clients they secured themselves. However, the police did give me some information I think you will find intriguing." What she then told Tiffany caused her to gasp and a tear ran from her eye. *How dare he?*

Tiffany hadn't heard from Mrs. Tolliver or her husband, and she was worried. Neither she nor her lawyer knew very much about the young judge named Christopher Green who was assigned to handle all of Judge Malone's previous cases. This was her second time in this courtroom, but this time she didn't have a throng of supporters. Tee, Lenice, and Lenora were all absent, but her parents and William were there. She was grateful for that. Tiffany prayed daily that God would give her the opportunity to repair the damage she caused to her friendships. She scanned the room. There were also two police officers in the room in addition to the bailiff. She wondered why they were there. She also recognized two news reporters from local TV stations. Cameras were not allowed in court, but the media for some reason thought that "The Memphis Madame's" child custody hearing was newsworthy. The news that her charges were dropped had not been announced yet. Tiffany found it quite disturbing that they were so quick to report bad news but slow to report good news. Quincy and his wife were sitting to her left with their lawyer. She refused to look at them. As far as she was concerned, they were little demons trying to separate her from her son.

The bailiff's voice rang out loud and strong. "All rise for the Honorable Judge Larry Malone."

What was he doing here? He was supposed to be in Europe with his wife. Tiffany knew she could never reveal her ties to Judge Malone or he would have to excuse himself from her case. Her face remained solemn but on the inside, she was elated.

Judge Malone entered and took a seat. His skin was darker than the last time she saw him. This was likely because of the many sunny excursions he and his wife enjoyed while frolicking overseas. He banged the gavel. "Court is now in session. Judge Green was called away unexpectedly, and I was asked to come out of retirement temporarily to cover his cases. I can't say that I am happy to be here when I am supposed to be in Europe, but I'm here. I understand we are here today to determine if Ms. Tiffany Tate should retain sole custody of the minor, Quincy Albert Tate, or if custody should be given to the father, Mr. Quincy Matthews. I must state that this is not criminal court. I am not here to determine Ms. Tate's guilt or innocence regarding any of the charges that may or may not be against her at this time. My only job is to determine what is in the best interest of the child."

He looked at her lawyer. "Attorney Willis, we'll begin with you."

"Your Honor, we are asking that Mr. Matthews' petition for custody by denied based on the fact that there is no evidence that Tiffany Tate is an unfit parent. The prostitution case against her in California has been dropped. An investigation by the Malibu Police Department revealed that she was not running a prostitution ring nor has she participated in the unlawful act of prostitution. Even if the charges hadn't been dropped, there still would be no proof my client is an unfit parent. She has been a stellar mother throughout young Quincy's life. She makes sure he is well fed, well clothed, well educated, and has provided a stable home environment for the youth. Child Service has interviewed her, young Quincy and inspected her home and all were found to be in good standing. We do realize that her work schedule can get hectic from time to time, but her parents also help her take care of Quincy, providing support when necessary. Furthermore, I have additional information that questions Mr. Tate's judgment.

"Really? Let's hear this evidence," said Judge Malone.

"Your Honor, I have in my hand two signed statements by the rape victim and her sister, who were allegedly engaging in prostitution while employed by Ms. Tate's company. I ask the courts to let me keep their identity a secret because of the sensitivity of this case. A woman has been brutally violated. Upon their arrest, both women began cooperating with the authorities and willingly supplied them with information that has cleared Ms. Tate of any wrongdoing because she was completely ignorant to their illegal activities. They also provided a list of their prostitution patrons."

Attorney Willis walked up to the judge's bench and handed him a manila folder. "On the third page you will find that they both confessed to having sex with Mr. Matthews on at least three different occasions. Their threesomes would take place at hotels and even in his Midtown office. The last one took place as early as last week. Although both young ladies are now living in California, Mr. Matthews flew them back to Memphis for his own private pleasure."

"That's a lie!" shouted Quincy.

Judge Malone banged his gavel. "I will have order in my court. Mr. Matthews, this statement was made by those two young ladies while in the custody of the Malibu police. This is a signed affidavit, which is as good as if they were sitting in court testifying. If you take issue with anything said, you will have to argue as to whether it is true or not during your trial. However, under the circumstances, I have no choice but to grant Ms. Tate custody of Quincy Albert Tate. He should be returned to her immediately. Your visitation is suspended pending an investigation by Child Services to determine if your home is still a suitable environment for young Quincy. I was actually made aware of these pending charges before I walked in here. I understand that there are officers here waiting to take you into custody. Officers, you may proceed. Two police officers stood, walked over to Quincy, placed him in handcuffs and read him his Miranda rights. His wife sat in the courtroom and cried as she watched in horror. "This concludes this court." Judge Malone banged his gavel again.

Tiffany cried and mouthed "thank you" to Judge Malone from behind the desk she and her lawyer shared. She then turned around and hugged her lawyer, William, and her parents. She was rejoicing over her victory, but she felt terrible for Quincy's wife. Hadn't she been embarrassed enough by him? First, an open affair that produced a child, and now prostitution with girls who were around the same age as their oldest daughter. He was probably with the twins when he didn't come home last week. She wanted custody of her son but not at the cost of him losing his father. She wanted the information about him sleeping with the twins made public to keep Quincy from getting custody, not to have him arrested.

Several news reporters tried to approach her for an interview as she left the courtroom. Tiffany had, had enough of the media. Her lawyer shielded her from them and ushered her from the courtoom. Once they were alone, Tiffany shared her concerns with her attorney.

"Tiffany, don't worry," said Attorney Willis. "He'll probably make bail tomorrow. If I had to guess, his charges will be for solicitation and transporting prostitutes across state lines. Quincy has money and no prior criminal record so I doubt he'll see any jail time. He'll probably have to pay a fine, be placed on probation, and given community service. This is not your fault. He was the one who decided he wanted a romp in the hay with your employees. They knew he was their boss's former lover and baby daddy. You should be upset with all of them, not concerned. Quincy's getting exactly what he deserved."

"But it will be at the expense of my child. He loves his father and spending time with his stepmother and sisters. Why couldn't you just have told him what we had on him and gotten him to drop the case?"

"I had nothing to do with that. I took an oath to uphold the law, and he broke it. Besides, it was only a matter of time before he got arrested anyway. Do you think Malibu PD didn't share these affidavits with Memphis PD? I understand how you feel, but this isn't your fault. So, don't beat yourself up about it." Little did Tiffany know, Attorney Willis was planning to run for Quincy's seat on the city council, and with him out of the picture she was almost guaranteed to win. The publicity during this case would also increase her chances.

Tiffany shook her head. This was yet another scandal she would have to try to shield her son from. She would have to explain to him why he couldn't spend time with his father for a few weeks. Although she was sure visitation would be reinstated after the investigation. He was actually a pretty decent father, but he was a horrible husband. A visit to her son's therapist would probably do him some good. She would make the appointment when she got home.

Tiffany was grateful to God, Judge Malone, and Mrs. Tolliver. Thanks to them, her son would be home with her where he belonged.

Chapter 84

Second Thoughts

Lenice looked out of the window at the Italian architecture in awe. She had never been to Italy and under different circumstances she would have been happy to be there. When they arrived it was night time. She was now dressed in a negligee made of the most delicate silk she ever felt. The lingerie was in their suite lying on the king-sized bed inside a beautifully wrapped box when she arrived. Their suite was massive. It contained a private pool, a patio and a bar. Her new husband exited the bathroom in what appeared to be a smoking jacket with pajamas underneath. He looked like the quintessential old man. It was beginning to sink in that she was married to this old man. He poured each of them a glass of champagne. Lenice began to panic. What had she done?

She suddenly wished she was home with James instead of with Brighton. Did she really agree to spend only God knows how long with a man she didn't love for money? He was worth at least $200 million, but at that moment it didn't matter. She began to hyperventilate.

"My love, what's wrong?" said Brighton.

Lenice gasped for air. She couldn't breathe, and she couldn't talk. It was obvious that Brighton didn't know what to do. She would have to save herself. Lenice managed to make her way to her carry-on bag and found her inhaler.

Once her breaths were steady, she said, "Brighton, I can't do this."

"Do what?"

"This. This marriage, this arrangement, this sexual act—with you."

Brighton let out a loud sigh. "I was afraid this would happen. Darling, I'm sure it's just honeymoon jitters. This is what we're going to do. I'm going to go for a stroll. While I'm gone, you think about us some more. When I return, you tell me your decision. I hope you'll change your mind. I would hate to have taken that Viagra for no reason." Brighton licked his lips and moved in closer to kiss her. She closed her eyes. His lips were still dry and thin.

"Before I go, let's propose a toast," he said and handed Lenice a glass of champagne. She had already downed three of them and welcomed another one.

"To family and a lifetime of happiness."

Lenice lightly touched her glass against his without saying a word and drank all its contents in one gulp. She hoped her buzz would kick in quickly to blur the activities of this evening.

She didn't care how many walks Brighton took. She wasn't going to change her mind. Marrying him was a mistake, and the horrid churning in her stomach which was now accompanied by a painful pounding in her head was all the confirmation she needed.

Chapter 85

Stokes, Stokes & Stokes

The Stokes men filed into the office. Michael, Maxwell, and his father introduced themselves to Sean.

"Well, now that you all are here can I go?" asked Sheba. "I'm late for my hair appointment. I might lose my slot if I don't hurry up and get there."

"That's fine. You can go, Sheba. I won't be needing you anymore today," said Michael.

"Sure thing, boss." Sheba grabbed her purse and ran out the door.

"Your assistant is nice. She even went and got me something to eat." Sean finished shoving the remnants of a sub sandwich into his mouth.

Michael noticed that he spoke with the same smooth inflections as his sister. He even moved his mouth like hers when forming the words.

Sean didn't look at all like Michael expected. He was a short man with a thin build. He had an almond complexion. Becca could have easily passed for white, but Sean took after his father, and it was quite obvious that African American was in his heritage. He wore a blue baseball cap that was pulled down low over his eyes. Michael couldn't see his entire face, but there seemed to be no resemblance to Becca.

Sean held his jaw rigid as if he were upset. Michael wondered what was bothering him.

He wiped his fingers on a napkin and took a swig of his iced tea. "Well, I'm here, now, so maybe you can call off Deputy Dog."

Michael was taken aback by the venom in his voice. He assumed he was referring to Dr. Foster.

"No need to be hostile. I thought it would be nice for my niece to know the other side of her family. I hired her to find you."

"Michelle is the only reason I'm here. I'd like to get to know the only connection I have to the woman you had murdered," said Sean.

"How can you say that? Dr. Foster killed Becca because she tried to stab me and my wife."

"Deputy Dog killed my sister? I wish I had known that when she came to my apartment. I would have returned the favor," said Sean.

Michael felt anger rising within him. He had no idea where Dr. Foster was, and for all he knew, Sean had something to do with her disappearance.

"I think you need to calm down, son," said Michael, Sr. "It's understandable that you are upset at the loss of a loved one, but neither Michael nor Dr. Foster are to blame. Your sister was sick. She was put in an institution to get some help, but she obviously didn't want it."

"I think you need to focus on what's left and what's important," said Maxwell. "And that's my daughter. I don't have any problem with you being a part of her life if I think you can add something of value to it, but with the way you're behaving now, I don't see that you can."

Michael's phone rang. It was Maverick. He excused himself to answer it. "Michael, you need to wrap that up. McKenzie called. Becca called him and told him where she wanted to meet for the drop. He's on his way now," said Maverick.

Michael, Sr.'s phone rang as well. It was Michael's mother, and she was talking a mile a minute. "Calm down, Vanessa. What's wrong?" Michael, Sr. couldn't make out what his wife was saying, but the loud tone of her voice made it obvious she was upset about something. He listened a few more minutes and finally understood. "Are you sure? Did you call the police? I'll tell Maxwell and Junior. We'll be home as soon as we can. I'll call you back."

Michael, Sr. returned to the room. "Boys, I don't know how to tell you this. Michelle is missing. Vanessa said she and Tomeka took her to House of Fun to cheer her up. She was still a little upset because we wouldn't let her come with us. The last time they saw her, she was playing in the game with all the little balls. Tomeka left her to go to the bathroom, and when she came back, she was gone," said Michael, Sr.

"Where was her security?" yelled Michael.

"You didn't take care of my sister, and now you can't even take care of her child. It's obvious that she doesn't need to be with you people. You wanted to meet me, and now you have." Sean pulled business card from his back pocket and put it on the table. "Here's my number. Call me if I can be of some help. I see this is a waste of time. I have another appointment."

Maxwell turned to him. "Did you have anything to do with this? I find it strange that you should surface and she suddenly comes up missing."

"Don't be stupid. I'm here in Memphis. How did I take her from here? Don't blame me because you can't keep up with your child."

Maxwell lunged at Sean. Michael, Sr. grabbed him before he could touch him.

"Calm down, Max. Hitting him won't solve anything. We'll find her. Michael, can you call your friends for help?"

Sean laughed and walked toward the door. No one tried to stop him from leaving because no one wanted him around. He opened the door and slammed it so hard one of the paintings Lenora hung fell from the wall.

"I'll make those calls right now, Pop." Michael went to the break room to call Maverick. He had to help him.

Maverick told Michael to stay put. He had everything under control, but Michael needed to trust him. Michael, Maxwell, and his father sat over an hour waiting impatiently in the lobby of MiTee Management. Once again, everything in Michael's life felt out of his control. He had no idea what his wife was doing. His niece was missing, and the woman who was ruining his life was still at large. He had to do something. Sitting around and waiting for things to happen was foreign to him. He was the type of guy who made things happen. He got up to make himself a pot of coffee. He heard a loud crash and twirled around to see Sheba flying through the glass door, into the office, followed by Sean. Maverick opened what was left of the door and walked in behind them with an assault rifle aimed at both of them. He was followed by Jade and Bass.

Michael sprang to help Sheba who was on the floor. She had several cuts on her body and was bleeding.

"What's wrong with you?" yelled Michael.

"He bit me," growled Maverick.

"He?" Michael looked more closely at Sheba. Her lace front wig was separated from her forehead revealing the cornrows that were hidden underneath. Gone was her soft feminine appeal. It was replaced by someone with an attitude who looked ready to fight. "Who are you?" asked Michael.

Sheba jumped up and hit Michael squarely in the jaw. Michael's body fell back, but he was caught by his father and brother. They helped him to his feet and all three stood there amazed at the strength that came from that little body. Clad in a canary yellow pants suit, Sheba was holding both fists up and bouncing around like a boxer inside a ring. She was waiting for Michael to retaliate.

"I've been wanting to do that for a very long time. C'mon take your best shot. I got more where that came from," she hissed. Gone was the sweet light voice they were used to. She was indeed a he.

Maverick cocked his gun. "Make one more move and I'm going to blow your false eyelashes off."

"No, don't shoot him." Sean ran and flung his arms around Sheba. "Baby, calm down. It's over. We'll be okay, but you've got to recognize when you've lost; it's over." Michael was confused. Now, Sean sounded like a woman, and he was stroking Sheba's face like they were lovers.

Maverick came over and grabbed Sheba by the neck. "Meet Becca's brother, Sean. You've been looking for him, but he found you a long time ago. And this woman pretending to be a man is his wife, Carla."

It was hard to believe that the "woman" Michael and Tee trusted to help them run their company was out to get them. Sean was very convincing as a woman. Michael noticed that she didn't have much of a figure a while ago, but Sheba didn't need curves to do a good job. He had a lot of questions.

"Who was making the calls?" asked Michael.

Sean laughed. "Hello, Binky," he said. "Did you really think I was still alive? Your beloved Dr. Foster killed me, remember, but I took care of her. How does that saying go, 'an eye for eye?' How about a life for a life? Ha ha ha!"

That voice sent a chill through Michael. It was a perfect impersonation of Becca, but it was coming from the person he used to think was Sheba.

"Pretty good, right?" said Sean. "I've been imitating my sister since I was 16. I used to call my high school and tell them I was sick. I can even sign her signature."

Jade tried to help Michael make sense of it all. "Sean suffers from multiple personality disorder. It seems that both he and Sheba believe that Becca is their sister. You actually had *two* siblings seeking revenge on you. In his mind, they believe that they are partners. We believe that Becca may be one of his personalities as well."

"*We* hate you," said Sean and spit at Michael.

"How did you figure it out?" asked Michael.

"We didn't," said Maverick. "Cult did. I sent him to see if he could get some more information out of the wife. While he was sitting in the house talking to her, he noticed that the woman sitting in the living room closely resembled the woman in the pictures with the kids that were scattered around the house, but it wasn't her. Like most women, she was attracted to Cult. He used that to do what he does best—make women bare their soul to him. She confessed that she was only pretending to be her sister while her sister tried to work out her marriage with her estranged husband who suffered from multiple personality disorder. She even had pictures of what Sean looked like when he took on the personality of a woman. Cult sent me the picture today. To make sure it was him we waited until he tried to meet Mac to get some more money. Seems you and your wife don't pay very well, Michael. Sean, Sheba, or whoever he is, didn't make enough to pay for him and his wife's life here and to make sure his kids were adequately taken care of in Cincinnati. Mac was their fundraiser. They used his money to buy surveillance equipment to spy on you. They also used the money to pay to have the rec room at that treatment facility dedicated to Becca."

The entire time Maverick spoke, Sean's wife was still clutching him for dear life. He wriggled away from her and said, "Go stand over there." He pointed toward the wall. "Nothing is going to happen to us." Maverick, Jade, and Bass all had their guns drawn in case either one of them made any sudden moves.

Maxwell wanted to know if they had any ties to his daughter's kidnapping. "Where's my daughter?" he yelled.

Sean laughed. "Maxwell, darling, I haven't the faintest idea where my niece is. If you can't take care of her, perhaps you should give her to me. We'll take excellent care of her."

Jade spoke again. "She's fine, sir. We realized that the next phase of their plan was to kidnap Michelle. We took her before they had a chance to. We didn't know when it was going to happen, but we knew it was probably soon. He was truly planning to ruin your life by attacking everyone you loved. However, you messed up the key component of his plan when you hid Tee. If I had to guess, he was going to ruin your reputation, then your marriage, and take Michelle. Then, after he felt he had tortured you enough, he was going to kill you."

Sean didn't say a word. He merely looked at Michael with a sinister smile.

"The two of them are the reason you can't sleep at night," said Maverick. "You have a decision to make, Michael. We can dispose of them for you and make sure they never bother you again, or we can call the police. The call is yours."

Michael looked at both of them. They were responsible for his broken marriage and the loss of his best friend. He wanted nothing better than to know that they would never bother him or his family again, but he couldn't commit murder. He walked over to Sean and punched him in the face several times. The weight of his fists and his anger were massive and rendered Sean unable to fight back. "That was for Peter and Dr. Foster. Lock them up. I want them brought up on every charge imaginable." Sean stood up holding his jaw. It was broken.

Jade pulled out her cell phone to call the police. "As you wish, sir. By the way, Dr. Foster is not dead. Sean shot her and left her for dead, but Cult found her and got her to a hospital. She's in stable condition and the doctors are optimistic about her recovery.

Michael looked at Maverick. "Thank you."

"My pleasure. You're a better man than me, because if it were me both of them would be in the bottom of the Mississippi River right about now."

Carla was still standing by the wall next to a light switch. She watched as she and her husband's hard work unraveled in front of her. Sean promised her that if she helped him avenge his sister he would come home, get some help for his mental problems, and they could be a family once again. They had two kids, and she wanted them to know what it was like to have a mother and father in the home. She knew what they were doing was wrong, but she didn't care. She yearned for the man she used to know. The one with only one personality that made her fall in love with him and treated her like a queen. She was willing to do whatever it took to get him back. It seemed as if that would never happen.

Sean looked at her and winked. That was her cue. She flipped the switch and once engulfed in darkness she grabbed Jade's gun and fired three shots in what she hoped was the right direction. They both agreed that no matter what happened, Michael had to die. It was their way of vindicating Becca. Sean told her that was the only way he would forgive her for separating him and her sister many years ago. It was her disdain for Becca's former life as a prostitute that kept them from communicating most of his adult life. He held it over her head every day.

Jade reacted quickly. She completed a roundhouse kick that sent Carla sprawling to the floor. She hit her head and was knocked out cold. Jade turned the lights back on to survey the damage. Sean, Michael, and Maxwell were on the floor. Sean was screaming at the top of his lungs in a woman's voice. "I been hit! Oh God, I been hit!"

Maxwell was writhing in pain with a blood-covered hand pressed against his shoulder. He had never endured such agony. The burn of the bullet as it ripped through his body was almost unbearable. Michael placed his arm around him and held him tightly. He whispered words of comfort to him. Michael, Sr. tried to survey the wound but Maxwell wouldn't stop moving long enough to let him do it.

The person Michael once knew as Sheba continued to scream as blood oozed from the chest area. Maverick ran over to Sean, took off his jacket and pressed it tightly to his chest trying to stop the bleeding. Bass called 911. "Binky! Binky, help me!" he screamed in a voice that sounded like Becca. Michael didn't move. It wasn't Sheba or Becca on that floor. Sheba didn't exist and Becca was dead; it was Sean, a psychotic man who refused to seek help for his illness. Sean turned his head and looked at Michael. It was obvious that he and the personalities that lived inside him were dying. In his final moments, it was Becca who surfaced to say good bye. "All I ever wanted to do was love you, Binky. Take good care of Michelle for me and tell her I love her. Loving you and having her was the best thing I ever did. I just wanted us to be a family." Tears streamed from Sean's eyes as he took his final breath. His eyes rolled into his head. Maverick took his hand and closed his eyelids.

Chapter 86

Family First

"Mr. Rupert, I need to have the week off," said Lenora.

"Why?" he asked.

"My sister is in Italy on her honeymoon and something bad has happened. I have to go to her."

"Lenora, I hate to hear that. Is your husband going?"

"No, he just started a new job and can't take time off yet."

"Do you want me to come with you?"

Lenora was surprised by his question. "No. I'm married. That would be inappropriate."

Mr. Rupert laughed. "You wouldn't be the first married woman I've gone out of town with. You really shouldn't travel to foreign countries alone. That could be dangerous. I know you like me, Lenora, and I like you. Let me help you."

Lenora was already at the airport. She didn't have time for this.

"Mr. Rupert, I'm sorry if I gave you the wrong impression, but I'm a happily married woman. I do not appreciate these unwanted advances. I don't think the Montessori school review board or the EEOC would like them either."

Mr. Rupert cleared his throat. "Lenora, what are you talking about? I was merely expressing concern for you as an employee. Take all the time you need. I hope your sister is okay. Have a safe flight. Goodbye."

Lenora put her phone away and gave the ticket agent her identification. She needed a flight to Italy as soon as possible. She received a frantic call from Lenice asking her to come to Italy right away. She was in the hospital. Something very bad had happened, and she needed Lenora to come help her. Even though Lenora didn't approve of her marriage, there was no way she could deny her sister's request. Her heart went out to Lenice. There was no quick way to get to Italy so she had to hope that God would keep her sister and her husband safe in a foreign country. She said a prayer asking God to make everything all right.

Chapter 87

Am I Dreaming?

Tee woke up and put on shorts and a t-shirt. She wasn't feeling well and figured fresh air would do her some good. She made her way down the steps and into the kitchen where she opened the refrigerator door to get some orange juice before she walked outside. It wasn't in its normal place on the top shelf. She scanned the other shelves and the door. She still couldn't find it. That was odd. She sat in the kitchen with Ms. Marita while she squeezed it yesterday. Who would be so selfish to drink an entire pitcher of orange juice before the next morning?

"Is this what you're looking for?"

That voice sent Tee spinning around to make sure her ears weren't deceiving her. "Michael?" she said. Her eyes drank in the vision of utter bliss that was sitting on a stool in front of the kitchen island drinking a tall glass of orange juice with the pitcher nearby. She ran to him and flung her arms around his body. He bent his head and met her lips with his. Tee devoured his mouth. If she was dreaming she was going to make the most of it before she woke up, but this had to be real because no one made her heart flutter like her husband, and no one's touch made her weak in the knees like his.

She broke her mouth away from his. There was something she needed to know. She was breathless from the veraciousness of their kiss. "Is it over?" she panted.

"It's over. No one is going to ever bother us again. Becca's brother and his wife were the ones harassing us. Sean is dead, and his wife is in jail. She was trying to kill me and accidentally shot him instead. She also shot Maxwell, but thankfully, it was only a flesh wound. He'll be fine, but you should have seen the way he was acting. You would have thought he was about to die. They will never bother us again. I'm here to celebrate! Teresa is taking a flight home tomorrow, and you and I are going to stay here for a few more days and have a second honeymoon."

"Pinch me," said Tee.

"Why?"

"I'm still not sure I'm not dreaming."

He kissed her again. "If you're dreaming, I don't want you to wake up, so I'm not going to pinch you." He took his wife by the hand and led her to the sitting room. Michael whispered softly in her ear as they padded across the floor covered with plush carpet. "I promised you forever and a day, Beautiful. Do you think you can handle me for that long?"

"I know I can, Handsome. I wouldn't have it any other way."

"Tee, how do you feel about more kids?"

Tee laughed. "We haven't gotten this one out yet, and you're thinking about more?"

"I guess you have a point, but I have my reasons for asking."

"Do tell, Mr. Stokes."

"Will do, Mrs. Stokes."

Michael and Tee sat down and discussed their plans for a Becca-free future. The next morning Teresa went home and Michael and Tee began a much needed vacation. Unfortunately, their island escape was short-lived. On day three, they received an urgent call from Teresa. They needed to come home. Something was wrong with Lenice.

Chapter 88

Ashes to Ashes, Dust to Dust

"Dearly beloved, we are gathered here today to celebrate the life of one of God's servants," said Pastor Alex. Lenice stared blankly ahead. Her thoughts were so loud they drowned out all other sounds. She saw lips moving but heard very few words. She sat motionless as dirt was thrown on Brighton's casket. Lenice couldn't believe that her husband of less than a week was dead.

"Ashes to ashes, dust to dust . . ." said Pastor Alex.

The night of their honeymoon Brighton suffered a massive heart attack during his walk. According to the doctors, it was a result of the Viagra pills he took that day. He took twice the recommended dosage for a medication that wasn't recommended for men with high blood pressure. He was rushed to the hospital. By the time Lenice got to the hospital he was unconscious. Two days later he passed.

Lenice was free of him, but she wasn't happy he was dead. She blamed herself. If she hadn't married him, this wouldn't have happened. His wanting to make love to her killed him. During the funeral, Lenice shed tears uncontrollably as his friends and family and employees stood to say a few words about him. They resented her, and she could see it in their faces as they passed her to make their way back to their seats. As far as they were concerned, she was an opportunist or worse, a gold digger. Many of them wondered if she killed him. Lenice resented and hated herself more than they ever could. She didn't listen to God, and she didn't listen to her sister when they told her not to marry him. She didn't love him, but she was very fond of him.

Lenice was now the richest woman in Memphis and the owner of a multimillion-dollar technology company that she had no idea how to run. One of her first orders of business was to find someone who was good with numbers who she could trust to help her with it. Herman would be great for the IT side, but he wasn't a numbers cruncher.

The graveside ceremony was beautiful, but she felt like a stranger at her own husband's funeral. She wouldn't have gotten through it if it hadn't been for her own friends and family. Although most of them never met Brighton, they came to support her. They flanked her on both sides and sent hateful stares back at all who felt bold enough to send them her way. Lenora and Herman, Tee and Michael, Tiffany and William, as well as Teresa and Zach attended.

After the repast, Lenice told everyone she wanted to be alone. Lenora insisted on coming with her, but she refused her sister's offer. The only company she planned to have that night was Webster. He was dressed in a black doggy suit to signify the solemn occasion and sat in Lenice's lap throughout the ceremony. He brought her comfort. She told her driver to take her home to her town house. She had no desire to spend the night in their massive home in Arlington, Tennessee, without him. She would rather sleep in the secure comfort of her own bed.

As the driver pulled in front of her home she saw James putting something in her mailbox. She rolled down the window.

"Hello, James."

"Hey, Lenice. I didn't expect you to be here, but I didn't know where to send the card I got you so I brought it here. I knew your things were still inside, so I figured you would return here eventually. I certainly didn't think it would be tonight. I'm sorry about your husband's death."

"I didn't want to be in that big ole house by myself. Tonight, I prefer the familiarity of my own home. Thank you for the card; that's very sweet."

"It's nothing. I wanted you to know that you still have friends who love and care for you."

"I owe you an apology, James," said Lenice.

"No, you don't. We ended things, and that's what happens when you end things. People have the option to see other people. We both moved on. Don't you dare be sorry."

"But I am. I'm sorry because I hurt you. You deserved better. Just because someone hurt me didn't give me the right to pass that pain on to someone else. You're a good man. Your girlfriend is very lucky."

"I don't have a girlfriend anymore. She wasn't right for me. We called it quits a couple of days ago."

"That's too bad. I was wrong, James. I should have never let you go. I was scared to love again. I was scared that my insecurities might somehow cause me to hurt you," said Lenice.

"Are you still scared?" he asked.

"Yes. But Brighton's death taught me that tomorrow isn't promised. You have to maximize each moment. I'm now willing to look past my fear and try to let someone love me and give it in return . . . if he'll let me."

"The fact that I'm here must tell you something," said James.

He opened the door and helped Lenice from the limo. Even in mourning she looked stunning to him. The black dress with her matching hat and veil made her look as if she went to a photo shoot rather than to bury her husband. The soft curve of the cotton accented the curves in her body. James tried not to stare.

Lenice recognized that familiar blush. She suddenly knew exactly who she wanted to help run her company and possibly her life. Who better than a certified accountant who loved her?

"Thank you, James. How would you like a new job?"

"Depends. Does it come with great benefits?"

"The best."

"When do I start?"

"Immediately."

"Sounds like a plan to me."

James escorted her inside the house.

Chapter 89

Two months later . . .

Over 300 women stared at Tee as she stood on stage sharing her testimony during the I'm A Good Woman Empowerment Conference. Once she returned to work, the entire planning committee agreed that Tee should be the keynote speaker. She had a powerful story of perseverance, strength, and what could happen when you trust in God. She was now giving all the women in the room the harrowing details of how a mentally ill woman and her family tried to end hers. The audience sat quietly, hanging on to her every word. Some of them wept; others raised their hands in glory to God, and some thanked God that nothing like that had ever happened to them. At the end of her testimony, Tee flashed a picture on the screen of her family. It was of a very pregnant Tee with Michael III growing inside her, Michael, Momma Pearl, and two almond-skinned children with green eyes and bright smiles. She explained how she and Michael were in the process of adopting Carla and Sean's children, Destiny and Blake.

Michael did not want anyone else to suffer pain because of Becca. Their father was deceased, and their mother was sentenced to 30 years in prison for the role she played in their father's plan for revenge, his murder, as well as the assault on Michael and the blackmail of Mac. Their aunt said she had no desire to raise two children on her own. Destiny and Blake would have ended up in foster care, and neither Michael nor Tee wanted that. They were sweet children, and they brought so much joy to their home. Each night, Tee and Michael prayed over them, asking God to shield them from any remnants of mental illness that may live within their DNA. They hoped their love would get them through any sense of abandonment the children were feeling.

So far, Blake and Destiny were adjusting as well as could be expected for two children who were uprooted from everything they knew and sent to live with strangers. Michael and Tee were blessed, and they were more than happy to share their blessings with two gorgeous gifts from God. Momma Pearl moved in with them to help raise their brood. There was no room for all of them in the condo. Lenice was kind enough to give them the house in Arlington. It was much too big for her and Webster.

Tee raised both hands to the heavens and said, "With God, all things are possible. He'll never forsake you, and He'll never leave you. Can I get an amen?" Woman all over the room answered her with a loud and strong "AMEN!"

After the conference, Tee and her planning committee went out to celebrate the success of their first major event. She looked around the table at those she loved and meditated for a moment on how far God had brought them.

Teresa was sober and back at work helping to keep the streets of Memphis safe. Tee and Tiffany repaired their friendship. Tiffany was now engaged to William, and he recently accepted a position as senior pastor at a church in Little Rock, Arkansas. They planned to wed and relocate there by the end of the month. Tiffany was hurriedly planning her dream wedding. Tee and agreed to serve as her matrons of honor. Lenice was now happier than ever. She was dating James and learning how to run her deceased husband's company. James took over as chief financial officer and was making changes to ensure the company stayed in business for years to come.

Lenora was probably the happiest of all. Herman was doing extremely well at her sister's company. He was promoted to head of IT and was back to being the primary breadwinner of his home and feeling quite proud of himself. Their marriage was doing better than ever. He and Lenora no longer had to worry about money and were once again communicating openly with one another. Lenora's new career as an artist was flourishing as well. After an article ran about her artistic talent, she held an art showing and sold several paintings. Each one sold for at least $2,000 and she received several requests to paint original pieces for businesses as well as individuals. The task she took the most joy in was preparing the nursery for the fourth child she and Herman were expecting. She also quit her job at the school to focus on her art full-time.

Tee grew teary eyed while thinking about how blessed she and her friends were. "Thank you, Father. My cup runneth over," she whispered before she went around the table and hugged every woman there.

THE END

Stay Connected

Websites
www.jaehendersonauthor.com
www.imagoodwoman.com

Facebook Fan Page
www.facebook.com/imagoodwoman

Twitter
www.twitter.com/imagoodwoman

YouTube
www.youtube.com/jaehenderson

Blog: My Side of the Single Life
Imagoodwoman2.blogspot.com

Email
Imagoodwoman2@yahoo.com

Book Clubs
For book club discussion questions visit,
www.jaehendersonauthor.com

Be sure to check out Jae Henderson's short inspirational ebook series "Things Every Good Woman Should Know."